Praise for *Mister White* by John C. Foster

"*MISTER WHITE* is a potent and hypnotic brew that blends horror, espionage and mystery. Foster has written the kind of book that keeps the genre fresh and alive and will make fans cheer. Books like this are the reason I love horror fiction."

— Ray Garton, Grand Master of Horror Award winner and Bram Stoker Award-nominated author of *Live Girls* and *Scissors*

"*MISTER WHITE* is like Stephen King's *The Stand* meets Ian Fleming's James Bond with Graham Masterton's *The Manitou* thrown in for good measure. It's frenetically paced, spectacularly gory and eerie as hell. Highly recommended!"

— John F.D. Taff, Bram Stoker Award-nominated author of *The End in All Beginnings*

"The most thrilling thing about Foster's sweeping thriller *MISTER WHITE* is how well it's written. If the idea is to put powerful words to paper, then Foster does it. And if the idea is to then use those words to pulley-up walls around a willing reader, trapping him or her in the world of *MISTER WHITE*, Foster does that, too."

— Josh Malerman, Bram Stoker Award-nominated author of the international bestselling *Bird Box*

"John C. Foster's *MISTER WHITE* is a lightning-paced, globetrotting mashup of espionage, adventure and truly disturbing occult horror. Fun and nasty in all the right places."

— Paul Tremblay, Bram Stoker Award-nominated author of the *New York Times* bestselling *A Head Full of Ghosts*

"John C. Foster keeps you turning the pages with prose as propulsive as a bullet. *MISTER WHITE* is a skillful blend of horror and international intrigue, Ian Fleming by way of Stephen King. An impressive, accomplished novel you won't soon forget."

— Nicholas Kaufmann, Thriller Award-nominated author of *Dying is My Business* and *Die and S̶ ̶D̶ead*

MISTER
WHITE

THE NOVEL

JOHN C. FOSTER

GREY MATTER
PRESS

MISTER WHITE
ISBN-13 978-1-940658-60-5
ISBN-10 1-940658-60-8
First Trade Paperback Edition - April 2016

Novel Copyright © 2016 John C. Foster
Design Copyright © 2016 Grey Matter Press

GREY MATTER
P R E S S

Grey Matter Press
greymatterpress.com
donotspeakhisname.com
facebook.com/greymatterpress
twitter.com/greymatterpress
shopgreymatterpress.com

DEDICATION

I remember the poem, Dad. I'll never quit.

MISTER
WHITE

THE NOVEL

CHAPTER ONE

- 1 -

"Who is Mister White?"

There was a pause and a crackle of static over the phone. Abel was about to speak again when the connection was severed.

"Um einen weiteren Anruf tätigen, legen Sie bitte—"

Abel hung up before the mechanical, feminine voice could finish telling him how to make another call. He turned back toward the crowd in the dimly lit bar, letting his gaze wander from face to face, his eyes stinging from the haze of smoke hovering beneath the low ceiling. He was grinning faintly and chuckling, as if he had just finished listening to a clever story.

He returned to his spot at the bar and ordered another beer. "Bitte," he said to the stocky bartender when a fresh pint glass was placed before him, adding another wet circle to the collection of moist rings that reminded him vaguely of the Olympic symbol.

Who is Mister White?
Click.

He sipped, licking the foam off his upper lip and nodding at a man holding court with a stein in one hairy fist. He was at ease. A somewhat familiar face around this part of Schweden-platz in the center of the city. It was warm inside, and everyone was talking themselves into having at least one more drink before heading out into the snow.

Abel turned, leaning one elbow on the bar, another happy regular at Das Hupfen Schwein. He didn't look Austrian, but his wardrobe and hair seemed as though it was possible he came from Ireland or Scandinavia, and his flawless German refuted any possibility he was American.

He forced himself to sip slowly, relaxing his shoulders, outwardly at ease.

"Danke," he said to the barman's back, catching a glimpse of himself in the mirror behind the bar. Good. He projected relaxation.

He looked anything but afraid.

- 2 -

The train clacked and rattled as it raced southbound along underground tracks toward the outskirts of Vienna. It was late, and only a few second-shift workers returning home shared the coach with Abel. A big man reading the newspaper. A couple of city workers in stained coveralls hanging from the overhead rail. A woman in a domestic's uniform sitting across from him.

Abel sank onto the bench, wrinkling his nose at a rank under-smell that infected the atmosphere on the car. He had already stepped off the train twice and boarded the next in line, keeping an eye out for familiar faces and postures. Indicators of interest.

There was nothing. Nothing at all out of place, but he still felt on edge. Maybe it was the smell.

"Who is Mister White?" He muttered in English, looking up to see the domestic eyeing him with a flat stare. He glanced over to see the two city workers giving him the once-over as well. Or were they?

He forced himself to look away, studying the laces on his shoes and the slush puddle forming around them from the melting snow. He looked up and heard the men in their coveralls talking to each other in guttural German. When he glanced across the aisle, the woman was still staring at him.

Abel closed his eyes, playing the language game to distract himself, listening to the two men. Austrians, by and large, had a liquid sound to their speech, and he placed them as immigrants from the eastern part of Germany.

He suddenly opened his eyes, and the woman was leaning her head back against the glass window, sleeping. A slight string of drool adorned the corner of her mouth. He noticed that the floor beneath her feet was bone dry and wondered how long she had been riding the train.

Who is Mister White?

Click.

Is it time to leave Vienna? He asked himself. *To shift the operation to another city?* He pictured Munich in the spring and chased that image with a memory of sipping brandy on the shore of Lake Geneva.

The car went black and Abel jerked in his seat, sweat beading on his forehead. The roar of wheels on tracks smothered his hearing, and he looked desperately to the left as something moved at the corner of his vision.

The lights flickered back on and Abel blinked, already aware that something was different. *The big man with the paper, where had he gone?* Abel heard the metallic slide of the door at the end of the car as it closed and could vaguely make out the big man walking into the next car.

He sucked in a deep breath and let it out slowly, calming himself. He thought of the dinner he would have after the drop. A backstreet restaurant that kept its kitchen open late and served the most amazing platters of pork shoulder with roasted apples and spaetzle.

"Nachte station, Simmering," a voice barked from the speakers.

Abel rose and grabbed a hanging strap, fumbling to close the buttons on his long coat.

The woman was watching him again. Dark skinned, hair escaping from the imprisoning bun on the back of her head. She hadn't bothered to wipe the saliva from her mouth.

"Fuck you," Abel said with a congenial smile as he picked up his briefcase from the seat. "Have a fucking fuckity night."

The doors slid open and he stepped out onto the platform. A moment later the train hissed into motion and roared away. He caught a quick glimpse of the woman staring at him through the window, upraised middle finger pressed against the glass. Then he was alone on the platform.

In the silence that followed the vanishing train, Abel knelt and placed his briefcase on the ground, pretending to tie his shoe while he carefully scanned his surroundings.

It was darker than the platforms near Vienna's nightspots. Dingier. Crumpled fast food wrappers and soft drink bottles were scattered about. Curling posters on the walls advertised performances that had gone dark a year ago, and he smelled the odor of finely aged urine.

The familiar disorder, at least by Austrian standards, reassured him. Simmering, the last stop on the line, attracted some visitors, but never eager ones.

Graveyards don't attract eager visitors.

- 3 -

Abel pulled his collar tight to keep the falling snow off of his neck and worked the pick into the lock with numb fingers. By the time he heard the click of the mechanism release, he had aged several decades, his hair and beard coated with a dusting of white.

He slid through the maintenance gate and pulled it closed behind him.

The Zentralfriedhof was the largest graveyard in Vienna, home to the disintegrating remains of Beethoven and Brahms. Abel trudged in the opposite direction of those notables, ghosting between marble gravestones gone blue in the dark, the falling snow shrouding him, muffling his footsteps. As he descended deeper into the sea of the dead, the perimeter lights faded and the shadows seemed to melt and flow into dark lakes across his path.

It was said that there were more dead in Vienna than living, and Abel found the Zentralfriedhof a perfect place to conduct business. He had worked with the Koecks before and knew that meeting in the cemetery would give the couple a not-so-subtle thrill.

The muffled crunch of his shoes through the snow faded as a sudden gust of wind blew a white curtain into his eyes. Wiping the wet coldness away, Abel was startled to see a tall figure staring down at him.

"Jesus," he said, the realization that he stood before a stone angel not coming swiftly enough to douse a surge of adrenaline.

He started forward impulsively, as if to curse at the angel, then stopped.

Crunch.

Abel turned slowly in place, rewinding the mental audio file and replaying it again. Had it been his own footstep, the sound distorted by the increasingly heavy snowfall?

Unaware, he backed into the stone angel and looked straight up as his back met marble. It was a dark figure against the white snowfall, hook-nosed and deep-eyed. Judging.

Abel jerked away and his nose wrinkled as he again smelled the rank scent from the train. A third-world odor of rotting flesh, blackened toes and gangrene.

"Ridiculous," he muttered. He was working himself up like a kid waiting for ghost stories around a campfire. Still, he thought he might take his coat to the dry cleaners tomorrow because the odor seemed to be sticking with him.

"Abel? Sin sie das?" A woman's voice floated through the night.

Abel grunted in disgust. *Amateurs*. Of course it was him, who else would be out here in this weather?

"Ja, ja," he said, breaking his own silence. Masha hadn't shouted yet, but she might if she was getting nervous, and the silly bitch had used his name.

He crunched his way toward the sound, thinking of the Go Bag back at his flat and the heavy automatic hidden inside among the cash and identification cards. Only amateurs carried weapons in his profession—or so he had been taught—but he kept one for a rainy day or a snowy night.

"Abel? Sin sie das?"

Abel stopped, the hair on the back of his neck prickling. Something was wrong with the question.

He began to back away from the voice when he heard the rapid footfalls of steps behind him. He spun around, catching a quick glimpse of a white face that seemed to float in the darkness. Abel blinked snow from his eyes and looked again, but the row between the gravestones was now empty.

"Abel? Sin sie das?" The voice came again from beyond a vast marble mausoleum. *Abel? Is that you?* Asked in exactly the same way, with exactly the same volume.

Break contact right now.

Abel darted into another row, moving quickly away from the voice, not returning to his path of entry. He caught a slither of movement from the corner of his eye and heard a loud cry followed by a splash. The gurgling death throes were unmistakable.

Panic seeping in, Abel reversed directions and ran through the rows of gravestones. He slipped and landed hard, the briefcase jarred from his grip.

Fuck it. He left it where it fell, scrambling on hands and knees.

"Abel? Sin sie das?"

"Shit," he said as he realized he had been herded back to the meeting point. He clawed his way to his feet, determined to sprint past whatever might be waiting for him. He ran, coat streaming, darting around the corner of the mausoleum.

"Oh hell," he said to Masha. His feet slid out from under him as he tried to stop and he fell again, the breath knocked from his lungs.

Masha had been crucified against the back of the mausoleum, railroad spikes driven through her outstretched wrists. Her chest was covered by a red bib flowing from the tear in her throat. A flashlight planted in the snow at her feet threw its light upward, transforming her expression into a ghoulish mask and causing the freezing blood on her blouse to glisten like rubies.

"Abel? Sin—"

"No…" he moaned over the recorded voice emanating from her coat pocket.

Abel turned away from her, crawling through the snow, the bonds holding back his panic shattered. A pair of boots blocked his path, and he looked up to see the white face floating in the night.

"Don't," he shouted in the instant before the shadows swarmed him.

There was a bright flash of pain, then darkness.

- 4 -

A familiar rumble became identifiable, and Abel fought a surge of nausea, his head throbbing. He felt like he was coming off of a three-day bender, but that didn't seem right.

He opened his eyes just in time to see a young couple watching him before he doubled over, retching.

"Verdammt ekelhaft," the girl said, her face wrinkling in disgust.

"Lässt uns gehen," the boy said, grabbing her arm and pulling her towards the door to the next car.

He looked down at the string of vomit stretching from his mouth to the bench, his nose choked with a sweet, antiseptic smell.

I'm on a train, he thought, and then, *chloroform*.

Abel sat up, clutching his aching head. His pants were wet with snowmelt and he shivered, struggling to clear the mental fog from his memory.

He wiped yellow bile from his mouth as the puddle of puke sent streamers down the bench towards his briefcase.

"Shit."

The door to the next car opened and a member of the Polizei stepped onto the car. He had the look of a man off duty, carrying his hat, tie undone.

"Bist du betrunken?" He snapped, eyes narrowing.

Abel shook his head, "Not drunk. Sick."

The cop gave him a doubtful look. "Sie, die sich sauber."

"I will. I'll use my coat." Abel realized he was speaking English and made a mental effort to switch languages.

He picked up his briefcase and something sloshed inside as he placed it on his lap. He had fumbled off his coat and was sopping up the vomit when he felt a warm wetness on his thigh. Red liquid was seeping from the briefcase.

Abel looked up instinctively at the Polizei officer, but the civil servant had turned away in disgust, and Abel quickly used his coat to smear away the blood.

As the train pulled into the lighted platform of the next station, the cop muttered a disgusted command over his shoulder. "Nach hause gehen und schlafen sie ab." *Go home and sleep it off.*

He got off the train and Abel tensed when another man stepped on, but the odor drove him back out in search of another car.

As the train resumed its clamorous transit, Abel looked down at his briefcase. *What the hell happened tonight?*

Trembling fingers worked the clasp open and he lifted the lid.

The severed human foot was resting in a sticky soup of blood. An amazing amount of blood. It dripped like red rain from the upper lid and Abel let out a high-pitched keening sound.

He remembered everything.

- 5 -

Abel's walk from the underground station to his flat was a paranoid dream set in motion. Every face turned to watch him, eyes shadowy pits like Masha's. White snow hats looked like skulls, and a man in a light-colored balaclava nearly gave him a heart attack when he stepped out of a doorway.

The befouled coat was in a public wastebasket somewhere

behind him. He shivered as the snow coated his shoulders and cold reached through his sweater to drag icy claws across his ribs. He grimly hung onto his briefcase, unsure what forensic telltales he had left on it, hearing the foot thump and slosh as the case swung from his hand.

He wondered if the foot belonged to Masha or her husband, Ernst.

Abel considered heading straight out of the city. It was the safest tactical move, but with no money and identification, he wouldn't get far. And he would likely freeze to death before long anyway. He had to risk returning to his flat, but when he came in sight of it, he couldn't force his feet to carry him across the street.

"Sie kann hier nicht schlafen." *You can't sleep there*, a voice barked at Abel from a window and he lurched out of the doorway he had been huddling in, a frozen marionette with tangled strings.

He stood in the street until headlights blazed through the increasing snowfall and a horn blared at him. Then he stumbled across the road towards home.

- 6 -

"I'm surprised to see you alive," a gravelly voice said from the dark room.

Abel froze, staring at the single red eye glaring at him. As his vision adjusted, he made out the hulking shape of the Fat Man. A dog began barking furiously in the apartment next door, the racket carrying easily through the thin walls.

"You hung up on me," Abel said, trying to sniff past the smell of the other's cigarette smoke to detect the odor of gangrene.

"You don't look well," the Fat Man said.

Abel turned on a reading light, but the Fat Man sitting at Abel's desk remained in shadows.

"Who is Mister White?" Abel asked, setting the briefcase down on one guest chair as he sat in the other. The Fat Man held out the pack of cigarettes, but Abel shook his head, afraid to show his shaking hands.

"Where did you hear that name?" the Fat Man asked.

"You know who he is then?"

"If you found his name, then it is already too late."

"Who is he?" Abel asked, breathing deep. There was no rotting smell. He thought he might be safe for the moment.

"Why don't you ask Mr. Bierce?" the Fat Man suggested.

Abel flinched at the name. "Tell me who he is."

"When you called, I thought it certain you would meet him tonight."

"Would I be alive if I had?"

The Fat Man's bald head shook slowly, connected to his massive shoulders by drooping jowls. "No." He exhaled a cloud of smoke. "But you do not look well."

Abel shrugged. "Amateurs," he said. "I'll have that cigarette now."

The Fat Man rose and offered him the pack. Abel slipped one free, his trembling almost unnoticeable.

"I will have a drink and you will as well," the Fat Man said, fetching a bottle of brandy and two glasses from a shelf.

Abel lit and the Fat Man poured before moving to sit on the edge of the desk. He wore a three-piece suit, very old world, the glittering length of a gold watch chain stretching across the immense expanse of his vest.

Abel had heard that he suffered from gout and wondered if he carried a gun.

"I will speak and you will listen, and then we will plan. You have heard the name of Mister White and you are already on borrowed time."

"You said that already."

Abel dragged deep, the smoke mixing terribly with the bilious taste in his mouth as if giving it life, making it airborne. He sipped and swirled the brandy, sighing as the warmth slid down his throat and through his chest.

"Who watches the watchers?" The Fat Man mused, carefully tasting his brandy. "A rhetorical question, but important in that it juxtaposes with my next question. When you were young, did you eat your peas and Brussels sprouts?"

Abel raised an eyebrow, finishing his glass. "Was that rhetorical too?"

"Did you clean your room? Did you mind your mother?"

"Do we have time for this?" Abel asked, pouring another for himself and wondering how many the big man had drunk already.

"What did your mother say when you did not mind her?"

Abel started to interrupt again, but the grim expression in the other man's eyes belied the levity of the questions.

Exhaling smoke, the Fat Man spoke through the cloud. "Never mind, I shall tell you what my mother said. She said that she would tell Mr. Haeckel and he would pay me a visit when I went to sleep."

The Fat Man stood and began pacing, his steps heavy. "He was an old man who lived several houses down the street, hideously maimed in an industrial accident and blind in one eye. Just an old man, yet my friends and I crafted terrible tales about him and ascribed powers to his ill-fitting glass eye in its bed of yellow pus. It got to the point where none of us would so much as walk past his house if we were alone."

He paused to look out the window at the street below.

"I had forgotten Mr. Haeckel until just recently, convinced I had left him behind with distance and years. But I realized with your call tonight that he was not left behind at all."

The Fat Man turned around and his face had gone slack with horror, so dramatically that Abel thought he was having a stroke.

"Mister White is the Boogeyman," the Fat Man whispered. "Like Mr. Haeckel long ago, but all too real."

Abel stood and slammed his drink down on the desk, sloshing amber liquid onto the dark wood. "What the hell is this?"

"You and I have not eaten our Brussels sprouts. But worse for you, Abel, *you* have not cleaned your room or minded your mother, and I'm afraid she—or he, in this case—told Mister White."

"You're fucking insane," Abel said, heading around the desk for the drawer hiding his Go Bag.

"Who watches the watchers?" the Fat Man asked. "And who do they tell when an operative goes bad? Very, very bad?"

Leather satchel in hand, Abel looked up to see the Fat Man pointing a small, black pistol at him, tiny in his giant fist.

"Put the bag down on the table and sit behind the desk," the Fat Man said. "When Mister White arrives, I will give you to him and tell him what you have done."

"You're dirty—" The pistol jerked sharply and Abel stopped speaking.

"Not like you, my boy, not like you, and I will be able to explain my own involvement away into nothing. Now sit."

Abel dropped the bag on the desk and sat in the chair, still disturbingly warm from his unexpected guest.

The Fat Man moved around the desk and topped off Abel's drink. "Finish this, if you wish. Have more. I'm not sure it will help, though, when Mister White comes for you." He slid the drink to Abel, leaving a wet trail. "But it might."

Abel downed the drink in one long swallow that set his throat on fire and eyes watering. When he looked up, the fat man was staring down at the briefcase on the guest chair.

"Why is this dripping?" he asked.

Abel's mouth twisted into a tight smile as the Fat Man bent to fumble open the catch with his free hand and lift the lid. A coppery musk of blood filled the room as he staggered back, eyes wide.

"Mister White is already here," Abel said.

"But...but...you're still alive."

Abel leaned back in the soft chair. "Maybe he wants you too, Herr Gruebel."

The Fat Man lifted the pistol and considered risking a shot, then turned and fled out the front door. Abel heard his thundering steps in the hall and then on the stairs.

- 7 -

The clock struck midnight, and Abel stirred in the tiny cone of light from the reading lamp. The level in the bottle had descended considerably, and he sat with an empty glass in one hand, a 9mm Spanish Llama pistol in the other.

Two hours had passed, and he had not heard a sound, save for the building creaking in the wind.

"Fuck you, Mister White."

He stood, having utterly failed to make sense of the evening. It felt as if he were trapped in one of the CIA's Cold War LSD experiments. The brandy didn't help, but he needed it to steady his nerves.

He carried the briefcase into the tiny bathroom and tossed the thing into the claw-foot tub, where he proceeded to douse it with rubbing alcohol, brandy and anything else that he thought might burn.

Smashing the smoke detector with the butt of the Llama, he lit a match and tossed it into the tub.

A cloud of bright flame whooshed up and he staggered back in surprise. Anyone looking in the tub would see the remains of the case, and forensics would be able to find blood traces, but any tells he had left on it would be gone. The apartment itself was under a false name and untraceable to him, no matter if he went to Geneva or Munich.

Once he was certain the fire was contained in the tub, he moved through the flat, grabbing essentials for his flight. The aroma of roasting pork wafted from the bathroom, and he briefly pictured pied du cochon—baked pig's foot—the chef's specialty at his backstreet haunt. His stomach rumbled, and he realized he had not eaten since lunch before remembering what was cooking in his tub.

Abel doubled over and vomited a hot stream of bile and brandy.

He had meant to stay and feed the small, charred bones of the foot into his toilet, but urgency won out over tradecraft and he took a jacket and hat out of his closet instead.

"Goodbye, Vienna," he said with a last look around the flat. Go Bag in hand and pistol in his jacket pocket, he stepped into the hall and pulled the door shut behind him.

"Es riecht lecker," an old woman's voice drifted down the hall. *It smells delicious.* Abel turned to see his neighbor peeking out of her door. She backed into the apartment as a series of barks erupted behind her. "Er wird nicht aufhören." *He won't stop.*

"I'll leave a plate outside your door when it's finished cooking," Abel said over his shoulder before hurrying down two flights of stairs to the street door. "Don't let the dog get it."

Munich or Geneva, hell, even Stockholm, whichever has the first flight out.

He stepped out into the cramped street, and his ears pricked up at a distant, panting sound. He glanced into the alley adjacent to his building.

A grotesque Buddha sat cross-legged in the snow, his bald head glistening as the flakes melted on his scalp. He was globular, morbidly obese, his immense stomach plumped out to absurd proportions on his thighs, and his skin was so white it was nearly blue.

The illusion of his snow Buddha-hood would have been complete if the Fat Man had not been silently weeping.

Abel pulled the pistol from his pocket and held it low by his side, stopping a good ten feet from the naked man.

"What the hell are you doing?" Abel said.

The fat man looked up and struggled to open his eyes against lashes that had frozen shut with tears.

"I...I...I...," he stammered through chattering teeth.

Abel noticed a dark discoloration in the snow beneath the Fat Man as he lifted his huge belly with both hands, revealing the railroad spikes driven through both of his crossed ankles and into the ground.

"Puh...puh...please..." he whispered, but Abel was already running away from him towards the main thoroughfare. His hat flew off his head and he didn't break stride, consumed with an overriding, animal need to escape.

A taxi was idling at the curb as a couple disembarked. Abel nearly ran them down in his haste to catch it.

"Flughafen," Abel barked.

As the taxi pulled away from the curb, Abel was gripped with the conviction that Mister White was driving the car. That the head he could make out only in silhouette would turn around and he would see a pallid, murderous face staring back at him. He pressed the barrel of the Llama against the back of the driver's seat and asked, "Mister White?"

"Huh?" the driver asked.

"You heard me, Mister White."

An oncoming car flashed headlights across the taxi's windshield, and Abel saw the man's dark skin and Rastafarian hair.

"Jesus," Abel said as he shuddered and sank back into the seat. The ride was slow and almost peaceful, the snow diffusing the city lights into a sea of glowing orbs. The car's heaters embraced him with their warmth, and he unbuttoned his coat with one hand, stuffing the pistol back in his pocket, soothed by the metronomic sweep of the windshield wipers.

The old-fashioned ringing startled him, and it took him several moments to realize it was a telephone sounding off beside him.

Abel frantically patted the car seat looking for the source

The ringing stopped.

"Was ist das?" The driver asked over his shoulder.

"A cell phone," Abel said as his questing fingers picked up the rectangle of smooth plastic. "Excuse me," he said, switching to German. "Es ist ein handy."

It twisted in his hand and Abel almost dropped it. But it was just the vibration as it began ringing again.

The screen read CALLER UNKNOWN. Abel wanted to throw it out the window.

"Is it yours?" the driver asked.

"Nein."

The driver held his hand back over the front seat and Abel handed it forward. The driver answered the phone, "Hallo?"

After a minute of conversation the driver hung up and pulled cautiously to the curb, sliding a little despite his care.

"What the hell are you doing?" Abel said.

The driver smiled and held up a hand in a *relax* gesture. "De last passengers, dey left it in de car."

His English was worse than his German.

Light filled the vehicle as another pulled up behind them. Abel twisted to see another taxi slide to a stop.

"Dey follow the GPS," the driver said, already getting out of the car. The door slammed shut, and Abel was frozen with indecision.

Steal the taxi? Wait for the driver? Get out and run? His thinking was muddied by terror, and he wished he had not consumed so much brandy. *Get out and shoot them all?*

His breath fogged the rear window as he tried to watch his driver talking to the person who emerged from the other car. He wiped at it frantically, leaving smears, obscuring the figures.

Anything could be happening back there.

Normally he would immediately follow training and take the simplest route to break contact, but he was terrified into immobility. Utterly uncertain. It was as if he had been manipulated into a position where his years of experience were useless.

He reached for the door handle and pulled, but the door was locked. Holding the gun, he fumbled at the door until he found the button and heard it unlock. He reached for the handle just as the driver's door opened with a blast of cold air, the driver huddling inside quickly.

Abel pivoted in his seat and lifted his pistol. "All right, Mister—"

The Rastafarian cab driver turned, eyes white and huge as he saw the pistol.

"Drive," Abel said.

"What? You can have—"

"Drive or I'll blow your motherfucking head off!" Spit flew from Abel's mouth.

The driver turned and keyed the ignition, starter engine screaming as he turned it over too long in his panic.

"Drive!"

The driver stomped on the gas and the tires spun up a rooster tail of slush. Suddenly they caught and the car surged forward, fishtailing.

Right into the path of an oncoming lumber truck.

Abel screamed as he looked at the blinding headlights and the half-seen grille grinning like a mouth full of metal teeth.

The sound of the head-on collision was like nothing he had ever heard, and he slammed into the back of the front seat, teeth clacking shut on his tongue, ribs cracking, vaguely aware of the taxi rocketing backward in an uncontrolled spin until it crashed into an immovable object and hurled out a deadly swath of hub caps, shards of metal and exploding tires.

Stunned, Abel was unable to give any meaning to the time it took to pull himself up from the back seat. He wiped at something stuck in his hair. His mouth was filled with the taste of pennies, and a steady spatter of hot liquid hit the back of the front seat as he beheld the driver.

A two-by-four had crashed through the windshield like a spear, impaling the driver through his mouth and penetrating out the back of his skull, exploding like a brain, blood and bone grenade, until the wood lodged itself in the rear window. The impaled Rastafarian hung from the two-by-four, eyes still open wide and white.

Abel dragged himself across the seat to the door and used both trembling hands to open it. He sprawled forward into the snow, his hands shooting out to either side in the slippery wet, landing face first in the road with his feet still tangled inside the vehicle.

It took years to pull himself completely from the wreckage until he flopped full-length in the road. In the next century he was able to lift his head by painful degrees, focusing his eyes with a herculean effort.

He saw a pair of black boots surrounded by white, just inches from his nose.

He tried to say, "No."

CHAPTER
TWO

Bare branches scratched at the windowpane as the Russian countryside huddled under its first major snowstorm of the season. Warm in his study, Lewis sipped his tea and watched the video from the dead-drop website as his calico cat Piotr patrolled the perimeter of the room.

A naked man sat inside a mirrored cube maybe ten feet on a side. His face was black and blue, nose horribly swollen and crusted with blood. His pale ribs showed contusions indicating the likelihood of broken bones. There was no escape for the prisoner from the sight of his own degradation.

Lewis had seen such injuries before. Seen them in person in his younger days. But the years had rendered the memories diffuse, and seeing wounds in such glistening detail made him shift nervously in his seat.

According to the time code running at the bottom of the screen, it had been two days since the man had awakened to find a straight razor beside him and heard the first emotionless command from what Lewis took to calling "The Voice."

"Shave off every inch of hair from your body, Abel."

Lewis started at the name and leaned close to the screen.

After hours of pleading and pounding on the walls, Abel complied, weeping and trembling. When he missed a spot, The

Voice was there to remind him. As a result, he was left with scratches over much of his body. His eyebrows were scabbed hyphens, and his groin looked like hamburger.

"Very good," The Voice said when the grooming was finished. "I would like you to think for a while on this question. How much of yourself will you give away to stay alive, and at what point does your life cease to matter?"

The camera shifted angles constantly during the next two recorded days, often shooting from underneath the cube where the blood smears were turning brown and the increasingly indiscreet puddles of urine dried.

Lewis played back the video frame by frame after the razor disappeared and noticed a brief discrepancy in the time code, but did not see The Voice. He accidentally let his gaze wander over the picture of his family on his desk. He turned it facedown.

When heavy wire cutters appeared on the reflective floor, Lewis rewound the video again, but The Voice remained a ghost. Abel awoke and cried tearlessly, without sound. Lewis suspected he was too dehydrated to produce either.

"Do you have an answer to my question?" The Voice asked.

"Please let me go. Can't you please let me go?" Abel asked, turning around and around until he was weaving dizzily.

"Is the answer one finger from your left hand? If it is, I will give you water."

"No! Please!" Abel screamed hoarsely and struggled to his feet. "Let me go…"

"I can't, Abel. You will be an example for others."

According to the time code, Abel cut the pinky off his left hand four hours and thirteen minutes later.

"Jesus Christ," Lewis muttered, his long finger trembling as he pressed the pause button. He jerked when the phone on his desk rang. The light indicated it was his business line, not the secure line. He ignored it.

Abel was watered and his wounds were bandaged. The time code showed another longer gap and Lewis realized that The Voice was concealing his identity, disrupting the feed while he attended to his prisoner.

When Abel was asked to cut off a second finger, he held out for only an hour, rocking himself like someone in the throes of severe dementia.

"Now write, Abel. Confess."

Lewis watched as the man on screen used the bloody stump of his second finger to scrawl a crude graffiti on the walls. Abel wrote and wrote until he was on his knees. Line after line of confession deviating into large, looping whorls of blood and tiny, cryptic scratches on the glass. Lewis felt his own pulse begin to race as he copied, to the best of his ability, what Abel was writing. Even under duress Abel was employing a code, and Lewis was able to extract a chilling name from the bloody script.

There was more in the confession, and it would take a specialist to get it all. But there would never be a specialist. Lewis had already decided to burn his notes once he learned everything he could.

Finally, Abel collapsed into a fetal position mumbling, "Killmekillmekillme."

"I can't kill you yet. Forensics would indicate when you had died, and we have more work to do before."

Lewis had watched the video with such concentration that he began to lose track of time and courted the absurd notion that he was somehow trapped inside the cell with Abel. When a calendar reminder popped up on screen, Lewis was dragged back into the present and placed a call to his wife and daughter in New York. He lied about weather interfering with his ability to make a video connection, unwilling to see Cat on the same screen that displayed Abel's disintegration. He hung up after several minutes, unable to remember the conversation beyond a sense of disquiet when he asked to speak to his daughter and Cat said, "Hedde's out."

He placed another call and cancelled a dinner meeting.

Long after he should have been asleep, Lewis crept through the house and retrieved a 9mm Makarov semi-automatic from the box in the bedroom closet. He took a quiet shower to wash away a rank sweat, the small pistol safe inside a plastic baggy on the soap dish. He emptied Piotr's bowl and scooped in wet food from a fresh can, unable to remember when he last saw his tiny companion.

He awoke some time later with the orange light of dawn filtering through the window, confused, hand pawing through papers on his desk until they closed over the automatic. Gun in hand, he stumbled to the kitchen and put on a pot of coffee—thick, black stuff gifted to him by a friend in Istanbul. Inhaling the steam as it rose from a cup, hot enough to burn his hand, Lewis stopped in the living room to pluck the old double-barrel shotgun from its rack over the mantle.

The oiled, black length of the rifle was backed by a carved, wooden stock and ornately worked triggers. Even Lewis, not really a gun aficionado, had admired its elegance when he first laid eyes on it. The Moscow official who had given it to him said its previous owner was Prince Mikhail Sergeevich Lopuhin, arrested and shot by the Bolsheviks in 1918. Antique though it was, the weapon was in perfect working order. Lewis felt comforted by the grim weight of it and leaned it against the wall of his study near the door before returning to his desk.

Abel made it through the remaining fingers on his left hand over the next few days, bandages and water appearing when he was a good boy. The words on the walls had run and were now like ruins buried beneath dried brown streaks.

On the fifth day, according to the time code, Abel picked up one of the stiffening fingers from the floor and ate it.

"Dear God," Lewis said.

He had taken to keeping the blinds down and checking the perimeter security system every half hour or so, seeking reassurance from the green LED display. He wished he had a dog. The pistol was in the pocket of a heavy sweater he had been wearing non-stop, and it clanked against the kitchen counter during rare trips outside his study to make another pot of coffee.

The video continued. "Consider the question, Abel," The Voice said. "Is the answer your left foot? Or a phone number?"

The footage jumped again and now Abel was screaming at a wall, as if The Voice had just been inside the cube with him. He looked emaciated and crookbacked, almost subhuman. He turned to a cell phone on the floor, but couldn't hold it with his mangled hand. Ultimately, he wedged it between his knees and dialed a number.

The footage blurred and the time code jumped. The image steadied on Abel shaking a small hatchet in his right fist. His first blow was clumsy, tearing a flap of skin off the corner of his forehead. He staggered and fell but bounced up with manic energy. Abel's second blow, even one handed, drove the steel head of the hatchet into the thin bone at his right temple with surprising force and he collapsed in a heap, red sludge seeping from the wound.

The time code indicated eight minutes of twitching before Abel went completely still.

Lewis hit pause and covered his eyes, trying to gather his thoughts and banish his fear. He rewound the footage until the image of Abel crouching over the cell phone appeared. Lewis paused it, using agency software to isolate and zoom in on the phone's damnably small screen. Either the camera's resolution or the software was insufficient and the enlarged number remained an indistinct blur.

Lewis returned to his place in the video, thankfully near the end. He hit play, unaware of the reluctant moan drifting from his own mouth.

Rigor mortis had begun to twist and stiffen Abel's corpse when Lewis noticed the tell-tale blur of yet another break in the recording. Automatically he ran the footage back frame by frame.

Lewis sat up straight in his chair, knocking over a glass of water.

The reflections made it nearly impossible to tell, and the light in the mirrored room had been turned off, but Lewis could make out the blurry outline of a too-white face that seemed to float disembodied, staring directly into the camera.

Lewis crumpled his paper notes into a glass ashtray, lighting them with a wooden match. The ball of paper curled and twisted like a live thing as it burned, and he turned away from the acrid smoke.

The phone rang and startled a small sound from him.

The business line again, not his secure line.

Lewis grabbed the shotgun and strode into the dining room where he opened the glass door of a dark wood liquor cabinet and removed a slender bottle. Fat, wet flakes of snow were blowing against the expansive windows, and the darkness of the woods beyond seemed to writhe in a constant state of indiscernible motion. He retreated from the windows, returning to his study with the bottle to pour a shot of pepper vodka, downing it as he dialed the secure phone. The bloom of heat expanded through his torso and spread a warm blanket across his seething mind while he waited for the clicks and sounds indicating a secure international connection.

"Secure connection," Lewis said.

"Connection secure," a clipped voice on the other end responded.

"Bierce, it's me," he said. "Something, I don't know how to describe it, came into one of the dead-drop web sites. I'm sending it to you encrypted."

"Who sent it?" Bierce asked. His thin voice sounded hollow, as if heard through a tin can and wire set up.

"That's just it. I don't know."

"But how did they access—"

"I know, I know. Listen, it came to the site because it was meant to be seen. It's a warning. It says so right in the fucking footage."

"A warning against what?"

Lewis poured himself another drink and downed it, hissing against the fire. This was a subject he had been meaning to broach with his superior but, until now, had not found a politic way to do so. Present circumstances were not taking his feelings into account, it would seem.

He tipped the glass over and rolled the cut crystal beneath his finger across the black maple desk. A thin trail of liquid slid into the wood grain.

"Are you there?" Bierce asked.

"It was Abel on the video, sir."

"Abel?"

"Yes," Lewis said, the icy hug of fear settling around his rib cage. "Sir, I've been aware for some time—"

"Not on the phone," Bierce cut him off. "Not even on a secure line."

The glass slipped from his wet fingers and rolled off the desk. Lewis ignored the crack of breaking glass.

"The things this son of a bitch did to him…" Lewis said.

"Send it," Bierce said. Lewis heard the note of worry in his superior's voice.

"As soon as I get off the line. But one question…"

"Yes?"

"I think our bad boy made a mistake," Lewis said. "I got a quick look at him, only one, but maybe Tech can do something with it. And I think there was a name coded into the confession Abel was writing."

"Who is it?"

Lewis nodded even though the other man couldn't see him.

"Exactly," he said. "Who is Mister White?"

"What did you say?"

"I said who is Mister Whi—"

"Stop talking," Bierce interrupted.

"What?"

"Consider yourself beyond sanction and get out of there right now."

The call abruptly disconnected, and Lewis was left standing in his dark office listening to a dial tone.

CHAPTER
THREE

Lewis redialed Bierce's direct line, but the phone on the other end rang with no answer. He hung up, brow twisted with worry. *What the hell was going on?*

He began to reach for the vodka bottle again but stopped himself as he heard a sound upstairs.

"Knock it off," he whispered to himself, but cocked his head to listen. The dacha, which could easily be described as rustically luxurious, and in which Lewis entertained the elite of St. Petersburg in the warmer months, was suddenly full of unfamiliar sounds and threatening shadows.

Lewis caught a flash of crimson in the dark window and spun to look at the perimeter security controls on the wall.

The LED display was flashing red.

Lewis crossed the room and snatched up the shotgun leaning against the wall. The house shuddered as a snowy gust crashed against it.

He quietly thumbed back both hammers on the weapon, barrels aimed at the floor as he put his back to the wall near the doorway. A chill line of sweat trickled down his spine and he forced himself to breathe.

This is ridiculous, he thought to himself, some rational part of his brain insisting that he had been worked into a nervous state by the horrifying video footage.

But Bierce was not a man to play games.

Lewis stepped into the hall, eyes darting in every direction. With a near silent slide-shuffle in his sock-covered feet, he moved towards the front door where he kept his heavy coat and snow boots. A Russian winter was lethal without protection.

He stopped in mid-step, muscles tensing as Piotr yowled from somewhere on the second story and flooded his bloodstream with adrenaline.

Break contact.

Lewis bolted for the kitchen, away from the obvious exit at the door. With no effort to remain quiet, he crawled up onto the counter and forced up the window over the sink. Long icicles hung like bars in front of the opening, but Lewis dove through them in an explosion of shimmering shards, landing heavily in a puff of white and losing his grip on the shotgun. He came up in a crouch and raked his hands across the snow but the weapon had disappeared.

"Son of a bitch," he hissed, writing off the long-arm. He looked around, trying to see everywhere at once, eyes straining through the falling white curtain to locate the threat.

Every clump of snow resting on a pine bough was the pallid face of Mister White. He heard death in the rustle of the trees.

Lewis rose and bulled straight for the tree line, knees pumping high as he plowed through two feet of snow. He made no effort to zig-zag or present an elusive target. Long-unused lessons blazed to the front of his thinking. Complexity was death. Simplicity was survival. His twin goals were distance and speed.

It had been more than a decade since Lewis worked as a true field agent, and his desk-jockey lungs were straining before he reached the shelter of the woods. His thighs burned with the effort, and he had to repeatedly wipe his eyes clean to see.

It was fifteen degrees out, sometime after midnight. He wore jeans, a sweater and socks. He carried a pistol with eight rounds in the magazine. He had no money, car keys or identification.

By the time Lewis ducked under the first branches and entered the forest, his feet were numb blocks of ice and he was losing feeling in his fingers.

CHAPTER FOUR

- 1 -

Zoya wanted more cocaine. She stayed in bed until Evgeny was snoring lustily, feeling him drying on the inside of her thigh. When she was sure he was sound asleep, she rolled over and fished a small glassine baggy out of the nightstand.

Empty. She ticked it with a finger to see if any powder remained, but she vaguely remember that she had already dipped her finger in before they had sex, rubbing the powder along her gums before sucking Evgeny's cock. It made things taste better.

She slipped out of bed, pleased at the bounce of her breasts. If Evgeny knew she was closer to thirty than the twenty-three she claimed to be, he'd throw her out on her ass. Zoya glanced back at his massive belly covered in a pelt of iron hair. She would convert him into a husband soon or have to move on, and each year that passed made that more difficult. She would not return to the village of Zheleznogorsk to become a shrunken babushka, dying a slow death under gray skies in the middle of nowhere.

But with the blow roaring through her body, she flew above future concerns. She grabbed her robe and padded, barefoot, towards the stairs.

Wind rattled the windows downstairs and Zoya pulled the robe around herself as goosebumps broke out over her body. It was freezing on the first floor.

She hurried into the kitchen where she had left her bag, vague on remembering whether or not she had bought more cocaine earlier, but hopeful. It wasn't until she had the bag on the butcher block table and was rummaging through it with both hands that she noticed the sliding glass door leading to the back deck was open a crack. She had just enough time to straighten up before she registered intense cold behind her and felt a body made of ice press against her back. Iron-hard arms—*ice* arms—wrapped around her and a hand colder than death pressed across her mouth.

"Nyet," she said against the frigid palm as she turned to see a white face made of winter beside her own. Ice clung to his cheeks and his hair was made of snow. Zoya screamed and bucked, but the hand muffled her cry. Something slammed into her lower back, stunning her before she was forced forward over the butcher block.

In a split second she was back in Zheleznogorsk a child listening to the old women talk of the Strigoi—the men without warmth who stole out of the night to drink in the heat of a living body.

The gun pressing against her temple brought her back into the present.

"Zatknis!" the Strigoi hissed, and she stopped trying to scream. "If you scream I will kill you. If you struggle I will kill you. Nod if you understand." His Russian reeked of the St. Petersburg elite. Her automatic envy brushed away the fear clouding her thinking. She nodded.

"I am your neighbor from up the road. I will not kill you if you do as I say," the Strigoi said. "I will make you rich if you do as I say, do you understand?"

"Da," she whispered into his palm.

Zoya registered his trembling body and heard his teeth chattering. She became aware of the familiar position she was in and slid backward, pressing her ass into him.

Blinding pain flashed through her skull and she reached up to find hot wetness in her hair. Tiny red drops spattered on the table.

The Strigoi held the small black pistol in front of her face, and she felt his warm breath on her ear. "Next time, I kill you and take what I need without your help."

She nodded, mouth clamped shut. It was all she could do not to cry out when he jerked her up straight. He spun her about to face him, and she opened her eyes as she felt the barrel of the pistol pressed to her forehead.

"Do you want to live?" he asked.

She studied him, noting the snow melting out of his hair and the ice running from his cheeks. His eyes were dark hollows.

"Da," she said quietly.

"Do you want to be rich?" he asked. She recognized him now. The neighbor who traveled often. Evgeny thought he was American and possibly a criminal.

"Da," she said again. She understood this kind of conversation, pistol and all.

"Take me to your computer."

She led him down the dark hallway to the study, not making an effort to hold down the natural sway of her hips.

"Where is Evgeny?" the American criminal Strigoi asked from behind her.

"He is upstairs. Drunk. He will not awaken," she said.

In the study he pushed her towards Evgeny's massive, oaken desk.

"Log me in," he said, and she sat, booting up the computer. She checked to see if he was looking at her tits, revealed through the opening in her robe. He wasn't.

"There's a security system on my house. I'll give you the entry code and the combination for the safe in my bedroom," he said. "Fifty thousand American inside, about the same in rubles and euros. You can have that and anything else you want. I won't be coming back."

She looked at him, her eyes wide and blue. "I thought you were Strigoi tonight, come to take my warmth. Instead you are a friend come to give me a way out of here."

"Get up," he said, gesturing with the pistol. She moved aside and he crouched in front of the computer, rapidly opening up an email program.

He typed a quick note.

HI CAT,

HEADBAND

LOVE YOU,
LEWIS

"Who is Cat?" Zoya asked. She could read English well enough.

The Strigoi American criminal neighbor sent the email and closed down the program. "I need a coat and boots. Hat. You do too. I'm taking the car, and you're coming with me. I'll drop you off a few minutes away from here. Whether you tell Evgeny about the safe or not is up to you."

"I will not tell him."

The melting man looked her over and nodded. "What will you say about the car?"

"I tell him Strigoi come and take it," Zoya said in English. She had no intention of ever having to tell that fat pig Evgeny anything ever again.

Lewis stood and aimed the pistol at her heart and the fear filled Zoya once more.

- 2 -

Lewis sat in the passenger seat, warm in a long, black overcoat and Russian hat. He completed the ensemble with a thin pair of black leather gloves and insulated boots, thankful for Evgeny's expensive taste in clothing.

He held the Makarov on Zoya the entire time as she carefully piloted the Mercedes sedan through the storm. Twice she slid and the heavy car glanced off the six-foot snowbanks lining the road.

"Sorry," Zoya said. Lewis made no comment, but the gun never wavered.

Far from a hindrance, the promise of money transformed Zoya into a quick-thinking partner as she had loaded the trunk with unasked-for items such as snowshoes, fresh water and dried sausages. A thermos full of hot coffee rested on the seat beside him. Evgeny's mistress had a mercenary's instinct for scenting new opportunity, and the winds of change were blowing.

"Stop here," he said. She nodded and pulled the vehicle to the side of the road.

"Stick to the road and you'll be at my house in no time," Lewis said. "Keys to my car are in my desk drawer."

"Spaseeba," she said, her voice low, buttoning her coat and pulling on a pair of gloves. She opened the door and a skirl of wind carried snowflakes inside. "Good luck, Strigoi."

"Go," Lewis said.

She closed the door without another word, and then he was alone in the warm car, listening to the hiss of air from the heaters and the comforting rumble of the engine. It was a good car with all-weather tires and a full tank of gas.

I hope you check your email, Cat, Lewis thought. He fought down a wave of panic. He still had no idea what was going on, but he sensed that he needed speed more than information at the moment. He could only control what he could control. Right now, that meant not making obvious choices. St. Petersburg air and rail facilities could be watched. He had to make a decision.

Cat is smart. She and Hedde will be all right.

"I'm coming, baby," he said.

He was two hundred miles from Finland. Finland gave him options.

Lewis decided.

CHAPTER FIVE

- 1 -

"You have a great ass," Jim slurred, and Cat had to bite back a scream before she made it into the bathroom and slapped at the light switch, missing it twice before the row of bulbs over the mirror blinded her and she flinched back.

The feeling had swept over her like a tidal wave while Jim was fucking her, pressing her face first into the mattress in a way that had once seemed violently sexy but was now smothering; the slap of his pelvis against her buttocks not raunchy but laughable.

"Come for me, baby," he kept whispering in her ear, and it was all she could do to fake it, consumed with the idea that the asshole fucking her still hadn't figured out she wouldn't orgasm when he came at her from behind.

She was so incredibly sad.

She braced her palms on the sink and looked at herself, not surprised to see the wet gleam of her eyes beneath a mess of dark hair. She looked haunted and feral, like something out of Dickens, if Dickens had written about cheating wives.

"God…"

The sordid tackiness of the affair had once been both shield and sword against her loneliness. An anger-fed solution to the increasing distance between Lew and herself. A counter to the growing conviction that he was leaving her, had already left her, was in love with another woman. She hadn't seen Jim since before Lew's last trip home. Had told Jim that it was over, a fling. "Let's be grown-ups and enjoy it for what it was," she had said back then, a model of suburban sophistication.

"I knew you'd call again," Jim had told her when she dialed his number from memory after Lew's last call. Distracted Lew. Not listening Lew.

She ran the water and wetted a tissue to wipe herself clean, forcing herself to watch the inelegant task in the mirror. Her nipples were hurting and she looked in his medicine cabinet for some sort of skin cream, but couldn't find anything besides a bottle of men's hair color and Tylenol.

Jim had picked up where they left off, but from the first moment when he peeled up her shirt, it was all wrong. The sight and smell of him, the taste of his cock, the hand smacking her ass, dirty fun that turned out to be just dirt. She felt like a kid who had been playing in the dark only to have the lights switched on and discover she was in a dumpster. Everything about the aftermath of their sex was awful. The reek of his cologne, the red skin of her inner thighs where his rough beard hurt her, the stale beer and cigarette taste of his tongue.

Cat doubled over and wretched up a thin stream of tequila-flavored bile into the sink, cupping her hand to lift water to her mouth.

"Quite a life you've carved out for yourself, Cat," she said to her naked reflection and did the best she could to record every detail about the single unhappiest moment in her life.

Green fingers of mold crawled up the corners of his coffin-like shower stall and Cat decided she could wait until she got home to wash away his stink, even if she had to drive with the window down.

- 2 -

The strains of "Long Cool Woman in a Black Dress" blended with the hiss of air through her open window as she piloted the Jeep Cherokee towards home. She'd stabbed the radio buttons at random, unable to handle the silence or her usual NPR talk radio. She needed something to keep her tethered, afraid of the incredible numbness spreading throughout her mind. The idea that her marriage had likely drifted beyond the point of no return was too enormous, too terrifying to face head on.

There was no single, catastrophic event that came to mind as having set the course towards where she found herself. It was, instead, a series of small decisions and minor cowardices—death by a thousand cuts. The loneliness when Lew started working overseas again. Hedde entering high school, throwing up walls where there had once been open roads between mother and daughter. The decision to work as a consultant from home instead of having the companionship of an office. Isolation had bred not a desire for contact, but a need to turn even further inward.

She looked up and realized she had no idea how long she had been parked in the strip mall. No recollection of pulling over. It was no coincidence that she had parked in front of a liquor store. Day drinking was a new event in her life, but every small, burning sip screamed a warning at her that she had chosen to ignore.

"I don't want it to be over."

The voice wasn't hers. Couldn't be hers. It reminded her of Hedde when she was younger, when she still let them hold her hand, when she still talked to them. *Them*. Cat and Lew. God, she remembered how cool she thought they sounded the first time she'd heard someone else describe them as a couple. The thing is, they *had* been cool. They had been fun. It wasn't fake. It was real. Had been real.

"I don't like this." That same small voice.

A sudden, barking sob burst from her and she wiped at her eyes with the heels of her hands, smearing dark eyeliner, not caring. She threw the Jeep into reverse and nearly backed into a compact car entering the lot, ignoring the irate honk of the horn as she peeled out of the parking lot.

Her phone beeped to let her know there was an incoming message, but she didn't feel solid enough behind the wheel to check it and had zero interest in being hounded about copy deadlines. What was it her friend had said? *There is a fuck I cannot give*. She pulled into a Dunkin' Donuts drive-thru for a necessary cup of coffee and had forgotten about the unread email by the time she pulled into the A&P to pick up groceries for dinner.

- 3 -

HEADBAND.

White light flooded across her vision and a rushing noise filled her ears as the phone tumbled from Cat's grasp.

For a moment, everything ceased.

She gradually became aware of the wetness soaking into the seat of her jeans and found herself sitting on the linoleum floor of her kitchen in a puddle of orange juice, the gloaming of the room relieved by the strident white light of the open refrigerator and the blue glow of her phone.

"No, no, no, no, no, no..."

She pawed amidst the sticky shards of the broken juice bottle and scooped up the dripping phone, noting the jagged lightning bolt that had ripped across the screen, convinced that it was broken, that she had hallucinated, hoping desperately, oh please, that she had not seen the word.

HEADBAND.

A hum arose from the refrigerator and a gust of cool air struck her as the machine struggled to maintain temperature. Cat glanced at her hand and plucked a sliver of glass from the meat below her thumb, absently sucking on it. She tasted like orange juice and copper pennies.

Slowly she rose and began collecting broken glass. She pursed her lips, wondering if she had another pair of clean jeans or if she would need to dig through the laundry.

HEADBAND.

A sound was building inside her, a sound that terrified her. She could feel it swirling, a tornado she was afraid to let out. If she gave in to that sound, she might never stop.

She broke down the key letters from the word Lewis had made her memorize. He had smiled when he told her, but he had been annoyingly persistent until she had played along. A bored Lewis Edgar was a noisy Lewis Edgar, and she was used to his need for minor amusements.

"Okay," she had finally said. "BAND is for bank." She had stolen the bowl of popcorn back from him.

"Hey," he said, grabbing another handful. "Give me the location and box number," he continued through a mouthful.

"Just write it down—"

He waved her quiet. "Never write this down anywhere."

Cat had seen that quick tightness in his jaw and gave in, reciting back the information.

"What's first?"

"Get Hedde," she said. "This isn't much of a code. It might even be a terrible code."

"Doesn't need to hold up under scrutiny for any length, but does need to be easy to remember no matter what the situation."

She forced a too-big handful of popcorn in her mouth and chewed as if it were perfectly normal, despite looking like a chipmunk.

"C'mon, Cat." She couldn't resist his earnest expression.

"Okay, okay," she said, swallowing between okays. "Needy bastard."

"You've grabbed Hedde and hit the bank. Now what?"

"But you can't stand Uncle Gerard."

"It's a good place to go," Lewis said, rising from the couch. She liked the strong line of his shoulder and still thought he had a nice butt, even if he complained that he was out of shape.

"You have to be serious here for a sec, Cat."

"Okay. I mean, I am."

"If you hear this word on the phone, if you get an email from me with this word, just do it, okay? Don't wait around, just follow protocol until I can get in touch with you."

His tone had annoyed her, although a more honest answer might be that he had frightened her. "It's a little 007, don't you think?"

He had stopped what he called the "skulking stuff" when they got married, became "just another office guy." When she pressed him, he told her his job was something like a cross between an ambassador and a Hollywood agent, one of those people that puts together a package of actors and money with a script before a movie gets made. Whenever she tried to dig into his time before her, asked if he'd ever done some movie-worthy undercover stuff, he'd say, "Nope." Lying to her, knowing she knew but not budging an inch.

"HEADBAND," she said, "is stupid."

He smiled. "I know. Just humor me, okay?"

"Okay. If I get the word, I'll drop everything and follow protocol."

Drop everything, that's a laugh. She was cleaning up orange juice from the floor.

"Oh God," she said, dropping the sopping paper towels with a splat. She ran to the counter and grabbed her shoulder bag and keys, then stopped. A terrible feeling gripped her. A penetrating fear that invaded the sunlit safety of her kitchen. Her *family's* kitchen.

Something was really happening.

She grabbed the plastic container full of cat food and tore it off, setting the entire thing on the floor for Mozart.

Hedde.

She grabbed her coat and banged out through the storm door, following the path the neighbor kid had shoveled to get to the car. The Jeep Cherokee had four-wheel drive, one of those things Lew had insisted on.

Get Hedde, then the bank.

She yanked open the driver's side door and stopped, looking around. The afternoon sun reflected blindingly off the white snow covering every rooftop and lawn on the block. Melting icicles hung from eves, refracting light in a kaleidoscope of colors. Billy Pelletier was building a snowman in his front yard. He waved and shouted something at her that she couldn't quite make out.

How can something bad be happening now? she thought. *It's not even that cold out.*

She pulled herself up into the Jeep and pulled the door shut, keying the ignition. The dashboard clock read 2:15 p.m.

If I don't get there soon, Hedde will disappear until supper time.

Cat twisted in the seat and backed carefully down the driveway. There were a lot of little kids like Billy Pelletier on their block, and you could never tell when they'd be right behind you.

In the street she stopped, both hands on the wheel. She was shaking. HEADBAND. She thought she was about to cry and shifted into DRIVE.

Lew, where are you?

CHAPTER
SIX

- 1 -

They thought she was gay. They thought she did drugs. They thought she was "Most Likely to Become a Serial Killer." The fact that the other kids were wrong about everything provided no relief from their contempt, the weight of which Hedde carried with shoulders hunched up to her ears, arms held down straight at her sides as if pushing off the earth.

Okay, she occasionally considered becoming a serial killer, but it probably wasn't in the cards.

She favored long skirts so out of fashion they belonged in yellowed photographs, and wool sweaters, always heavy, always gray, though she varied between pullovers and cardigans. Her boots were scavenged from vintage stores where she paid boutique prices for drab leather, and she cut her own hair when it grew too long. A snip in the front and black hair hit the sink to reveal her eyes. Two or three snips across the back to keep it from falling past her shoulder blades.

They called her Wednesday Addams and Lizzie Borden but lacked the rhyming ability to do much with either. She called them morons and counted them even.

"Did you bring it?" Hedde asked as the circle of girls in the smoking area parted and reformed around her, placing her at the center of the listing gazebo, with its peeling paint and graffiti scars. She saw the glitter of hate in their eyes and scowled back at them from beneath her jagged bangs. She knew the smokers by sight, but today there were new faces in the crowd. Susie Chambers who drew a fucking heart over the *i* in her name. The Abercrombie & Fitch set walking on the wild side.

"Here it is," Sorsha said, pulling a plastic sandwich baggie from the pocket of her green army coat.

"The money," Hedde said.

"Oh, here."

Sorsha pulled a crumpled twenty from her jeans pocket and Hedde snatched it from her hand, making it vanish.

"Okay," Hedde said and took the baggie with its disgusting, sticky mess inside. She produced a pencil from her book bag then let the bag slip from her shoulder to crash on the ground. Feet shifted around her and she realized they were nervous.

"You know if you used these all the time you wouldn't be in this jam," Hedde said.

"C'mon," Sorsha pleaded.

Susie-with-a-heart whispered something about not being such a slut and Sorsha's face went beet red.

Hedde knelt on the ground and fished the messy condom from the bag with the tip of her pencil, grimacing at the stale bleach stink of it.

"All right, do it," Hedde said and handed her grandfather's straight razor to Sorsha, who accepted it as if it would wheel in her hand and slash her.

"Holy shit," one of the girls gasped as Sorsha cut off a thick lock of hair and offered it to Hedde, who quickly fashioned it into a circle that she lowered around the prophylactic before laying the two objects on the dirt.

"This will bind his seed," Hedde said as she pulled a slim flask from her bag. "He won't be able to get you pregnant." She unscrewed the lid and took a swig of tequila, eyes watering before she lowered her face over the fetish and dribbled the liquid from between her puckered lips.

"Can I have a hit?" Some wit.

"Shut up." Some frightened rabbit.

The circle shifted around her when she pulled out the book of matches and struck one alight.

"Don't you need to say anything?" Sorsha asked.

"No," Hedde said.

She lowered the match to the bundle, and a blue flame licked across the alcohol for a brief moment before the hair flared brightly. Everyone recoiled from the smell.

"They used to burn people like you in Salem," Susie-with-a-heart said.

"No they didn't." Hedde looked up from beneath her bangs. She stood, lifting her book bag onto her shoulder and taking a step towards the taller girl. The in-crowd shuffled back. "They used to hang us."

The school bell rang and postponed the confrontation. Hedde moved with the swirling mass of students back towards the low, brick building. Among them but not of them, so consumed with her own thoughts and the lingering awfulness of the tequila on her tongue, that she failed to see her mom's green Jeep screeching into the parking lot.

- 2 -

Cat was approaching the entrance to the high school when the metal double doors boomed open and a horde of teenage boys piled out, a singular mass with dozens of arms, legs and mouths. They streamed around her on either side as she frantically looked for a familiar face.

"Have you seen Hedde?" She asked a passing boy, touching his arm. "Hedde Edgar?"

He shook his head and exchanged loaded looks with a buddy as they continued on. Cat was reaching for the door handle when she heard a burst of cruel laughter behind her, and she looked over her shoulder to see half a dozen older boys looking at her with vulpine grins.

What the hell is happening?

She took a deep breath, fighting down the growing paranoia that was eclipsing her ability to think. She felt muscles pull in her back as she grabbed both doors and dragged them open, stepping through into the dark entrance hall. The bank of overhead fluorescents was buzzing ineffectively. A step ladder had been set up beneath them, but she saw no sign of a custodian. She cast a look back and caught the red glow of the EXIT sign above the doors she had just passed through.

"Can I help you?"

Cat turned too quickly and blurted, "What?"

An older woman with a horrendous pile of immobile hair leaned down to the gap at the bottom of the window and repeated the question.

"Yes, I need to find my daughter immediately," she said.

"And you are?"

"Cat...Catherine Edgar. Her mother."

"And your daughter is?"

"Hedde Edgar," she said, placing both hands on the counter and forcing herself not to scream.

"And the reason you need to—"

There's been a headband.

"There's been a family emergency," Cat said. A manic hilarity threatened her, and she wondered how Miss Beehive 1962 would react to the word HEADBAND. She felt her smile grow plastic as the woman moved several papers aside and produced a clip board with a sign-in sheet.

"Sign in here."

"Do you have a pen?"

- 3 -

Cat stalked the halls of Rifton High, making no effort to hide her desperation. The few students not in class gave her wide berth. One student noted to a friend that Mrs. Edgar, "Looked intense."

The innocent rows of bright blue lockers and the windowed doors into empty classrooms screamed silent threats at Cat. She knew it was ridiculous, but she couldn't stop thinking about those disturbed boys in Colorado who went on a shooting rampage at their school. Of course Lew wouldn't have sent her the message HEADBAND because of something as prosaic as children murdering children.

A detached, clinical part of Cat's mind was stunned at how unhinged Lew's coded message had left her. There was only one reason that it could have stepped on the accelerator and roared past worry, past fear and straight into panic. She believed that her family was in mortal danger. She believed that somewhere on the other side of the world, where she could not help him, her husband's life was in jeopardy. All of her jokes about his past life in Foreign Service were laid bare, exposed for the feeble things they were, fig leaves pathetically draped over her very real fear. *Lew is in Russia, for God's sake.*

The cafeteria doors were up ahead and Cat paused to get control. She didn't want to frighten Hedde.

- 4 -

Study hall was an unending series of sniffles, squeaking chairs and the occasional calls for silence. Sitting alone in a far corner of the cafeteria, Hedde was scratching her pencil back and forth across a page of algebra notes as her mind entered a familiar fugue. When she was younger, she called this state her "listening place." Now she didn't bother to name it, only welcomed it when it came over her.

When Cat strode in and saw half a dozen kids scattered about the lunch tables, surrounded by books and papers, Hedde dropped her head as if to hide.

"Hedde," she called out. Heads rose around the room, looking up at the odd disturbance. "Hedde, come here right now."

Oh my God, what is she doing? Hedde thought as she hurried to gather her things, hoping to escape the tittering scrutiny of her classmates with as little damage as possible.

"Give me some Hedde," someone sang out in a falsetto voice, and she ducked her face, hurrying away before she realized her mistake and spun back to snatch her notebook from the table.

She paused a moment before slapping the notebook shut.

There, in her own broken handwriting, the scribbles had decided to form a word: MOM.

- 5 -

Cat pulled out of the parking lot and onto Milk Street, Hedde safely in the back seat. A confused roar filled her ears, and she struggled to remember the protocol she was supposed to follow.

The bank. A lock box at the bank.

She turned left at the light, checking her rearview mirror for anything out of order. Not that she had any idea what to look for.

Hedde was listing a litany of complaints, but Cat could barely hear them as she struggled to choke back a sob.

CHAPTER SEVEN

- 1 -

The bank was in a small town a few miles from the Vermont border. A one-story brick affair on a street lined with many other one-story buildings. The tallest structure Hedde could see was a steeple dominating the circular park in the center of town. She felt a pressure growing in her chest, even worse than she felt at home. A trapped feeling, imagining a long life of work in a FedEx store, or waiting tables at a sports bar. The screaming need to escape, always thrumming below the surface in Hedde's thoughts, was bad enough where they lived in Westchester County. In this burg it burned in her like a fever.

"Here we are," her mother said.

Like most kids, Hedde was well-attuned to the emotional state of her parents. Something in her mother's voice sounded like a guitar string stretched to breaking, and while she hadn't expected constructive responses to her earlier complaints, the complete lack of explanation left her cold.

Cat pulled the Jeep into one of the diagonal spots on the street and opened the door. "Stay right here," she said. "I'll only be a minute."

"It's El Mysterioso, isn't it?"

Cat tensed as if expecting a blow. "Don't call him that."

"Are we leaving dad?"

"No, honey. Never."

Cat turned around and her melting, plastic smile sent tendrils of unease worming through Hedde's stomach.

"I'll be right back," Cat said.

The slamming car door seemed to echo for several minutes in the quiet.

Her hair's a mess. She never goes out like that, and there's a big stain on the ass of her jeans. Not to mention that she looks batshit crazy.

"Screw him," Hedde said, jamming the earbud back into place and slumping into the corner of her seat.

- 2 -

Cat stood in the privacy booth with the heavy length of the metal safety deposit box on the counter in front of her. It was a combination lock, not a key lock, and it took her three tries before she rotated the numbers to the correct position. She felt like Pandora on the verge of a terrible mistake.

"Lew, I'm not ready," she complained to the emptiness. The closed box offered no answers.

Her left hand crept up to her mouth. "Like a Band-Aid," she muttered, and pulled the top of the box open.

"Oh God," she said.

A black .38 revolver lay on top of several envelopes. The greasy, metal truth of the gun took her breath away. It was an inelegant thing, demonstrating a pure, functional ugliness. It was not her life.

She reached out, almost dazed, and picked up the weapon in her right hand.

The surprising weight of the gun was undeniable. *All of this is really happening.* Six brass shells winked from inside the cylinder. The words Smith & Wesson were stamped into the metal along the short barrel.

She placed it next to the box.

The envelope beneath it had her name typed on it, so she opened it and dumped the contents on the counter.

A New Hampshire driver's license with her picture on it carried the name STELLA DUMAIN and she started to cry, smiling in spite of herself. *Stella?* She thought. *Really, Lew? Stella?* He hated the film and refused to see a stage performance. "Brando talks like he has a mouth full of oatmeal," was his refrain every time she brought it up. She felt his jest in the choice of the name. It was as if he were standing in the small privacy booth with her.

A US passport and two credit cards were also under the same name, as was a typed note. She set that aside and lifted a thick envelope from the box, knowing it was cash before she opened it.

"Sweet Jesus," she muttered, thumbing through the bills. She flashed briefly to an image of herself in a glittering dress on the arm of a gangster. This was not a life of groceries and copywriting and a daughter who was secretly smoking cigarettes.

She stuffed the envelope into an inner pocket of her coat and picked up the folded note.

CAT,

1. RUN FAST. STAY ALIVE.

The note began to tremble in her hand and Cat stilled herself with an effort.

2. NO SAFETY ON GUN.
POINT AND SHOOT. DO NOT HESITATE.

"Oh God, Lew, what *is* this?"

3. DESTROY ALL CELL PHONES.
CAN TRACK BY GPS. THEY ARE LISTENING.
USE THIS PHONE ONLY.

An older model cell phone was in the box.

4. GO TO GERARD'S. LISTEN TO GERARD.
DO NOT LEAVE GERARD'S.

5. DO NOT USE EMAIL.
THEY ARE WATCHING.

6. PROTECT YOURSELF. PROTECT OUR BABY.

I LOVE YOU.
LEW

At the bottom of the note was a handwritten sentence, Lew's jagged penmanship unmistakable.

I AM COMING.

CHAPTER EIGHT

Evgeny rolled onto his back and bellowed, "Zoya!" The effort made his head pound, and he sat up with a groan of effort and a ripping flatulence.

I feel terrible, he thought, a sentiment so common that he barely noticed it anymore.

"Zoya!"

Evgeny staggered to the bathroom of the opulent bedroom to puke in a gold-lined sink and piss in the antique tub. In the silence following his various efforts at excretion, he noticed that the wind had died down, and a glance out the window told him the storm had stopped.

Pulling on a silk kimono, he lumbered towards the stairs and made his way down, hand on the rail for balance.

"Zoya!"

The air downstairs was ice cold and Evgeny felt his balls tighten, forcing him to belt the kimono closed over his massive belly.

The sliding glass door was open.

"Durak," he muttered. *Stupid*. He plodded barefoot across the cold floor and was reaching for the door when his foot slipped on slick tiles.

Evgeny fell hard and lay stunned on the floor for nearly a minute before he registered the wet smear he was resting in.

He struggled awkwardly to a sitting position and noticed, with dawning horror, the red dripping from his palms.

"Govno," he swore, staggering upright to see that a trail of blood led out through the sliding door and onto the snow beyond.

Evgeny shut the sliding door and locked it, then lumbered for the phone in his study and discovered why Zoya wasn't answering him.

The woman's severed head was resting upright on the desk where his computer should be. Her eyelids had been stapled open, and he recoiled from the dead stare of the milky orbs.

A sudden, massive blow struck him in the chest, and Evgeny clutched himself, squeezing the meat of his chest between white knuckles as he fell into the doorway. He made it three steps into the hall before falling to his knees, his face ashen.

"Pomogi myne," he whispered. *Help me.*

Blackness swirled around the edges of his vision as he fumbled for the medical alert bracelet on his left wrist.

His last thought was, *Did I push the button?* before unconsciousness took him.

CHAPTER
NINE

- 1 -

Chambers trailed the pale man along Washington DC's National Mall, passing a crowd of tourists braving the winter weather. He thought the man might be an albino afflicted with alopecia, rendering him completely hairless. The suit and overcoat contributed to the idea, a faint gray that matched his wintry eyes. Chambers suspected that, seen quickly, the man's face would be a featureless blur. Not a bad trait for a spy.

"Bierce?"

The pale man turned and Chambers saw the dusty hint of stubble on his brows. He felt a chill that had nothing to do with the season. *What kind of man shaves off his eyebrows?*

"I'm Chambers."

Neither man offered their hand.

"Have we met?" Bierce asked.

"No."

Bierce's gray overcoat hung in neat lines. Chambers wore a beige London Fog. The tourists milling around them displayed a panoply of colors.

"Lewis Edgar is one of yours?" Chambers asked.

Bierce studied the naked branches of a cherry tree as they passed beneath.

"Russian authorities have an all-points out for him in relation to a homicide," Chambers said. A portly man, he was breathing more heavily than Bierce. "Neighbor found his girlfriend's severed head as a good morning present and promptly had a heart attack. Emergency arrived and called the police who followed a blood trail through the woods to Edgar's house. They found the rest of the girlfriend there."

"Any idea where Edgar is?" Bierce asked with a brief smile. Chambers noticed that his teeth were unusually small and regular.

"I was about to ask you the same thing. They, uh, have an idea he is one of ours."

"Of course they do," Bierce said. "We know who they are and they know who we are, and we all go about our business quietly."

"Until one of ours chops a girl's head off," Chambers said, coughing into his hand. He fished out a roll of Hall's from his pocket and grimaced as he put a lozenge on his tongue. *Lemon my ass*, he thought.

Bierce stopped and fixed an unblinking gaze on the shorter man.

"Lewis Edgar did not do this. He's a family man."

"Speaking of family, the Bureau would like to bring them in. See if Edgar has been in touch."

Bierce nodded. "By all means."

"And you'll call me if he contacts you?" Chambers kept his tone casual, but like many in the Federal Bureau of Investigation, he disliked dealing with spooks and all of their shadowy bullshit.

"I'll be in touch," Bierce said, turning to leave. A hand on his arm stopped him. Chambers smiled.

"If you were going to bet, you think the Russians will catch him?" Chambers asked.

"I don't gamble."

Chambers's smile widened as he sensed how much his presence offended Bierce. "What I want to know...is Edgar any good?"

Bierce eased his arm free from Chambers's hand.

"Years ago, he was in Chechnya for a while, but now he buys and sells things and listens for us. He's a family man, as I said, and has settled into a job suitable to his familial responsibilities."

"So he's not gonna get away?"

"He didn't do this thing."

"Not what I asked."

Chambers let the silence stretch out a bit before turning to look up at the Washington Monument. "You know, I barely even notice that thing anymore."

He walked away and was soon lost in the crowd.

Bierce sat down on an empty bench and thought about the strange call he had received last night immediately after hanging up on Edgar. There had been no voice on the other end, yet Bierce found himself unable to hang up.

Instead, he had listened to the sound of quiet breathing from thousands of miles away.

- 2 -

The decision was made as soon as Chambers walked away, but Bierce remained on the bench. To anyone watching, he was a man unhurried, unworried. Still, when a shadow fell over the bright crowds, he cast a gaze skyward, fighting back a shiver as a cloud slid across the sun.

He walked to the L'Enfant plaza metro stop at Maryland and 7th Street, pausing to purchase a coffee from a sidewalk vendor and using the moment to look around in the event Chambers had friends. His mind was working rapidly, despite the unruffled demeanor he had presented to the FBI man.

While he sipped he availed himself of the least unpleasant of the public phones at the station.

"We have a problem," he said. The remainder of the terse conversation boiled down to a single sentence from his superiors: *Your problem, deal with it.*

The special nature of Bierce's duties made him pariah. If his project went off the rails, no one would come near him.

He closed his eyes as he replaced the receiver in the cradle, wondering if Lewis Edgar had felt the same trill of fear when his superior, Bierce himself, had cut him loose.

He dialed a new number, and after identifying himself and being relayed to a broker, relayed a string of interspersed digits and letters. "Move it immediately," he said.

"Consider it done. I'll have the new account information—"

Bierce interrupted him. "I will call you for the information." He hung up.

Riding the escalator down amidst a chattering flock of tourists in bright plumage, interspersed with government employees in various shades of gray, Bierce felt as if the clean, autumn air was replaced by something thicker. More than the result of too many people gathered together below ground. He hesitated a moment as the escalator neared the bottom and the stairs beneath his feet were hurled towards chewing metal—

Bierce shook off the image and stood taller, unconsciously straightening his tie, navigating around the throngs of the confused as he contemplated what-ifs.

He emerged from the metro three stops later amidst a crowd of loud young men with sagging pants and oversized, puffy winter coats, ignoring the casual insults, "Hey, Marshmallow Man" and "Yo, Snowflake, where the summer gone?" He accidentally kicked a bottle and they laughed as it shattered against a drain grate.

Bierce had walked for only one block north before a cab responded to his raised hand, and he took that to the imposing edifice of Saint Matthew's Cathedral. He entered a throng of tourists outside the double doors and wondered if it was merely his mood or had even the tourists grown more somber? His ear caught something that might have been Hungarian, and he wrote off the lack of chatter as a reflection of Eastern Europe, not his task.

Face obscured by the clouds of his breath, he used the visitors as a scraper to remove any tails before hurrying towards a couple just exiting a cab at the curb.

"Hold that for me please?"

They did and he slid onto the still-warm vinyl of the backseat, cracking the window, despite the cold, as a salve for the driver's body odor. They wound their way southeast, the driver admirably using his horn on both crowded and open streets as the buildings shrunk into squat things with peeling paint, and the statues grew more obscure, until eventually they left the landmarks and government buildings behind altogether.

At one intersection a legless man in a wheelchair waited on the corner, bundled in layers, his jutting stumps wrapped in beach towels secured with mismatched belts. Bierce started when he realized the man was staring back at him through the window of the cab. Nearby, a crowd was gathered outside of a liquor store, half-heartedly jeering a woman wheeling a shopping cart. Bierce was struck by the visible process of the city's decay since leaving Chambers and the opulence of DC's National Mall. He struggled to write it off as urban blight and not a result of *Him*. And still, an unquiet part of his mind wondered if *His* presence created decay, or if the state of locales in decline drew *Him*, like the rotting nectar for some unholy bee.

"Here?" the driver asked when they pulled up to the cracked sidewalk in front of the old, three-story building with a Chinese take-out restaurant and bail bondsmen advertising in bright neon in the plate glass windows of the first floor.

Bierce shook off his thoughts, mindful of them now, bracing himself against their return.

"Thank you," he said, holding a twenty over the front seat. "Keep the change." He tried not to react to the sight of the cabbie's yellow, phlegmatic eyes but saw the man's lip curl in disdain and knew he had failed.

Bierce produced a key as he approached the narrow, metal fire door between the two businesses, grimacing as he stepped over a sticky red mess of discarded barbecue and turned the key in the lock before stepping into darkness. The space reeked of rancid grease from the take-out place and something less tangible, yet uglier, from the bail bondsman, but he paid neither any heed.

A weak light flickered into being overhead when he flipped the wall switch, and Bierce ascended the narrow staircase, the toe of his shoe catching more than once on the cracked linoleum. At the top was another locked door, this one with pebbled glass and the faded lettering of a long-dead business. He brushed cobwebs off a mezuzah affixed to the doorframe.

If Bierce had a romantic train of thought he might have imagined the space as the office of a former private investigator, a Sam Spade type who entertained tough-talking dames and broken-down men, whiskey drinkers and cigarette smokers. He was not a romantic, however, and inserted yet another key into the lock with nary a stir of his imagination.

The air was stale and his passage stirred up dust, which he took as a positive sign that the office had entertained no visitors since his last check. Bierce removed a handkerchief from an inner pocket and held it over his nose as he closed the door. He glanced around the dim space, noting the absence of light from the windows before producing a small flashlight in his right hand.

It was a dismal space of yellowing walls and floor tiles, their corners curling with age. Dust and a vaguely oily miasma lingered in the air and had settled over the two metal desks and ancient swivel chairs with chewed seat cushions. A dirty, black wastebasket sat next to one desk, and a lonely fly hovered over it, likely starving but drawn to old smells. The window shades had been fixed in place with thumbtacks, and Bierce ran a finger over the bottom of each. They were secure.

It was a colorless place, uninteresting enough to be almost deliberately so. The faded wall calendar displayed a frigate from the age of sail and showed anyone who cared which day was which in August of 1998.

Bierce placed his handkerchief on the floor on front of the metal file cabinet and lowered one knee onto it before pulling out the bottom drawer, wheels squeaking on the runners. Only a careful eye would note that the drawer was not long enough to account for the depth of the file cabinet.

He winced at the gritty feel of the floor as he braced himself on one palm and aimed the light into the empty cave left by the drawer, and then placed the flashlight on the ground, reaching past it to turn the combination of the small safe hidden within the recesses of the cabinet.

Removing the files took only a moment, but they slipped from his fingers as he stood and several sheets of old paper slid free. He snatched up the flashlight and played the beam across the floor, chasing the fluttering ghost shapes see-sawing through the air.

Two were easily located, but a third glided silently beneath a desk and he had to crawl after it, ignoring the dirt griming the knees of his trousers. Shipping paperwork for a large crate, six feet by fifteen feet. Faded customs stamps circa 1948. He fed it back into the file and rose again.

There were two more objects he required.

He crouched and reached in blindly as demanded by the awkward angle, as tense as a trout noodler reaching into a swampy river hole beneath the water's surface. His fingers probed tentatively, as if at any moment he would feel the searing snap of a mouse trap, or worse, needle-sharp teeth. Instead they located a smooth object and he pulled it free—a small case in black leather, rounded and held closed by silver snaps. It bore a resemblance to a shaving kit his father—or, more likely, grandfather—might have carried.

Bierce sniffed against the dust, and a single bead of sweat dug a river through the grime that had settled on his temple. He reached inside, eyes closed and fingers splayed, until they felt the ugly warmth of the last item and pulled it free. It was always the last retrieved for reasons no one had ever explained. Bierce, in a rare moment of inebriation, had opined that it was last retrieved because it wanted to be last.

He had never shared the sentiment again for a variety of reasons.

It was a small book, perhaps the size of a young girl's diary, if young girls still kept diaries and if said diaries were bound in human skin.

Cut into the cover were words that he studiously avoided reading. It was wise to read only what was needed in this volume and no more.

Bierce was already heading for the door with his finds before remembering to turn back and close the safe, returning the file cabinet to its former, uninteresting appearance.

He paused again, slowly dragging the beam from his flashlight around the edges of the room, crouching to peer under the desks.

The file was intact. Nothing else had escaped. Still, he had to be careful. Bad luck, accidents and foolish happenstance hovered around these particular papers in an invisible cloud of unexpected possibilities.

Holding the file to his chest, he left the office and locked the door behind him, descending with more haste than he had used mere minutes before, vaguely aware that his pulse was racing by the time he emerged onto the sidewalk and closed the heavy fire door.

Sweat beaded on his upper lip and he wiped it away, frowning at the dirty smear on his fingers and thinking thoughts of corruption.

The light outside had grown grayer as the sun slid towards the west, and Bierce took a moment to glance around but detected no interest from the few derelicts on the street. Several blocks away, a man sang drunkenly as he rolled slowly up the sidewalk in a wheelchair. It was not the same man. Surely it was not.

Somewhere, a car horn bleated and Bierce set off on foot, dwelling on what-ifs and preparations for such.

CHAPTER
TEN

- 1 -

It was well past sundown when the Edgars reached Flintlock.

Empty storefronts with peeling FOR RENT signs lined either side of the street, and lifeless houses hunched under a heavy mantle of snow. The Jeep's tires crunched over frozen sand on the tar, so she knew there were some municipal services functioning, but there were no street lights to be seen, and the town seemed deserted.

She knew from the last letter Uncle Gerard had sent that recession had hit the northern New Hampshire town brutally hard. The textile mill, the area's main employer, had closed a decade before, and many of the residents that hung on after its closure were on public assistance. The town had enjoyed a brief respite when a group of Massachusetts developers built a winter resort in the nearby foothills, but a fire destroyed the property and it was not rebuilt.

More people left the town. Those that stayed hunkered down under the slate gray skies in the shadow of the mountains.

Gerard had ended the letter, "God does not smile on Flintlock."

Guilt washed through her in a wave as Cat realized that she had never written back. It was one of those things that she meant to get to, but between Lew's travels and growing worry about Hedde's estrangement, she never seemed to get around to it. A year had passed without her ever seriously thinking about her uncle.

Now she was planning to show up unannounced on his doorstep to beg for help.

Cat's eyes closed under the unrelenting weight of emotional exhaustion. It was only for a moment, but long enough to miss the patch of black ice that the sand had not reached.

She felt the slide in the pit of her stomach and wrenched the wheel over, but the tires found no traction on the slick surface and she hit the frozen snowbank with a loud crunch. Glass tinkled as her headlights shattered and she was wrenched hard against her safety belt. There was a hard thump against the back of her seat as Hedde was hurled into it.

"You okay?" Cat asked, unbuckling her belt to turn around. Hedde was picking herself up from the footwell.

"I'm fine," Hedde said with disgust.

Cat was stretched to the limit of her endurance and had only enough energy for basic functions.

The engine was still running, so she shifted into reverse and pressed her foot down on the gas pedal. The Jeep lurched, but even with four-wheel drive it couldn't pull itself free. The front tires were stuck, and the rear wheels spun on the frictionless ice.

Cat shook herself. The engine was racing and she eased her foot off the gas.

"If we still had cell phones we could call a tow truck," Hedde said.

Cat opened her mouth but found herself unable to speak. A sob wracked her body and she felt hot tears sting her eyes.

She leaned forward until her forehead rested on the steering wheel, and she began to weep.

- 2 -

Hedde touched the lump on her forehead and thought about getting out of the Jeep and just walking away into the night. Her mother had gone insane and thrown out her iPhone. Now she had stuck them in a snowbank and was crying like a lunatic.

Uncle Gerard the redneck. The townie's townie. God, she would kill for a cigarette, even a menthol.

She looked up at her window and saw a face pressed against the glass. For several long seconds every muscle in Hedde's body locked.

Then she screamed.

CHAPTER ELEVEN

- 1 -

The axe blade split a length of stove wood with a single blow, and the big man had to brace a boot on the stump before yanking the axe free.

He bent down and grabbed another length in one scarred hand, positioning it on the stump to stand upright. He grunted as he swung the axe and split the wood. Glowing embers drifted from the end of a hand-rolled cigarette dangling from the corner of his mouth.

It was a clear, cold night and moonlight painted his property in silvers and grays. The work and a checked flannel shirt were enough to keep him warm.

He freed the axe. Placed another piece of wood on the stump. Swung.

The stump was broad enough across to serve as a table top and squatted in the crooked shadow of its brother oak tree. Some years back, when the textile mill was still employing townsfolk, a man named Buddy LaChaise told a story about the stump, at that time a tree. He said it used to be called Dead Nigger Tree, the name reflecting an incident of violence involving the Underground Railroad.

"The dead niggers involved," as Buddy explained it, "escaped the South only to find that white men in the North didn't want their kind either."

Gerard had decided that he disliked both the story and the way Buddy told it. The discussion that followed had left Buddy LaChaise with a permanent limp, and that night the very same axe that was now splitting wood had chopped the tree off at the base.

Later it was whispered that the wrong tree had been chopped down, but it wasn't whispered often. Buddy LaChaise's limp saw to that.

Another stove length felt the bite of the axe and the man paused, leaving the blade buried in the stump. He slipped a metal flask from his back pocket and took a hit of Canadian Club, ambrosia of the North. The whiskey burned a path straight down to his stomach, and he wiped the back of his hand across his lips, feeling the whiskers grown in since he had last remembered to shave.

He stepped back from his work and glanced over the hillside and its incongruous forest of Christmas trees in carefully organized rows, poised like a phalanx of short evergreens ready to assault the jumbled forest beyond. They were coming in well, except for the Douglas firs. But he had a few nobles that topped eight feet, and most of the Frasers stood around six feet, which is where most of his customers wanted them. Claire Whitman at the MLO—Methodist Ladies Organization—had once suggested holding a tree cutting festival on Beaumont's land but was quickly talked out of it. She was new in town, after all, and didn't know any better.

Soon enough the trees would belong to anyone with fifty dollars and a saw, but for now they were his, and he enjoyed their squat presence and the clean smell they lent to the air around his home.

Gerard took another hit from his flask and hissed at the ugly taste. He didn't cut wood every night, but it had become an irregular ritual since the evening of LaChaise's story. If, as he had heard it whispered, the wrong tree had been cut down, he figured the murdered folks were most likely to let him know during dark hours, and he could set things right. That this was not a thought he shared went without saying, and no one ever asked him about his nocturnal wood-chopping habits. He was content to let the few townsfolk who even remembered he existed think him strange and bitter, knocking about in his big, drafty house on the hill.

Gerard Beaumont was a man built to be alone.

- 2 -

The dog started barking and Gerard stood up from his chair beside the fireplace, already pissed. He stopped to pull on his boots, but was otherwise wearing only jeans and a thermal undershirt when he banged out the front door to see headlights winding their way up his long driveway. He grabbed a big handful of salt crystals from the sack by the door, scattering them in a wide arc across the frozen walkway to give a little traction if he had to do the unthinkable and invite someone inside.

Detouring past the stump, he yanked the axe free before meeting the vehicle at the top of his driveway. The headlights blinded him as it pulled up and stopped behind the covered bulk of his ongoing automotive project, a 1969 Camaro.

Gerard threw an arm over his eyes.

"Turn off your goddamned lights," he said as the driver's side door opened. A moment later the lights went off and Gerard recognized the broad shouldered form of Giancarlo Messina, the local Catholic witch doctor.

"Gerry," Messina said.

"Father Messina, it's too goddamned late to cut a tree." Gerard said, blinking to get back his night vision. He had just realized that Messina was towing another vehicle when a door popped open and a woman leapt out.

"Found something of yours in a snowbank," Father Messina said, nodding back to the Jeep he was towing.

"Gerard," Cat said, running up to him and wrapping her arms around his middle, burying her face in his chest. He could feel her sobbing against him and was so surprised that it took him a moment to realize who she was.

"Cat?" Gerard said, awkwardly patting her back.

He looked up at the sound of another door opening and saw a teenager staring at him with fear in her eyes. The priest rested his hand on her shoulder and ushered her forward, speaking quietly.

"I'll unhook the Jeep," the priest said as Gerard looked down at the wild red hair of his niece.

"Best come inside," he said to the top of Cat's head.

CHAPTER
TWELVE

- 1 -

Uncle Gerard's smell filled the dimly lit kitchen. Sweat, whiskey and cigarettes competing with the more pleasant scent of the black iron woodstove in the corner. The chemical salt odor of canned soup was ingrained in the table and the exposed wood of the floor. Cat wondered how much of the stuff you had to eat to leave such an indelible scent.

"No way. Dad?" Hedde said, scorn writ large in the twist of her lip.

Uncle Gerard just grunted, reading the note Lewis had left for Cat. He held it out and Hedde snatched it.

"His work changed, but he never left Foreign Service," Cat said.

"This is total bullshit," Hedde said, looking up from the note and crumpling it.

Cat pulled the new passport and driver's license from her purse and tossed them on the table. Hedde picked them both up and her brows furrowed even deeper.

"And this," Cat said, laying the revolver on the table.

Uncle Gerard and Hedde reached for it at the same time, but the teenager pulled her hand back when the older man showed no sign of relinquishing the weapon. He expertly flipped open the cylinder and emptied the bullets onto the table, his thick fingers surprisingly nimble.

"These are meant to do some harm," he said, picking one up and examining it. "Hollow points." He fixed his eyes on Cat. "And you don't know anything else 'cept this note and the code word Lewis sent?"

"Just that he's in trouble and thinks we might be too," she said.

Gerard handed the empty pistol to Hedde, who balanced it on her palm, surprised at the weight.

"Dad hates guns," Hedde said.

"Then your father made a hard choice," Gerard said. "Sending you to me must've been a hard choice too."

"We'll only be here overnight—" Cat began, but a shake of Gerard's head silenced her.

"You'll be here until this thing is done," he said.

"But Dad's such a…such a…" She couldn't match the long-held image of her father with the cold reality of the pistol in her hand. "He throws dinner parties."

Gerard took the gun back and reloaded it, snapping the cylinder closed with a flick of his wrist. He slid it across the table to Cat.

"I don't want it."

"It's yours."

"When were you going to tell me he was in the CIA?" Hedde asked.

"You're father planned to tell you when you turned eighteen," Cat said.

Hedde sprang from her seat, eyes blurring. The chair toppled over and she made no move to catch it. "This is such bullshit."

She turned like an automaton and stalked from the kitchen with her palms pressed down by her sides. Cat rose when she heard the front door bang open.

Gerard waved Cat back to her seat. "Etienne," he said, voice thrumming deep in his chest.

Cat heard claws scrabble on wood and a dark shadow ambled into the kitchen, red tongue lolling from a black snout. He wore the scars on his face and a mangled ear like a record of his conquests.

"Find her," Gerard said, and the dog trotted from the room, claws clicking on the tile.

"Is this really happening?" Cat asked.

Gerard nodded.

- 2 -

Accustomed to solitary reflection, Gerard realized that he had spoken more in one evening than he had in the last month. It had been years since anyone had sat at the kitchen table with him.

He looked through the frost-covered panes of glass on the front door to see his niece divided into a thousand prisms as she sat on the stump beneath the hanging tree. A dark girl in some strange, old timey dress, as if she lived in a faded black-and-white picture. The black bulk of Etienne nosed at the hands covering her face and she shoved him away. The dog settled onto his haunches, watching her.

Family is family, even Cat's husband, Gerard thought. Even if Lewis did throw dinner parties.

CHAPTER
THIRTEEN

- 1 -

From the outside, passersby saw ancient ruins draped in a wintery white mantle. Inside, it smelled like a portable chemical toilet in the height of summer.

"Haluat seksiä hänen kanssaan?" the cadaverous Finn asked over the crashing death metal erupting from a brand new Bose speaker. He leaned over and placed a rolled euro note to his right nostril. In the flickering candlelight the shirtless dealer looked like a walking corpse, his eyes lost in deep sockets, his white-blond hair cut close to the scalp and invisible.

"Fuck her? She's dead," Lewis replied in Finnish.

The Finn snorted a line of coke off the low table and leaned back, eyes closing. He reached over, without looking, to the woman sprawled next to him on the stained couch and pinched a nipple through the bra she wore as a top.

"She's just resting," the Finn said.

Lewis glanced around the stone interior of the abandoned church. Violent graffiti covered the walls, and empty bottles and crumpled fast food wrappers littered the cracked tiles of the floor. One wall was charred by recent fire. He had been awake for close to two days, hurrying across the Finnish border and then searching for a man like the one in front of him.

"Like I said," the Finn spoke up, doling out another line of fine, powdery cocaine. "We don't do cars, Mr. Cop." He smiled, and receding gums gave his blackened teeth vulpine length.

Lewis shook his head and took the rolled euro. "If you were as heavy as I'd heard, you could move a car. Think of it as a test."

Lewis leaned over and inhaled expertly, the drug burning in his nasal passage. His eyes watered and he wiped away a drip of snot. When he looked up, the skeleton man was pointing a chromed revolver at him.

"I hate tests! I flunk tests!" The Finn screamed, laughing. "But I will take your car anyway, Mr. Cop."

Lewis shrugged.

"They used to hang people here, when the Soviets came," the Finn said, gesturing at the fire-blackened beams overhead. "How about we hang you and use you for target practice?"

Lewis leaned over and snorted the remainder of the white line off the table. "This is *good* shit," he said in a language of the north Caucasus region, keeping the desperate hope off of his face. "But your taste in music is just shit, period."

His seat squeaked as he turned to see the young Russian kid on guard by the door move into the candlelight. The pimple-faced twenty-something had his hand on the butt of a pistol jutting from the waistband of his jeans. The leather jacket he wore was covered with metal studs, and he had skipped the shirt beneath it. *Haut couture in the Scandinavian drug set*, Lewis thought.

"Aapo," he said to the dealer. Lewis thought the kid's name might have been Alex.

"What?" the dealer screamed, strings of spit flying from his fishlike lips. "I'm doing business with Mr. Cop!"

The guard hesitated, eyes darting between Lewis and his boss, before he circled around and whispered in the dealer's ear. Lewis leaned back, relaxed, his hand closer to his pocket. He realized that what he had thought were intricate, blue tattoos on the dealer's bare torso were actually a network of prominent veins.

The dealer looked angry and whispered back. Lewis heard the word "Chechnya" mentioned more than once as he eased the pistol from his pocket. They hadn't even removed his coat when they frisked him, and the small weapon had been easy to keep hidden.

"Bullshit," the dealer said, turning to Lewis. The cadaverous eyes went wide in the split second before Lewis shot the young guard in the knee. The half-dressed girl on the couch opened her eyes and screamed louder than the writhing man on the floor. She sprang up, racing from the room without a backward glance.

Lewis stared down the barrel of the Finn's huge weapon, his own discreet automatic held steady on the other's chest. The guard continued to wail.

Abruptly, the Finn smiled. "See, she's not dead. You want to fuck her now, Mr. Chechen?"

Lewis smiled back. "Call me Strigoi."

- 2 -

The commuter train hurried along the tracks, passing safety lights that bathed the interior with periodic flashes of orange brilliance. Lewis slumped on a maroon bench in the dim car, just another weary traveler. He planned to convert the considerable amount of cocaine on his person into cash in Helsinki. Not only was the capital city home to a boisterous club and drug scene, it was a safe distance away from the Mercedes.

He was sure the expensive vehicle he had traded for the drugs had a tracking system built into it.

"Dammit," he muttered, wiping his dripping nose. He noticed a woman a few seats ahead of him was sitting sideways in her seat, staring at him. Her face was a mass of gray seams, eyes like bitter, black raisins buried in creases of fat beneath a surprisingly colorful hat from which a few white wisps of hair escaped. Orange light filled the car, and for a brief moment her shadow climbed up the wall behind her.

Lewis looked down at his lap.

He had achieved safe distance with speed and considerable luck. But he thought he could feel them, or *Him*, right on his heels, the rasping breath of Mister White hot on the back of his neck. Some fading, rational part of his mind knew that fatigue and shock were generating an internal wave of paranoia, but his rational mind was powerless to resist.

Above all he needed time to think. *What was happening? Who was Mister White? What did Abel have to do with anything? Why had Bierce warned him and then cut him loose?*

Abel.

Bierce.

"No," Lewis said under his breath.

Declared "beyond sanction" meant that Lewis did not dare contact any agency assets, and it also denied him access to agency resources. It left him alone and vulnerable.

Easy to clean up.

This was not agency, even if Bierce was involved. This smelled like freelance. It smelled like Abel. Lewis had already been looking at Abel, wondering why he had been allowed to color outside of the lines for so long.

Abel and Bierce.

And now it was being cleaned up, except Lewis was in the loop as well.

The sinking feeling he had was more than just a cocaine crash. It would take all of his experience, care and the funds he could scrape up to get him to Munich and the very important locker waiting for him there.

And then, if he was very, very lucky, he would make it to America.

Did you follow instructions, Cat? Are you all right?

The very idea of his family had taken on a surreal quality, far less real than the warm breath in his ear whispering wordless threats.

"Sätt en kula i huvudet." *Put a bullet in your head.* Lewis jerked around in his seat to see a young man with a blonde beard sitting in the row behind him, eyes closed and buds in his ears, muttering along to some Swedish musical monstrosity. He turned forward and slumped lower.

Lewis had shot a man just hours ago. He was smuggling drugs taped to his torso while his family, far away, was dealing with school and home. He had illegally crossed an international border and planned on crossing more before he was finished. He had sent his family fleeing from their safe haven and into a world he thought he had left behind.

It's all coming back too easily, he thought. The veil he had draped across the past turned out to be a gossamer thing and no protection at all.

As the drugs wore off, he felt the crash coming on and leaned his head back against the vibrating glass of the train's window.

He twitched awake at the next stop and sat up straight, confused until he saw the old woman in the brightly colored cap still staring at him. He closed his eyes again, aware of the weight of her regard until the swaying train worked its will on his tired body.

Tension drained away in waves, and the sound of the metal wheels clacking rapidly along the tracks lulled him into a troubled dream in which his family was being chased by faceless men for reasons they would not share.

CHAPTER
FOURTEEN

Alex drove a vintage Yugo like a racecar driver, sliding around icy turns, bouncing off the packed snowbanks and daring himself to get home with both headlights intact. The white walls blew past him so fast he could not make out any details. Trees were a blur and the stars overhead were streaking as if he was attaining light speed.

Fuck, it's only a Yugo, he thought. His leg hurt where the bullet had clipped it, but they made pills for that shit and he was flying high, the bandage around his knee crusted brown already.

"Maailma ilman Jumalaa," he screamed at the windshield. The title lyrics to Convulse's "World Without God." *Finnish death metal to beat all death metal. Fuck the Swedes.*

At twenty-one years old, Alex knew about death metal, selling drugs and the hell of serving in the Red Army's disgraceful ass-kicking in Chechnya.

Now he could add the selling of stolen luxury cars to that list.

He howled with laughter as he caught the corner of a snowbank and lost his left headlight. He knew fuck all about racecar driving, but fuck it!

Aapo would be pleased at how easily he had moved that Chechen's Mercedes. Maybe he would let him start his own sales, or at least fuck Narttu.

He skidded under a pair of leafless, overarching trees into the decrepit church's driveway, and his headlights picked up the stone structure rising from the snow. Narttu thought it was so old it was haunted, but Aapo said she did too much coke to know anything.

"World without God!" he screamed again, even though the next song was playing. He turned off the engine before reaching a complete stop, and the car lurched and farted as the music died.

The car door resisted when he tried to open it, so Alex hit it with a shoulder and it popped halfway open with a squeal. He slithered out.

"Shit," he said in Finnish. Cursing in his adopted language was still his strongest vocabulary. *Fucking knee hurts*. He pictured a line of white and a pile of pills and started limping for the side door they used to go in and out. The main congregation's doors had been boarded up a million years ago, and it was too hard to get the stuff off.

"Aapo," he called out to give the tweaky bastard some warning it was a friendly coming inside. He adjusted the pistol in his waistband as he limped, and he patted the rolls of cash in his jacket pocket.

The door was already cracked open an inch and he pulled it the rest of the way before the security breach caught his attention, but his knee hurt like hell and he wanted some pills.

"Hey Aapo—" he shouted before the rest of the greeting died in his throat.

The interior of the massive room was lit by a hellish orange light, and Alex saw that the little furniture they had was consumed by eager flames.

When he looked up and noticed Aapo, his mind refused to accept what he saw, and he blamed it on the drugs twisting his sight into nightmare.

The Finnish drug dealer's naked corpse dangled by the neck from an overhead beam and was melting like a plastic man softened in a microwave oven. His limbs hung too low. His arms were as long as his legs and *stretched* until they were easily five feet in length.

"Aapo?" But the dealer didn't respond. Aapo's tongue was a thick wad of meat protruding from his mouth, and his nearly bald head was black with retained blood.

Alex shook his head to erase the horrifying sight and only then noticed the massive stones tied by thick ropes around Aapo's wrists and ankles. As he watched, Alex heard a ripping noise as Aapo's right arm grew another six inches before separating completely at the elbow.

Alex opened his mouth to scream and was hit by a spray of red drops, gagging at the salty taste on his tongue. The stone and forearm hit the floor with a crash, and Aapo's hanging body spun wildly until the left arm tore free at the shoulder.

"Nyet, nyet," he blurted in his native Russian as he backpedaled. He heard the door slam shut behind him and spun about. Alex had a split second to make out a pale, featureless face atop a body made of shadow before he grabbed the pistol in his waistband and yanked, blowing off the tip of his penis and shattering the patella on his uninjured right knee.

He let out an animal bellow as he collapsed onto the flagstone floor, trying to clutch his wounded groin and knee at the same time, writhing like a grub covered in salt.

Alex, who knew about death metal and a few other things, did not actually know very much about pain. But shortly after he opened his eyes and saw the terrifying face hovering over his, Mister White instructed him.

CHAPTER FIFTEEN

- 1 -

An autumn breeze rustled the broad-leafed trees surrounding the Millhouse and scattered drifts of orange, yellow and brown across the grassy hillside. There were oaks, maples and hickories, old Virginia forest on protected Federal land that circled the fence line in the manner of ancient, natural guardians.

Ronald turned up the collar of his denim jacket and resumed raking near the rusted chain-link fence, gathering the fallen leaves in a series of piles leading downhill. He inhaled their musty odor while the rake worried at new calluses on his palms. Not long ago he would have balked at the thought of manual labor, a pear-shaped man with wide, wobbling buttocks, unaccustomed to physical exertion. But the directions on the bottle of clozapine caplets were quite clear. DO NOT OPERATE HEAVY MACHINERY. So he wielded his rake when the leaves fell and used a wheeled dolly when it was time to move feed or other goods about.

The sheep were clustered downslope between Ronald and the old Millhouse beside the pond. A small plaque beside the door stated that the Millhouse was a HISTORICAL LANDMARK erected in 1785. The outer shell of weathered boards and gray shingles certainly supported the deception. On rare occasions an ungrateful, questioning thought wormed its way up through the clouds of clozapine fog and Ronald wondered, *Why the deception?* If it was a government facility, as stated on the metal sign adorning the gate—FEDERAL PROPERTY: NO TRESPASS-ING—why the need to hide?

He leaned his weight on the rake and studied messages in the clouds of his breath, smiling in a wonder that had not faded in the months since he was called forth from the segregation unit to meet The Man who called himself Bierce. It was inside a windowless interview room that The Man had offered Ronald redemption. A caretaker was needed and he qualified for the position. That he was required to wear a tracking anklet didn't worry him at all. Anything was better than seg. Better? It was Shangri-fucking-La compared to that tiny cell with its lidless toilet and unyielding cot, his only access to the outside world a narrow slot in the door through which he was fed.

Care for the grounds, and care for the sheep and goats that trimmed the lawn with their endless chewing. When it came to the sheep, Ronald's primary job was to keep them from drowning themselves in the millpond. They were warm, curly-haired things with black faces peering out from thick, off-white wool and very, very dumb. Still, they never bit or kicked him. Instead, they crowded around him whenever he came outside, or bumped against him and nuzzled his ears when he sat on the old stone lip of the pond with his fishing pole.

The goats were another matter, but there were only three of them, and he had worked out an accord with the stunted brutes. "I'll leave you alone and you leave me alone." Like the sheep, however, they refused to enter the Millhouse. Ronald had learned the wisdom of flight early in life, and he retreated inside whenever the goats grew ornery.

He resumed his work, enjoying the scratch of the wooden teeth against the grass. After his third fall for kiddie pictures, he never expected to see the outside world again. Expected to die face down in a shower as a series of angry convicts ran a train on him, or a guard hit him one too many times with a lead-cored baton and caved in his fragile skull.

Then The Man offered Ronald a second chance, and he was one grateful sex offender.

A bat fluttered overhead, and Ronald saw the smiling disk of the sun sink below the western trees. He lowered his gaze to the Millhouse, the historical monument hidden in the woods.

"Shit, shit, shit."

His digital watch chimed, reminding him it was time for another pill. The pills were in the bathroom, and the bathroom was inside the Millhouse.

Inside.

"Shit," he said.

He told himself it was the time in segregation that made him reluctant to enter the building. After all, in the Millhouse he had all the food he could warm up in the microwave and near unlimited cable television. Each night, as he fell asleep on the couch, the moans and cries of pornography eased him into chemically lubricated dreams. So what if he wasn't allowed alcohol or marijuana? The clozapine made him feel pretty good. When The Man called all Ronald had to do was answer the old phone on the metal desk and report, "All's well."

The watch chimed again and Ronald's slack lips assumed a petulant twist. He had agreed to the medication as part of his work release program. Compared to prison, the rules of his new existence were simple, really.

Don't leave the grounds.

Don't touch the phone unless it was to report to The Man.

Don't explore the tunnels beneath the Millhouse.

- 2 -

Her voice: "But I didn't order a pizza."

His voice: "Lady, somebody ordered a meat lover's."

Voices from the old, blocky television squatting in the corner. Ronald came back to himself sitting astride the wheeled desk chair, around him the dispassionately ugly cinderblock front room outfitted in government ugly, circa 1950.

His chin was wet and he sat facing the doorway to the dark bedroom.

"What I really want is a big cock," the woman's voice said from the TV.

Ronald shifted and the wheels of the chair squeaked on the cement floor. Sometimes he lost time because of the clozapine.

Sound from the dark bedroom and Ronald sprang from his seat, the chair rolling backwards to bang against the old metal desk as he braved the black rectangle and thrust his arm into the dark, hand slapping against the painted cinderblock wall as if to attract attention, call something forth—

The light switch.

Fluorescents overhead flickered to life with an audible hum and threw unflattering light over the sparsely appointed bedroom with its single, unmade bunk and incongruous bookcase of religious tracts.

Tapping sounds echoed from the painted cluster of pipes that ran down one corner of the room and disappeared into the floor. Random noises. Water pressure. Not Morse code.

Ronald rubbed a hand across his comb-over and left the greasy black strands standing erect. "Aww, shit," he said. He had forgotten. Soon the pipes would start picking up random radio sounds. Disjointed voices that he could almost understand.

Ronald staggered past the couch with its rumpled pillow and blankets, where he had slept since that first unsettling night in the bedroom, during which the tapping and radio voices had kept him awake in an ecstasy of shivering terror. He bumped his shin against the coffee table and dislodged a CD jewel case, scattering crushed lines of clozapine on the floor.

"Shit!"

His boxer shorts strained across his wide backside as he bent and lifted a cardboard box from the metal shelves, lugged the case of dog food into the bedroom and dropped it on the floor below the hatch to the dumbwaiter. He pulled hard and the door came down, revealing an empty box into which he fed the cans of DAVE'S ALL NATURAL DOG FOOD. Closing it, he hummed TV theme songs while he pressed the red button to lower the tray. Faint moaning came from the actors on the television, and he wished he had remembered to turn up the volume before feeding time.

"This used to be a quarantine space for infectious disease research, defunct and unused for more than twenty years before we picked it up," The Man had told him. "But you will never have to go below to the quarantine area. You would not want to. It is dark, empty and very easy to become lost."

Ronald glanced at the bookcase against the wall. He had pushed it aside on that first day before he learned to fear the bedroom. Behind the bookcase of Bibles and Torahs and Bhagavad Gitas was a great metal door with an oblong keyhole in place of a handle.

After two minutes he heard a quiet thump when the tray hit bottom and couldn't help but wonder how far down the dumbwaiter went.

A flurry of taps rang from the water pipes and he slammed the dumbwaiter's hatch closed, backing away to the antiseptic safety of the front room, with its desk and microwave and tele-vision.

Dogs can't open boxes. Dogs can't open cans.

What am I feeding?

Don't explore the tunnels beneath the Millhouse.

There was no chance of Ronald ever going down there. No chance at all.

CHAPTER
SIXTEEN

- 1 -

A thin coating of ice covered the big house on the hill, steaming faintly in the bright morning light. The building was unused to so much warmth, with a fire burning in the front room and two extra bodies slumbering. A stranger's body slept in the guest bedroom, and a room that had never fulfilled its purpose did so now with a different child. The owner of the big place had laid out an air mattress in a dusty, upstairs room that he hadn't visited in years and ruminated on the idea of change.

- 2 -

The old building creaked and whispered its own strange logic.

It was a house used to quiet and loss, and it spoke to Hedde as she lay on the stiff mattress atop scratchy blankets her uncle had pulled from a closet. It was a small room with a floor of uneven boards and a single window through which moonlight flooded in, painting the nearly empty space in shades of blue. Hedde suspected the peeling old house was haunted.

A handmade crib stood in one corner, a box of wooden bars on tall legs covered with carved images but lacking a mattress. As far as Hedde knew, Uncle Gerard had never had a child, though he had once had a wife, and her quick mind saw a dark path to his taciturn personality. If she was right.

Hedde was always right.

She was right about her father spending more and more time away from home, right that he liked doing whatever he did overseas more than he liked living in a small town in Westchester. She was right that her mother was moving in another direction, like a planet breaking orbit from the sun. She was right to pull in her own tendrils, to fasten her seatbelt and assume crash position. She was right that something bad was coming that would hurt her.

She was right that somehow, in the space of a day, everything had changed. Something worse had happened, something that meant her father was in danger, enough danger to give her mother a gun and a note and money like she had only seen in movies. She was right in knowing that those tendrils she had thought retracted were still fully connected to her parents, and they opened her to hurt.

She did not want her father to go away. Did not want her mother to break orbit. She was filled with a fear that gathered in her belly with a sick heaviness, and so she stared at one of the only other features in the small room that was meant for another child.

An old, iron horseshoe hung over the door on a single nail, covered with rust but, she suspected, still potent. Old magic, protective magic. *Bene gris gris* to guard the child who slept in the room.

Her.

She sat up on the thin mattress in the corner of the room and pulled on her boots, lacing them up to the top.

The floor spoke as she crossed to the window, which opened with a protesting screech. Cold air rushed in and she felt the goosebumps break out on her arms. She shivered even as her eyes watered, casting mirages and prisms across the beautiful expanse of snow-covered land, the leafless branches of nearby trees limned in white, the hulking barn draped with a wintry blanket, as if in sleep it had pulled up the covers.

Below her, she heard a noise, an unsettling sound. She cocked her head to listen, but it wasn't repeated. Her eyes were drawn to the quiet barn and she wondered about its mystery, aware that she was distracting herself on purpose.

She shivered again and told herself that the icy wetness on her cheeks was simply the cold, not crying, she was too old to cry. Eventually the crying girl slipped out into the dark hallway and crept to the staircase, unable to avoid the constant chorus of the house announcing her every movement.

Her mother's gun was sitting dead center on the kitchen table and she picked it up, feeling the deadly weight of it, the ugly, bulldog attractiveness of the device. She played her fingers over its shape, careful to avoid the trigger, until she was able to find the lever that allowed the cylinder to slide out to one side. She rotated it with one finger, touching the visible ends of the bullets before snapping her wrist like Uncle Gerard. This proved harder than she thought, and she had to use her left hand to press the cylinder home until it clicked.

She placed the gun back on the table and went outside into the night.

- 3 -

What's in the barn?

Hedde stood in the yard looking over the pleasantly dilapidated structure, all gray wood with gaps between the boards and she recognized a postcard shot with the dark line of trees across the field behind it. She curled her hands into fists and sucked them up into her sleeves, but she was still cold.

Something's in there. Something that moved and made noise.

There was a shiny padlock securing the big front doors, the only thing new she could see in the whole yard, including the house and her uncle's old pickup truck.

Hedde stepped closer, her Doc Marten's punching holes in the crusting snow, and gave the padlock a tug.

Nothing.

She spit and wished for a cigarette, then kicked her way around the side of the barn until she found a conveniently placed crack. *Probably stores bodies in there*, she thought, picturing her uncle's axe buried in the big stump. *Mom took us to stay with a serial killer.*

Placing both hands against the wall, careful not to get splinters, she leaned in and placed her right eye against the crack, opening it wide in an effort to drink in more light.

It was dark, with a dim red glow coming from behind some sort of low wall. She could see the faint outline of piled junk and rusting farm machinery, all giant wheels and bent blades.

A low and ugly thunder rumbled from the darkness, and Hedde jerked back so suddenly she almost fell down.

What the...

She leaned closer, ready to spring away again, and peered again into the gloomy interior.

A shadow moved inside, emitting a deep sound like the bass at a rock concert, vibrating the fillings in her teeth.

"Zut alors!" she said, hopping back until she could see around to the front doors and the sturdy lock. *Is that supposed to keep people out, or something in?*

Snow crunched behind her and she spun to see the black form of Etienne standing utterly still, watching her from the front yard. The fur on his shoulders bristled and his upper lip raised, showing huge teeth, but he didn't make a sound. The big shepherd just watched her.

"It's okay, boy. It's okay," Hedde said, holding her hands out and backing away in a direction that let her keep an eye on both the dog and the barn. "Uncle Gerard doesn't want anyone to know what's in the barn? I won't go in the barn."

She backed onto the icy dirt of the driveway and felt a surprising sob catch in her throat. *What the fuck?* She fought it down with a wave of anger, aware that her attempt at distraction was failing. She felt a hot prickling behind her eyes and closed them against the return of tears. Blind, she backed into the old Camaro beneath its snowy cover.

Of course he has a Camaro. The disdainful thought was automatic, and she was beginning to think, undeserved. Shame joined the chorus calling for surrender to the thorny emotions jabbing at her wavering control.

Something wet nudged her hand, and she jerked away from Etienne, who trotted calmly over to the front door of the house and sat in the snow, watching her.

"Do you want to go inside?"

The tail thumped once and Etienne said something like, *whuff.*

"Do you understand me?"

Whuff. Etienne stood and turned in a circle, then sat down and stared at her as she crunched to his side and opened the door. He pushed past and she closed the door behind her as she followed the big dog upstairs. He paused in the hallway, head lifted and nose twitching, before trotting down to her room and going inside.

"Hey," Hedde said when she entered the room. "That's my mattress."

She closed the window and bent to untie her boots before kicking them off.

"Shove over," she said, wedging herself between the Shepherd and the wall, aware of his body heat and the thick animal smell of him. A strong smell, but not unpleasant once she got used to it.

"You gonna sleep up here?"

His tail thumped once.

Hedde settled in, one hand on the thick fur of Etienne's shoulder, eyes wide in the blue moon light.

- 4 -

Gerard opened the door quietly and looked into the girl's room, catching the glint of Etienne's eyes as the dog lifted his head to regard him. His niece was asleep, snoring quietly, and Gerard thought that was good. He had heard her moving through the house and the unmistakable click of the revolver's cylinder. He had watched through a window as she skulked in the yard and explored the outside of the barn. Even from a distance he could feel her need, her fear. But it was as if the part of him that understood such human things had burned out, an old motor long since gone to rust. He was quietly glad for Etienne. The dog understood better than he.

If Gerard was aware of conflicting emotions about entering a room that had remained undisturbed for so many years, he paid it no mind. He was so accustomed to ignoring the calls from that part of his wounded soul that he no longer heard them.

He heard them.

And so he was also unaware of the surprising warmth he felt on seeing a child in the room, sleeping with his trusted companion.

Etienne lowered his head and closed his eyes. Gerard, respecting the message, stepped back into the hall and quietly closed the door.

- 5 -

Hedde awoke to the smell of coffee and coughed when she discovered her face pressed into Etienne's thick coat. A long tongue lapped at her ear and she recoiled, pushing the big dog away.

"Gross! Move!"

Etienne trotted around the perimeter of the room before pausing at the door. Hedde crawled off the mattress, knees aching on the hard wood, until she could reach up and turn the knob.

The thunder of Etienne's charge downstairs faded as she pulled herself to her feet. She was still wiping sleep from her eyes when she shuffled into the kitchen and Uncle Gerard offered her a cup of steaming black liquid.

"Merci."

"De rien."

Hedde blew ripples across the surface of the coffee and glanced at the kitchen table. She saw a note in her mother's handwriting and fought down what might have been a frightfully adult sound of disgust. She didn't need to read the note to understand what it said.

"My mom's gone?"

"Yes."

"She took the gun?"

"She took the gun."

Gerard slid the paper towards her, but Hedde pushed it to the side and, after a moment, responded to his unasked question.

"Doesn't matter what's in it. She left."

Gerard grunted. "She said some things in there she wants you to know."

"I'll tell you what I know. I know that my dad has been gone more than he's been home the last two years. I know—I think I know—that mom is seeing someone. I know that they're going to get a divorce. And I know that they haven't said one thing to me about it."

Gerard sipped his coffee, pursing his lips against the heat. "Tough way to look at it."

"Tough thing to look at."

Gerard sat down in his seat and placed his works on the table, tapping a line of tobacco down the center of a cigarette paper.

"Can you make me one?" Hedde asked. Gerard gave her a steady look to which she replied, "I haven't been a kid since I was a kid."

He slid a small square of white paper over to her and handed over the tobacco.

"Like this," he said, demonstrating. "Now wet it."

Hedde's fingers were nimble and she rolled a competent cigarette on her first try.

Gerard struck a wooden match alight off the corner of the table and held it to his cigarette until he inhaled a hot stream of smoke. He offered the bright flame and Hedde leaned in, piloting the tip of her cigarette into the fire until it had achieved a healthy smolder.

"You know about lighting no more than two off one match?" Gerard asked.

"Bad luck," she said.

Man and girl attended to hot coffee and smoldering cigarettes in silence as the two ribbons of smoke intertwined overhead.

- 6 -

It had taken all of Cat's self-control to wait until she crossed the border into Vermont before pulling off the road in front of a white clapboard general store with two gas pumps in front.

She bought a coffee from the teenager at the counter and several dollars of quarters, which she loaded into a coat pocket as she eyed a glass jar full of enormous green pickles.

"Buck fifty," the kid said, and she looked at him in confusion before pushing out through the glass door.

The big ice machine next to her clunked and rattled as she fed quarters into the pay phone. The false comfort of the aromatic steam rising off the coffee was threatening her fragile composure. Cat deliberately scalded her tongue with a molten sip, a painful if expedient way to quell her rebellious emotions.

She had a good memory for numbers and was just handy with them in general. Lew always made her calculate the tip, and she rarely, if ever, used a calculator for anything. Still, the number she dialed was years old, and she was afraid she had bungled it even as the phone on the other end began to ring. She decided that if she had dialed in error, she would drive to another public phone in another town before trying again. Paranoia was nibbling at her and she didn't want to make herself memorable to the Guardian of Pickles by asking for more quarters.

Four rings. Five. She had blown it. Or the number had changed.

"Shit," she said.

"Bierce," a tinny voice said into her ear.

"Are you missing a pet?" she asked. Hearing the question aloud, she realized how stupid it sounded. Hell, it was too foolish to even be thought of as a code.

There was a long quiet marked only by breathing from the other end before Bierce responded. "I had one once, but it ran away and we never found it."

She closed her eyes. "Do you know who this is?"

"I think so." A pause. "Can you help me find mine?"

"That's what we need to talk about."

"We really do." Another pause. "It's cold, much better to talk inside."

Cat agreed and told him both where and how.

CHAPTER
SEVENTEEN

- 1 -

Herr Steiner took a last sip of tea and set the cup on its saucer, the delicate rattle of china folding itself into the wash of sound created by a living, breathing train. The clatter and roar of steel wheels on the rails, the *tock-tock-tock* of the individual railroad ties thundering up from below with machine gun speed. The constant whoosh of the air circulation system that made conversation something of an art, and the under-hum created by so much humanity in close proximity, the insect buzzing of a dozen European languages punctuated by the occasional cough or sneeze.

It was quite late, and the dining car of the Berlin Night Express was empty, so Herr Steiner took the moment of privacy in the long, table-filled car to collect himself as he searched the snow-covered countryside for the ruined convent, the remnant of some unnamed Nazi atrocity. He made a specific effort to watch for the crumbling stone on every trip, both to mark the distance they had traveled—the six-hour point of their ten-hour journey—and because such a thing should never be forgotten, even if Herr Steiner was the only one to remember.

He had been a conductor for eight years, eight years since his wife succumbed to an infection following a routine surgery, eight years of working through the night because he could no longer sleep in the dark. During those years, the living organism of the train sustained him and crowded out the shrieking voices inside his head. The routine of his duties kept him occupied and gave him a sense of purpose. If he was mildly bored, he enjoyed the occasional moment when he could assist a confused passenger or solve the minor problems that were brought to his attention.

Tonight he was uneasy.

The electric lamps dimmed, except for the running lights on the floor, and for a moment the rush of air quieted, as if to allow the clatter of wheel and tie their own musical solo. As the ferocious yellow light faded, it was replaced by the gentle, azure glow of the snowscape outside. These were special moments for Herr Steiner, and much as a child hopes that summer will never end, he always wished for a few extra seconds of darkness in which to enjoy a mystical atmosphere that seemed to have been created for him and him alone.

Not this night. This night he counted the seconds with mounting tension until the light and sound flooded back in.

It had begun with the goat. The bloody, ghost-furred goat.

The evening had been marred by the unusual since leaving the station in Sweden, all but one event unnoticed by the passengers but already causing enough muttering among the crew that Herr Steiner had spoken to the engineer about it, and the gossiping was silenced.

Not two miles south of Malmo, their point of departure, the engineer had told him, "We were entering a black woods where the leafless trees stab skyward like a forest of pikes."

Herr Steiner nodded, hiding surprise at words that spilled straight from the id of M.R. James or Algernon Blackwood, these from a man whose preferred reading material generally included a centerfold. But the grizzled engineer was entranced at the memory and it made Herr Steiner uneasy to see the old salt rattled.

"Its eyes, its damnable eyes. The forward light picked them out first. They glowed like shining coins over the tracks and I could see no body..." When the old man hesitated, Herr Steiner had rested a hand on his shoulder, concealing his growing concern. The engineer was not a man given to pause.

"It's me," the head conductor said, and the old man squared his shoulders as if pressing forward into a squall.

"There was no body," the engineer said. "I know you would think to tell me that its fur was so dark that it could not be seen against the night, but the thing was white as flour when we finally saw it. If you ask me..." And here he paused again, fixing his glittering eyes on Herr Steiner. "If you ask me, the body of the goat did not fill in behind those eyes until it had to, until it knew that the light should be showing a form."

"It?"

"The damnable goat," the engineer swore. "It stood without moving on the tracks, eyes red in our headlight, the rest of it little more than an outline. I sounded the horn and it reared back as if to butt the train in the instant before it was sucked beneath the wheels." He wiped a rag across the oily sweat on his forehead. "For a terrible moment I was certain that we would derail, but the train held."

The assistant engineer had slipped from the locomotive at the next stop to examine the front for damage, reporting blood and fur smeared across the bow of the car and a crack in the single, nose-mounted headlight. It wasn't until the next stop, owing to the need to keep on schedule, that they had been able to dispatch a crew with water and cleaning fluid to hastily wipe away the blood.

Herr Steiner replayed the conversation in his mind as he stood and placed his cap on his head, evening the brim over his eyes. The lights and sound in the food car dimmed again and he counted, "One-one thousand, two-one thousand…" The interruptions struck him as uncommonly frequent on this trip, and he wished for the damned journey to hurry up and be over.

He rebuttoned the top of his white uniform shirt and straightened his tie, nose wrinkling at the faint stink that remained in the car after the second incident. It was an unpleasant, organic smell loitering beneath the herb and roasted boar from the evening's dinner service.

The Belgian chef, another reliable man and something of a friend to Herr Steiner after so many years, assured the head conductor that he had personally inspected each carton of produce as it was loaded on board with the fish.

"I heard a scream and ran into the kitchen to see the sous chef reeling back from the refrigerated compartment as if she would be ill," the chef had told Herr Steiner. "When I ran to the open door and looked inside, I understood why."

The chef had slipped a metal flask from his apron pocket and unscrewed the cap, shivering as he slugged back brandy.

"No, thank you," Herr Steiner replied when the flask was offered. He had fit a lifetime of drinking into the months following Gretel's death and dared not return to that gloomy place. The chef knew this, and his lapse seemed yet another sign of his fear.

"Merde," the Belgian said. "The interior was covered with a grotesque, white fur, the mold of months," he continued. "The vegetables had become soft things, liquid sacks that burst at the slightest motion and released a brown liquid, like watery molasses." He paused for another bite at the flask. "And the fish…" he continued, turning away so that all Herr Steiner heard was the word "chewed."

"The stink, mon ami. I am ashamed to say I vomited, as did most of my staff. If an inspector had seen my kitchen then…" The chef shook his head. "I instructed my people to throw the rancid crates off the side of the train." He held up a hand. "I know, I know, but the corruption was so powerful, I was near to panic. Even now I can smell it."

The chef's eyes darted about in shame and Herr Steiner gripped his shoulder. "Then how did you prepare dinner?"

The Belgian laughed, a forced sound but better than the furtive posture of moments before. "Monsieur Henri Lefevre shot a four-hundred-pound boar and brought it onboard the train, asking me to store it in my freezer. I arranged for the Berlin Night Express to purchase his prize on very favorable terms."

"That was well done," Herr Steiner said, indicating that he would sign off on the purchase.

The panicked chef had worked a miracle with powdered instant potatoes and herbs, and no one but the kitchen crew and Herr Steiner knew anything was amiss. But the conductor, who was in no way superstitious, began to wonder if the night's journey was ill-fated.

He turned smartly and checked his reflection in the windows, his image given a sinuous quality by the passing winterscape outside.

Why he felt a need to check again on the status of the third incident he was not certain, but his general feeling of alarm was increasing as the evening went on. There had been a medical emergency on board the train. In the sleeper car.

Herr Steiner patted his pocket to assure himself he had the master key to the sleeping cabins, but paused to stare with curious alarm at the stiffening hairs on the back of his wrists. He could feel each individual hackle rise on the back of his neck.

"This is foolish," he chided his reflection in the window. The expression his reflection wore indicated some disagreement. "All right then."

Herr Steiner headed aft to check in on the dead man in cabin number eight.

- 2 -

Lewis's heart leapt into his throat as he stared down at the vibrating phone in his hand, at the picture of himself, asleep on the very bunk on which he was sitting.

"What?"

He leapt to his feet, lurching into the opposite wall as the train rocked while he pawed madly at the coat hanging on the back of the door. Seeing the door was locked but not believing it. How had someone snapped a picture of him sleeping?

He batted aside his pillow and clutched the pistol in a white-knuckled hand, pressing his face against the window to see outside. Winter chill flooded his nose from the icy glass, and he cursed wordlessly at the rolling blue-white landscape, with not even a single light visible in the distance.

He stepped back and caught the reflection of movement behind him.

The gun snapped up and he nearly shot his swaying coat. "Shit." He yanked the coat off the hook and tugged it on quickly, clumsily, some distant part of his mind telling him to slow down and do things right.

But the panic was rising. The phone buzzed in his hand and he threw it, chipping the window glass.

The damned thing was a burner phone. There was no way to trace it to him. Yet it buzzed and skittered on the floor like a mad beetle as someone tried to call him.

He snatched up the small valise containing all of the cash he had made selling the cocaine, but his head snapped skyward, trying to see through the slanting curve of the ceiling at the *clop-clop-clop* he heard overhead.

Hooves cantering on the roof.

A heavy thump came from the cabin next to him. Lewis gritted his teeth, flipped the lock and stepped into the hall with his gun leading.

And he almost put two rounds through the heart of the conductor.

He pretended to stumble, slipping the weapon into the valise while his free hand slapped against the row of windows to draw the other's gaze.

Herr Steiner glanced up as he closed the door to the sleeper car behind him. He regarded the disheveled man, his sleep-spiked hair and wild eyes.

"Guten abend," Herr Steiner said.

Lewis patted his spiky hair into place and lowered the valise. "Guten abend. Wann ist die nachste haltestelle?" He raised his voice to be heard over the clatter of the tracks.

"Zwanzig minuten," the conductor replied, touching the brim of his hat as Lewis turned sideways and squeezed against the windows to let him pass. Twenty minutes until the next stop. Too long.

Herr Steiner pressed his shoulders against the cabin doors as the passenger negotiated his way through the narrow corridor between the cabins and the windows on the port side of the train. The man was agitated, but that was nothing new for Herr Steiner, who had seen humanity in all of its forms on the Night Express. What was unusual was the pistol he believed he had seen for a fraction of an instant as the man stumbled. He had the unprofessional urge to halt the man with a hand on his arm and ask him if he had heard anything from the cabin next door.

The frightened man had emerged as if shot from a cannon from the adjacent unit, number seven.

Once they were past each other, Lewis hurried to the end of the sleeper car. He felt the conductor's gaze like a weight pressed between his shoulder blades as he opened the door and stepped into the deafening racket between cars. Sliding the door closed, he risked a glance through the smudged porthole and saw the conductor standing outside of what appeared to be his own cabin door, staring intently at the handle.

Lewis quickly stepped across the slippery metal floor and yanked open the door into the next passenger car, using his free hand to balance on seat backs as he passed between rows of sleeping passengers in the dim silver glow.

- 3 -

Herr Steiner faced the door to cabin eight and bounced the key in his palm, shifting slightly with the rolling motion of the train.

He looked up the car at the line of scalloped curtains fluttering in the wind that slipped through the window cracks. Could there be so much wind? The lace fringe had an oddly chewed look, as if they had recently been brought down from a dead relative's attic where moths had feasted on them over many years, laying eggs alongside nesting mice. He should write up a report on this shabby state. The Berlin Night Express had a reputation to maintain. In fact, an impromptu inspection of the entire train might be in order.

A bead of sweat slid slick as mercury down his temple, and without any sort of rational, psychological transition, Herr Steiner realized that he was terrified.

The tinkle of wind chimes reached his ears and his head whipped left and right, searching for the origin of the sound. *Chimes, or breaking glass?*

He thought of summoning his friend from the kitchen, but the Belgian chef was undoubtedly sleeping by now and quite possibly drunk. And what would the rest of the crew think when they heard that the head conductor required a hand to hold in the dark?

Unconsciously squaring his shoulders and tugging down the bottom of his uniform jacket, Herr Steiner shakily inserted the key into the lock with a quiet clatter and gave it a sharp twist to the left, the tumblers thundering within the mechanism as the door was unlocked.

"Right, then," he said, pushing open the door and stepping into the dark cabin. He felt along the wall for the switch and flipped it up.

The overhead lamp flared brilliantly and went out with a faint pop.

"Scheisse."

As Herr Steiner fished a steel lighter from his pocket, the door swung shut behind him and he nearly dropped it. He fumbled it open, very much aware that he was standing in the dim chamber with a corpse. He rolled the flint with enough force that blue sparks flew and a small flame sprang into being.

Herr Steiner held the lighter up near his head, pivoting slowly in a circle as he examined the cabin, noting nothing amiss, and the shape of the old man seemingly undisturbed beneath the cover Herr Steiner himself had pulled over his face.

He coughed violently and the lighter flame blew out. "Scheisse!" He backed into the wall opposite the bunk as he spun the wheel and the comforting flame returned.

The body beneath the sheet had not moved. Of course it had not moved. Still, more light would be beneficial.

He took one long step to the windows and yanked the cord that lifted the blind so that silver moonlight reflecting off the snow would enter the car.

Herr Steiner brought the lighter close to the fogged window and saw the beads of condensation on the interior. He extended an index finger and drew a quick arc.

"Nein," he said even as a terrible thought bubbled forth. "Nein!" He heard the slither of fabric and whirled about as the body beneath the sheet sat up.

- 4 -

The car was dark save for the parallel running lights on the floor and a few reading lights. Lewis moved quickly but carefully, trying not to bump seats and awaken anyone. He had decided to get off the train despite being far from any towns and did not want passengers to be able to place him if they were questioned later.

It was a car full of German and Belgian skiers returning home and Scandinavian tourists heading south where the days were longer and warmer. Here, a family slept in an ungainly pile of limbs and puffy coats; there, four nuns sat straight across in a row with veiled heads bowed. Whether asleep or in prayer, Lewis could not tell.

His fear had diminished to a background hum as his training reasserted itself. He plucked a draped scarf lightly from the back of one seat. A hat and gloves from the rack above a snoring old man. It would be cold and he would need the protection.

He reached the end of the car and peeked through the porthole before sliding the door half open and slipping through, pulling it shut behind him in one smooth motion. He was exhausted, his lack of conditioning resulting in sore muscles and stiff joints, but he was reaching into deep wells of experience.

He had been afraid before.

He had been hunted before.

He had survived.

A glance into the dining car showed empty tables. Lewis slipped inside, pulling the door shut behind him to cut off the rush of noise.

He became aware of the distinctive clink of silverware and noticed the flicker of a candle, obscured by the man eating alone at one table, facing away from him.

Lewis reached into the valise and his fingers found the butt of the pistol, but he did not draw it.

"Komm, Herr Edgar, mit mir." *Come, Mr. Edgar, join me.*

The voice was muffled but familiar, and Lewis took a step toward the diner, freeing the pistol from the valise and holding it down by his leg.

"A strange night, ja?"

Lewis stiffened at the English. He was certain he had spoken only German while onboard the train.

"Was war das?" Lewis asked, stepping closer and aiming the pistol at the neatly combed hair on the back of the diner's head. "In Deutsch, bitte."

The man was bent protectively over his plate in the manner of a starving beggar, sawing diligently with his right hand. Lewis heard a mewling sound that raised the hackles on his neck. A bloody steak knife was placed on the table and a fork picked up, all with the right hand. The man ate, the sound of his chewing sickening.

Lewis closed the distance until the barrel of his pistol was mere feet from the back of the man's head. He noticed dark stains on the white tablecloth near the knife and the conductor's cap resting on the table.

"Schau mich an," Lewis hissed. *Look at me.*

The man's shoulders twitched and he lowered the fork to rest on the plate as he turned, cheeks bulging as he chewed, eyes streaming tears.

The head conductor. Lewis flinched in surprise.

"How?" He blurted, only then noticing the man's ruined left hand resting on the plate. The conductor swallowed and picked up the knife without moving his eyes from Lewis.

He began sawing off another finger.

"What the fuck?" Lewis said.

"Please," Herr Steiner said, and Lewis made a sound as he heard a finger bone snap. Blood was a drunken smear of lipstick around Steiner's mouth. "Who is he?"

"Stop," Lewis said, stepping back.

"Who is Mister White?" Steiner asked, and Lewis bolted back the way he had come, banging through the door and skidding on the wet metal between cars until he careened into the entry of the first passenger car.

He threw a desperate glance over his shoulder, but Steiner had not left his table. By then, Lewis had the next door open and was stepping into the passenger car, dragging the door shut behind him.

The car was now empty and dark.

He searched in vain for a passenger and saw no luggage, no books or laptop computers. There were no jackets draped on seats or empty food cartons. He steadied himself against the nearest seat back, his feet invisible with the running lights out. His breath misted in the air and he heard the crackle of moisture freezing on the windows. A choosy, eldritch light entered the windows, outlining certain details, while leaving others entirely in shadow.

In the eerie illumination, Lewis saw that his initial assessment was incorrect. He could just make out the four nuns sitting in a row towards the rear of the car, unmoving beneath their black shawls.

The train shuddered and he stumbled, reaching out to catch himself on a seat back. A puff of dust arose as his palm slapped down and he recoiled, turning to flee.

He detected a flicker of motion through the porthole and pressed his face against the glass to see.

The door across from Lewis's car slid slowly open to reveal the dark maw of the dining car. A smear of white floated within the black until some deeper color, some greater density of darkness, filled the doorway.

His psyche short-circuited and he stumbled back before sliding into the aisle seat, paralyzed as he watched the handle of the door begin to turn. The pale moon of a face filled the porthole, unformed and terrifying behind the glass.

"No, no, no."

He lifted his weapon and fired blindly in the direction of the door. Three shots. Four. They were deafening in the enclosed space of the train car but shocked him from his lethargy so that he could roll to his knees and begin to crawl, dropping the pistol and valise. From behind him came the low keening sound of a wounded animal.

He heard the scrape of corrupted metal, the noise of whetstone against knife and rusting hinges opening with an avalanche of dust. The strength went out of his arms, fighting with all of his might not to collapse, groveling like a worm as—

Mister White.

—swept toward him.

He had no time for regrets, no time to conjure the face of his wife and child. There was no room even for fear as blinding white pain seared his mind.

The train rocked savagely to the side as if struck by artillery fire and light swept over Lewis as a rooster tail of sparks fountained up from the wheels, assaulting the windows with luminescent fury that threw crazed, rippling shadows about the compartment.

In his madness, Lewis could hear words.

"Quid erat agnum est nunc leo."

A whisper.

A scream.

Lewis slapped his hands over his ears as the train was rocked again, as if struck by a giant's palm.

The dark nuns rose.

"Quid erat agnum est nunc leo!"

The windows exploded outward and a cyclone of ice and snow screamed inside.

Quid erat agnum est nunc leo. What was the lamb is now the lion.

The nuns filed into the aisle and began to walk towards him. The terrible weight of their regard pressed him to the floor, peeling back his coat and shirt and skin and ribs to skewer the very heart of him with their absolute judgment. Every flaw in his character, every wicked decision, was mounted on a glass slide as a giant eye peered down at his soul through a microscope of impossible proportions.

Behind him, he heard a rumble so low and deep, a subsonic scream that twisted his insides and filled his mouth with bile as the first nun reached up with hands of withered flesh, of scar tissue, of bone, and lifted the black veil from her emaciated face. Her toothless mouth opened, as did her eyes, white and blind in the ever-dark, and from the bowels of the crone came a *sound*—

Are you all right? Are you okay?

It was a muffled voice, not by distance, but as if the speaker and Lewis were both underwater.

"Sind sie verletzt?" *Are you hurt?*

Lewis felt gentle fingers probing him and he reacted violently, sweeping his hands blindly as he opened his eyes and pain exploded throughout his battered body.

Illuminated by firelight, a bearded old man in a monk's cassock was backing away, eyes wide and fixed on the pistol in Lewis's right hand.

"Nicht bewegen," Lewis said, coughing against smoke as he pushed himself to a sitting position with his free hand.

The man held out his hands, fingers wide. "Nein," he said.

Lewis pushed up to one knee and stood, body swaying but gun aimed unwaveringly at the other man. Behind him, Lewis saw that the train had derailed, or at least partially so. One car had split in half. Jagged, open ends, both halves pointed towards his position in the snow beside the tracks, as if he had been fired from a cannon.

Quid erat agnum est nunc leo. The words filled Lewis's head and flooded from his mouth. The old man stiffened as if he had been struck across the face.

Lewis snatched the moment to look left and right. Not a single passenger besides himself had been ejected from the train. He searched for the pale-faced Mister White as a cold not born of winter chilled his blood.

"Nonnen," he said. *Nuns.*

The old man's eyes grew wider still, but Lewis was looking past him at the old flatbed truck with wooden boards lining both sides of the bed. It was running, door left ajar where it was parked on the snowy shoulder.

"Munich. Now," Lewis said, advancing with the pistol outstretched and herding the monk into the open driver's door before quickly rounding the vehicle and jerking open the passenger door with a squeal of hinges. As he stepped up onto the running board, he looked again at the flaming wreckage of the train car. Looming up behind it was the wavering black of mighty ruins.

He threw himself into his seat, burying the disbelief at what had happened onboard the train.

"Drive," he told the old monk, jabbing the gun into his ribs. Spitting snow, the truck lurched away from the train.

- 6 -

The old truck's heater rattled like a fan one step away from the trash bin, while producing little in the way of warmth. Lewis was reminded of a line from Shakespeare, something about sound and fury signifying nothing.

Then he caught sight of a featureless oval in the windshield and looked away, frightened of his own reflection.

"I am Lucien," the monk said, removing a hand from the wheel and holding it out. The truck slid a bit in the snow and Lewis grabbed the armrest.

"Christ, keep your hands on the wheel," he said.

"Yes," Lucien said, unperturbed, while righting the truck. "May I ask you a question?"

"I'll tell you the address when we get to Munich."

"No, no." Lucien made a sound that might have been a chuckle. "I merely wish to ask you, are you a good man?"

"No more talking."

Lucien raised a conciliatory hand. "I am sorry. It helps to keep me awake while driving. Normally I sleep now but was awakened by a call moments before the accident."

Lewis rubbed a hand over his face and said nothing.

"I am caretaker for the convent of Saint Emily de Vialar," Lucien continued, in his unruffled manner. "The ruins located on the other side of the tracks, at the site of the accident."

Lewis leaned his head back against the rest and listened, anything to distract him from what had happened aboard the train.

"In 1941, during the war, the four residents of St. Emily's raised their voice in protest against what they saw as the Vatican's capitulation and tacit acceptance of the genocide. For a brief while, their voice was heard, newspapers made in basements were handed out. You see, they did not approach the men of the surrounding villages, they spoke only to the women."

Lewis cracked the window an inch and lifted his chin for a sip of cold air to clear his head, but a buzzing had started that would not go away. He wondered if he had a concussion.

"The women spoke to each other across lines of drying laundry and huddled at market. They spoke to the schoolteachers who chafed under the new edict and finally, when it seemed as if a dam would burst, they spoke to those men who had not yet been sucked into the tide of war."

The old man drew in a breath and pushed it out, as if to lift a heavy burden.

"A great gathering occurred at the convent and the nonnen spoke eloquently and with passion to the crowd. And their truth was felt by all…and by the men of the Gestapo, who were among the audience, black uniforms covered in the wool of farmers."

Lewis placed the pistol in his lap and pressed fingertips to either temple, rubbing, but the buzzing only increased, as if a machine inside his skull had awakened and was spinning to life.

"Stop," Lewis said.

"The Gestapo held the crowd at gunpoint as they made an example of the four nonnen, shaming and violating them, breaking them in front of the people until each of the four was killed with fire and blade. The Gestapo did not kill the people, as expected, but allowed them to go forth and spread the word of what happened to those who spoke against the Reich." He paused and glanced at Lewis. "And this is why I ask if you are a good man because I would understand why the nonnen helped you tonight."

"The dead nuns?" Lewis asked, attempting a sneer.

"Dead in body but, clearly, not in spirit."

"Then you're shit out of luck, my friend, because I am nobody's idea of a good man."

"Nein," Lucien said with a shake of his head. "Then you are about some task that is good?"

"I'm running for my life."

"Running from what?"

"I...don't know." Lewis grabbed his head. "What the hell are you doing to me?"

Lucien patted Lewis on the leg. "Nothing, my friend, but you were touched by a miracle this night, and a man does not walk away from such an event without an awakening."

"Bullshit."

Lucien laughed. "Not bullshit. You have seen it and cannot call it so. Tell me, what did you see?"

Lewis rolled down the window and let the cold air slice into his sweating forehead. "I can't explain."

"You were at a moment of danger, of crisis, when the nonnen saved you?"

Lewis jerked back in his seat at the vividness of the memory. "God, yes."

"And was this danger the work of man?"

"I don't think it was." Lewis felt tears leaking from the corners of his eyes.

"Now, tell me what you are about," Lucien demanded.

"I'm running."

Lucien slammed his palm on the dashboard with a crack like wood striking wood. "Tell me what you are about!"

"I'm trying to get back to my family," Lewis said, choking back a confused sob. "I don't understand what's happening, but I think they're in danger, and I need to get to them."

Lucien let out a great sigh, and his tense features softened as he spoke so quietly that Lewis struggled to hear him over the rushing wind. "And what could be more holy a task than that?" Lucien hummed a snatch of music to himself and gave his passenger time to think before asking, "What is in Munich?"

"The train to Vienna."

"Ah, the train is terribly crowded," Lucien said. "But perhaps more comfortable than this aged chariot?" He patted the dashboard.

"Thank you," Lewis said.

As if in answer, the monk downshifted the truck and pulled to the side of the road.

"Hey," Lewis said, picking up the gun. "What the hell are you doing?"

Lucien smiled and gently pushed down the barrel of the pistol. "You have been touched by a miracle, by the nonnen of Saint Emily de Vialar."

And the buzzing opened inside Lewis Edgar's head and he knew the truth of the old man's words.

"The nonnen are saints of God and can see into a man's heart, but I must listen to words. You are not Catholic?"

"No," Lewis said.

"Then I will make this easy for you," Lucien said with a grin. "Tell me, my son, why you think you are a bad man?"

CHAPTER EIGHTEEN

- 1 -

Ronald slept deeply, having succumbed immediately to a dreamless state of exhaustion as soon as he stretched out on the couch. He lay in snoring slumber in the front room, shirt rucked up to reveal the pale bloat of his belly, the prone expanse of him lit by the unflattering flicker of the snarling television.

On three different occasions, sheep had fallen into the millpond and Ronald was forced to swim after them, clutching a fistful of sopping wool as he dragged them bleating and kicking to shore. Each time he had tied the offending animal to the trough with a length of rope, ignoring their plaintive cries. The three goats stared at the performance as if entertained, chewing their cud and regarding Ronald with glittering eyes.

"Fuck you," he had said, more than once. The chewing beasts had grinned back.

He had considered calling The Man to report the incidents, but ultimately rationalized that it was just the way of sheep to be so stupid. Clozapine was good for rationalization. And so he had fallen asleep, science fiction blaring onscreen, his frozen French bread pizza lying unfinished on the plate he had placed on the floor near the couch.

The front door rattled in its frame and Ronald jerked awake with a phlegmy snort. "Wha—"

Something struck it hard, and again the door banged in its frame.

Ronald sat up and made to rise but tripped with a foot twisted in his blankets. He fell headlong and cracked his chin against the unforgiving floor.

Bang!

The door shook and Ronald saw paint flecks fly free from the interior.

"Go away!" He shouted, blood flinging from a bitten and rapidly swelling tongue. "This is Fed—"

Bang!

The door rocked again.

BANG-BANG-BANG!

The impacts were coming faster, heavier than any fist, bony and hard unlike any human shoulder or boot. Warmth spread across the crotch of Ronald's sweat pants as he voided his bladder, and the door danced under the unimaginable assault.

"Stop it!" Ronald cried out, and at the sound the attack on the door doubled in ferocity. He heard an animal screaming, and before he knew it, he had backed into the pitch darkness of the interior room, hands pressed over his ears as he yelled, "Stopit-stopitstopitstopit!"

And, as if at his command, the door stopped shaking, the thunder stopped crashing. Crouched in the dark and straining to listen past the drumming pulse in his ears, he recoiled from a horrible stench, incredible in its magnitude. It was as if some great beast had entered the room. He spun in place without rising but could see nothing behind him. His mind flashed back to his childhood and the behind-the-scenes tour his Cub Scout pack had enjoyed at a traveling circus. He recalled the incredible bestial stink of the elephant trailers, a force so physically powerful he had felt dwarfed in its presence.

Ronald felt that now, something vast pressing against him, the hairs on his forearms standing straight even as his scrotum grew tight against his body.

He heard it then, in the quiet darkness. The ringing of an old phone and the eerie murmur he had heard so many times before, like a talk radio station, the volume turned down low but slowly increasing. His stomach roiled and he fought back the urge to vomit as his ears pricked at the familiar sounds. Somehow, he knew that in moments he would understand the words, understand what they were saying.

An explosion ripped through the interior room as the bookcase detonated, spattering the walls with the shrapnel of holy writ.

Ronald bolted for the front door, forgetting about the intruder outside until he had thrown the bolt and yanked the portal open, charging forth only to have his bare foot skid on something hot and wet, dumping him hard on his shoulders.

Ronald gasped, struggling for air, only gradually becoming aware of the warm liquid soaking through his t-shirt and sweats, and the rank, coppery stink of blood.

He sat up amidst the carnage, hiccupping for air as he took in the red wreckage of the three goats.

Awestruck, he turned to look at the door itself and saw the crimson-tinged dents they had made as they dashed their brains out against the metal.

Around him, the night was quiet. An owl hooted from the trees, and he felt goosebumps from the cold spring up along his exposed flesh.

"Oh shit," he said, using the doorjamb for balance as he climbed to his feet. He tottered inside leaving a trail of bloody footprints as he made for the phone.

His eyes strayed to the battle on-screen as he waited for the ringing phone on the other end to be answered. But he saw none of it, his mind's eye consumed with the sight of exposed bone and cottage-cheese brains.

A voicemail recording answered after an eternity, and Ronald waited for the beep. "Sir, something's happened. You gotta call me back."

Ronald was peeling off his blood-soaked clothes when the desk phone sounded, and he let out a shriek.

- 2 -

The headlights picked out a narrow funnel of visibility as Bierce navigated his Mercedes down back-country roads, the boles of trees on either side dancing past in unsettling, shimmering waves.

The file lay on the passenger seat beside him, beneath the black leather case with its array of silver snaps holding it in place. The horrid book bounced on the empty seat behind him as if it were a living thing chafing to be opened. The musty scent of its aged papers filled the car with a cloying atmosphere, lining his nostrils with a miasmal swampiness more suited to Louisiana bayou country than Virginia. He cracked the window and lifted his nose into the fresh stream of cold air.

He had received the three calls in rapid succession. The report from his own man that Lewis Edgar was wanted in connection to a multiple homicide in Finland. No sooner had he hung up the phone than it rang again carrying a warning from Chambers at the FBI. Lewis Edgar had been spotted at the site of a train accident in the German countryside and was wanted by local authorities for questioning. Chambers warned that connections would be made in short order and involvement by Interpol was inevitable. Did Bierce have any new information or means to contact Edgar?

And then the terrified call from Ronald.

It was happening.

Had happened.

Something unexpected.

Bierce was uncertain, frightfully aware of his lack of real experience in the matter. He had the notes from his predecessors, solutions for the unthinkable. What to do if Mister White had been deflected from his course or had somehow defied control. Paltry pieces of paper so utterly inadequate. He was expected to defuse a bomb with no actual experience, relying on scribbled anecdotes. The object was a secret even within the temple of silence that was the Central Intelligence Agency. Retrieved from Europe in the aftermath of Hitler's madness by agents of the OSS, and first employed by Americans during the crazed explorations of the Cold War—MK Ultra, drugs, psychic research, the occult.

But nobody truly understood it, only that it must be placated. Directed.

Madness. Madness. Madness.

It was dark, so dark beneath the trees, only a thin river of starry sky visible overhead. The night seemed to gather in the car with him until he flicked on the overhead light to dispel it, his own skull-like visage reflecting from the inside of the windshield.

He snapped off the dome light and gripped the wheel in white-knuckled hands, wishing for the hundredth time that he had never done business with Abel. That Abel had not decided to branch out yet further, jeopardizing everything.

Most of all, Bierce wished that he had found another solution for his wandering operative.

He should never have dispatched Mister White.

- 3 -

Bierce wheeled the Mercedes around in front of the Mill-house, pointing the nose uphill towards the still-open gate. His headlights illuminated the sheep clustered up on the hillside, as if the herd were trying to get as far away as possible from the house.

He pushed open the door and stepped out with the engine running, file under one arm. In the red of the taillights, he beheld the lumpy smear on the front step, and the shining footprints and wet streaks where Ronald had dragged the dead animals inside.

So he had at least achieved that much.

Bierce patted his jacket near his left armpit, not at all comforted by the flat hardness of the holstered .380 Smith & Wesson.

One last glance back at the rumbling Mercedes, dome light on and an irritating chime chiding him for leaving the driver's side door open. Seconds might be critical.

He knelt in the crimson light, feeling the tackiness of the blood soaking through the knees of his slacks. With the file and book tucked beneath his left arm, he undid the snaps on the case and unfolded it to reveal an array of stoppered vials and eye droppers, all color-coded. He filled the first dropper and dripped liquid on each palm, then rubbed them together with the thoroughness of a doctor scrubbing for surgery. The process was repeated with the next vial and this time he tilted back his head, wincing as he dripped liquid into his nostrils, which descended in thick coils down the back of his throat. The contents of the third vial were dripped onto his tongue, and that of the fourth were dripped onto his vulnerable eyeballs until the pain compelled him to close his lids and shake his head. He blinked for what might have been several minutes until the shining blur before him grew detailed and he could see once more.

He stood and pulled out of his pocket several salt packets taken from a fast food restaurant and, balancing like a drunken stork, sprinkled them liberally on the sticky soles of his shoes.

He blew out a breath he was unaware of holding and, in the macabre light, entered the Millhouse, his shoes grinding with each step.

A quick glance around revealed the squalor of a degenerate living in a single room. Bierce noted the bedding on the couch and determined that Ronald had been sleeping there. Proximity to the metal door in the bedroom was already unnerving the man. Faster than normal. Sooner than Ronald's predecessor. Either Ronald was weaker of mind—a distinct possibility—or the process of decay was accelerating. The clozapine should have shielded him longer. Bierce's own protections were, of course, too precious for a man such as Ronald.

A replacement would be needed.

"Ronald?" Bierce questioned the empty room. The caretaker had been instructed to return to the front room after taking the dead goats and a matching number of live ewes inside.

The trail of gore led through the door into the interior room, and Bierce beheld the wreckage of the interior as if witnessing the aftermath of a localized storm. The bookcase, which had once concealed the door to the lower levels, had been split in two as if by a giant axe, and the tomes themselves scattered about the room, pages still slipping and fluttering about in a wind he could not feel. He felt a subsonic pressure against his eardrums, an invisible chisel attempting to pry him open. The urge to flee grew to near irresistible levels, but he shook his head and sucked in several deep breaths to steady himself.

The great door to below stood open in invitation, a dark rectangle that could not be more frightening if it had been lined with teeth. Somewhere beyond, a faint light flickered, and Bierce breathed the tiniest sigh of relief. The notion of penetrating the lower levels in subterranean blackness with only a flashlight was almost unthinkable.

But Ronald had done it. Craven, twisted Ronald had ushered the livestock and deadstock through the door and down.

And had not come back.

Bierce bent and picked up one book, a quick glance revealing that each and every line of text was charred into illegibility. He tossed the holy text aside, its purpose complete. Or failed in its purpose, depending on point of view.

The red trail had gathered into a wide smear before the metal door that led below, growing sticky and dark. He could imagine Ronald's hesitation, the influence of the object chewing through the protective chemical haze of clozapine that was all that kept the caretaker from going mad.

Bierce patted the items under his arm in a last, futile gesture of security, and stepped through the dark doorway, following the trail of blood.

- 4 -

Bierce stood in shadow at the top of the great, grinding escalator and watched the metal teeth rolling down, ever down, each moving riser streaked with viscera and hideous, unnamable smears sprouting patches of blood-stiffened hair.

It was if the caretaker had driven his small herd not down the long escalator, but into the threshing viciousness of it. And still it rumbled contentedly, grinding and spreading, stretching and tearing, God's gentlest creatures not even recognizable as meat.

Mister White drew sustenance from the fear of his prey, but the meager notes in Bierce's possession indicated that, on occasions not entirely understood, he required more. The carnage of feeding. An abattoir.

Bierce panned the flashlight function of his phone across the moving stairs until he stepped onto the slick wetness of one, slipping, grabbing at the sliding rubber rail with a disgusted curse. Already he could feel the damp grue seeping through the salted leather of his shoes.

He steeled himself and descended in silence towards the flickering light, down the length of several ordinary escalators strung together, stories beneath Virginia's fertile green surface, to where the earth grew secretive.

Bierce had not lied when he sketched the facility's past for Ronald, though he had failed to color in the true horror of the place. America's proud tradition of medical experimentation on prison inmates had continued at this secret facility. An attempt to weaponize syphilis, the tactical plan being to insert infected operatives into Soviet submarine ports, whereupon they would convert eager young sailors into disease vectors on the closed confines of a submersible. Eliminate the submarine-born missile threat without firing a shot.

Remaining records indicated that forty-two prisoners had died during the experiment, screaming syphilitic madmen with decaying brains. Deemed unreliable, the weaponized strain remained under lock and key at the Center for Disease Control. The corpses had been fed to the onsite incinerator.

Wicked, unhallowed earth full of pain and memory, perfect to house the object.

Bierce shivered and panned his light along the descending

wall, frowning at the brown traces of graffiti. *They shouldn't have been up this far.*

He touched the gun through his jacket and told himself he was reassured by it.

The descent was timed to be exactly three-and-one-half minutes in length. At the three-minute mark, the uneven light from below had grown enough to reveal details, and Bierce involuntarily stepped back and up as he beheld the fleshy carnage at the base.

A red and lumpy slurry had formed at the bottom of the escalator where the collapsing stairs disappeared into the metal teeth of the landing plate, a churning, splattering mulch revealing here the white of bone, there the slap of fur-covered skin. Even as his stomach roiled at the sight, a thick butcher-shop stench assaulted his nostrils. Bierce slapped a hand over his nose and forced himself to breathe through his mouth, but he could feel the foulness of it crawling on his tongue.

He leapt over the ugly froth at the bottom, heels skidding in the ichor until he caught his balance, glancing down at the darkening cuffs of his slacks. He silently damned the men who had brought the object back from the hell of World War II as he removed a long iron key from his pocket.

He had hoped to discover Ronald waiting by this final gate, but the man was nowhere to be found.

Bierce approached the rusty metal mesh, feet sucking off the floor with each step. He inserted the key with a tiny clatter, his hand shaking, and turned it hard to the right.

Tumblers clicked inside the gate and he pushed it open with a horrendous screech, flakes of rust falling to the floor. Beyond the doorway he saw more bloody footsteps.

Bierce stepped through and closed the gate behind him, kicking aside a scattering of empty dog food cans. He listened for sound of the lock engaging before striding forward into madness.

- 5 -

Bierce covered his nose and muffled a cough. The smell beyond the security gate was an almost physical force combined of human body odor, horrendous flatulence, the acidic tang of urine and a nauseating under-smell of organic rot.

The corridor itself was narrow and windowless, the air unmoving. Only a few of the overhead fluorescents worked, and Bierce made out peeling paint and a filthy floor of black-and-white tiles stretching ahead to an intersection where a light strobed irregularly.

There was not a living soul in sight.

He thought briefly of calling out for Ronald but decided against it. The stillness of the place urged silence.

Bierce proceeded, heels peeling from the tiles as he stepped over a carefully arranged circle of empty dog food cans. A few fat flies buzzed sluggishly over the rancid containers, scattering as Bierce moved through their air space and reforming after he had passed.

He listened for voices and heard nothing. At the intersection he paused, listening again. The footprints had grown fainter and eventually vanished altogether.

The corridor to his left had only a single working light. It flickered off as he looked and plunged the hallway into pitch blackness. When it flashed alight again, Bierce made out open doorways on either side of the hall.

He glanced to his right and saw another hall lined with closed doors and a floor covered in dust. The rotting smell was stronger from that direction and Bierce recoiled, turning back.

A woman of pure white was watching him from twenty feet away. Nightgown, hair and skin reflected like dull alabaster.

"What?" Bierce said, startled.

The light flickered out and he took an involuntary step back, kicking through another circle of empty cans with an ungodly clatter.

"Hello?" he called out softly as the light snapped on. He wondered how much of her mind had been consumed, cored by Mister White's hunger for her fear.

The corridor was empty. Bierce stepped carefully down the hall to the place where the woman had stood, his feet brushing through curls of torn newspaper.

"Hello?" he said again as the light went out.

He froze, ears straining, and heard nothing until a buzz and snap heralded the return of the light. He continued forward.

The first several doors opened into cramped rooms with rusted furniture. His tension grew as the light stayed on, and he wondered when it would go out. Madness felt inevitable in such a place.

Instinct led him closer to the wall and he sidled carefully up to the next door, leaning around for a quick look.

"What—"

It looked like the inside of a dumpster. Faded food wrappers and ancient soda cans littered the floor, and an enormous pile of shredded newspaper was heaped in a far corner. The light overhead had been smashed, despite the protection of a wire cage.

The hall lights went out and Bierce pulled back in surprise. He was just gathering himself, straightening up, when he heard a loud rustling from inside the room.

Buzz-snap.

The light came on and Bierce froze.

The pile of newspapers had moved, halving the distance between the far corner and the door.

Bierce backpedaled, unnerved. When the light vanished again, he turned and took several long strides, not quite breaking into a run. The rustle behind him grew louder and then stopped. A word floated to him through the dark.

"Hello?"

An open double door was visible up ahead, dim light and a hissing sound emanating from it. Bierce hurried towards it, slipping around the corner to find himself in a large bathroom.

"Hello?" The voice was muffled but getting closer, and Bierce moved across the moldering bathroom towards the sound of flowing water. He had the vague memory of playing in an indoor pool, the shouts of the children amplified in the damp space.

The stench was staggering. His steps echoed as he pushed forward only out of a sudden and very real sense of danger until he skidded to a stop, at first not sure of what he was seeing.

The shower room was long and claustrophobic, with ten showerheads on each wall, long brown stains on the tiles beneath them. Bierce identified the hissing sound as coming from the single showerhead that was working, it's spray of dirty water striking the back of a woman's hospital gown, plastering it to her buttocks and legs as she swayed slightly from side to side, muttering.

He stopped in mid-motion, afraid to attract attention.

There were twelve of them. Soulless bodies standing in a circle, looking at something on the ground in their midst, something Bierce could not see. They swayed, out of synch with one another, slowly and clumsily shuffling around the circle until the woman had moved from under the spray and a man stepped into the blasting water, oblivious as it soaked through his gown.

Bierce held his breath and took a step backwards. He took another step, forcing his imagination away from the questions. *What was in the middle of the circle? What were they staring at?*

He stepped slightly to the left, out of the line of sight of anyone in the shower room, and released his breath. Even with his protections, to see what they saw would be to embrace the world as envisioned by Mister White, a sight that would surely drive him mad.

They were the embodiment of minds consumed. Bierce struggled to shore up the walls of his own sanity, refusing to consider the idea that if he was not exceedingly careful, one day he too might take a place in that circle and share their vision of Hell.

- 6 -

Her name was Bella and she thought she was dreaming when the man from outside entered the ward. As he approached, she saw his paleness and decided it was a trick. She fled, white hair streaming behind her. In her own room no one could find her. She was safe. She burrowed.

As she calmed herself, the man reminded her of streets and cars and ordering dinner at a restaurant. A world beyond here. She came to believe that this man was not *Him*. This one was a sad man, she decided, and a sad man would understand. A sad man would help her leave the ward.

It's a trick! It's a trick, and you know it, Bella.

"Hello?" His voice was clear and sounded so much of outside, of sanity, that she almost wept.

He'll think you're sick, Bella. Sick people don't leave the underground.

She moved closer along the floor, carefully. But he was gone, and she forced herself to uncurl from underneath the newspaper and slip quietly out into the hall. A wraith named Bella.

In the safety of the dark, she thought she answered him. "Hello?"

Why didn't he respond? Did she actually speak? She used her hands to open her mouth and tried again. "Hello?"

But he left her dark hallway and went into the shower place. She couldn't go any closer. Goosebumps erupted across her exposed arms and she shivered. She closed her eyes. A second? A minute? Time was becoming taffy, and she railed at the early warning sign of psychosis.

Open your eyes, girl. Open!

She used her fingers to peel her eyelids up and saw the back of the man as he strode quickly away.

NO!

With him departed distant dreams of sunlight on her skin and wind rustling her hair. Dreams, surely, because they could not be memories. There was no time before the now. She was of the underground and had always lived in the underground.

Lucidity—more a cruel tease than a friend of Bella's—chose that moment to slide away between the cracks. She dropped to her knees, crawling back down the flickering corridor to her burrow where she brushed aside debris and crawled inside a ring for safety, carefully setting upright the cans that had tipped.

As Bella—conscious Bella—grew smaller and smaller in her mind, she railed and fought. She screamed for him, screamed inside her diminishing mind.

"Hello!"

- 7 -

The unclean atmosphere grew noticeably thicker as Bierce approached the chamber that held the object. After eluding the woman in white, he had passed several more geometric shapes made from tin cans, shapes that tickled at his understanding. But he refused to address them consciously, terribly aware of the traps that existed in this subterranean place.

The people who lived here now had once lived in the light of day as he did, but they had not been careful as they cared for the facility and the object within. They had allowed themselves to consider, to ponder without suitable precautions, and thus were lost.

Bierce did not intend to join them.

He armed sweat from his upper lip with the gray sleeve of his jacket, aware of the growing damp beneath his armpits and in the crotch of his slacks. It was a soupy air, difficult to breathe, and his lungs labored from more than fear as he came to the unmarked door at the end of a long corridor.

Here he paused to remove the file from under his arm, opening it to remind himself of the page number he needed before compulsively closing it with a snap.

He straightened his spine, inhaled a long breath through his nose and pushed it back out through his mouth before taking the slimy doorknob in his free hand and pulling open the door. He strode through as if late for an executive meeting.

The chamber itself was not large, and a black excrescence had grown in biological patterns below the two air vents. It was a wet, mossy substance that sent tendrils across the crumbling acoustic tile of the ceiling and dangled from above like sickly Spanish moss.

A single tattered goat's hoof lay between Bierce and the object.

It was a tall, coffin-like box of rotting wood and peeling paint, covered in all manner of obscene graffiti with the word TELEFON inscribed at the top. It stank of fresh piss and lost hope, emitting a subliminal message of unwelcome.

Contained in the folder beneath Bierce's arm were photographs and a detailed study of every marking on the surface, an attempt to understand how the object had come to be what it was. That it was originally from Berlin they were certain, but other than that, the experts could not say.

Experts. They were children fumbling in the dark with atomic weapons. A team of would-be Oppenheimers illiterate in physics. They knew, to a limited extent, what it could do. But not why. Not how.

It was hideous, a Bavarian work of art gone awry, with severed wires dangling from the back like black hair from a wart. The semi-liquid moss hanging from the ceiling had reached down to touch the surface, or perhaps the phone box had reached up to spread its corruption. Bierce was struck again by a desire to reinstate the old emergency protocols that were designed to fill the corridors with benzene fumes and detonate the underground compound like a massive fuel-air bomb, incinerating everything inside in the event the weaponized syphilis escaped confinement.

Bierce pushed such thoughts away, clearing his mind before attending to the business at hand.

The booth's folding doors were pushed open and the interior was blacker than it had a right to be. Extending from within was a long cord connected to the tubular ear piece for the ancient candlestick phone it contained.

Ronald was inside listening to the phone, facing away from Bierce, hunched over as if his internal machinery had spun down to dormancy. He took the phone away from his ear with a meaty tearing sound, his mouth opening in a silent shriek as the cartilaginous organ was torn away from his skull. Rivulets of bright scarlet danced down the side of Ronald's neck as his anguished eyes met those of Bierce.

"It's for you, dear," Ronald said, before dropping the handset so that it swung back into the opaque interior with a whack. He shuffled out of the booth and patted Bierce on the shoulder as he moved past.

Bierce cleared his throat and opened the file once more,

committing the fourteen-digit number to memory, knowing from past experience that he would be unable to read once inside the dark space.

"Right, then..." Bierce said.

He carefully opened the book to the page he needed and committed the words to memory as he angled sideways into the phone booth, gagging at the palpable stench and closing the door behind him.

Ronald looked back at the phone booth, lips stretched in an idiot grin. With the door closed, he almost couldn't hear Bierce screaming.

CHAPTER
NINETEEN

- 1 -

"Morphine," the Fat Man slurred into the darkness as his consciousness swam up from the depths of Lethe. He was aware of the rank sweat pooling between his breasts and running down the folds of his flesh beneath the hospital gown as his body fought the infection.

He struggled to see past the bulk of his own middle to the heavily bandaged stumps at the end of his legs. Tears boiled from his eyes as he realized that the disfigurement was real, not a symptom of his unending nightmare.

I am in hospital in Landstrasse. I am in Vienna.

He groped for the call button as his eyes slid to the closet door, open just a crack. A hoarse whisper drifted forth from inside, "Herr Gruebel."

"No," he whispered as it swung open with a faint squeak of hinges and the shadows inside stirred. What he at first took to be the dim outline of a hanging coat stepped out and into the room. He drew in a breath to shout as the shadow flowed towards him, and the smothering white of a pillow was placed over his face.

- 2 -

Warmth flooded his extremities and lit his mind with heroin joy as Herr Gruebel opened his eyes to see the outline of an intruder beside his bed.

The intruder removed the syringe from an IV connected to the Fat Man's wrist and set it on the nightstand.

"You are not him," Herr Gruebel whispered.

"I am Strigoi," Lewis said, and his eyes flashed in the reflected light of the heart monitor. "Herr Gruebel, who is Mister White?"

The Fat Man flinched and waved a palsied hand. "To say that name is death." He glanced at the phone on the bedside table and closed his eyes. "He lurks and listens for his name and rides our own creations to follow us."

Lewis glanced at the phone. "Phones? There are phones everywhere."

"And so is he."

Slats of light from the sodium lamps outside slipped through the venetian blinds to illuminate unsettling features of Lewis's face. Hard eyes. Narrow lips. Unshaven jaw. Even as the opiate set his mind adrift, Gruebel knew he recognized in this man another denizen of the shadow world. A creeper of alleys and slitter of throats. A spy.

"He's after me. Tell me who he is."

"If he's after you, then I speak to a dead man."

"Why do you say that? He didn't kill you."

Gruebel released a long sigh. "As hunters will hang a pheasant until the meat grows high with flavor, so too may this one have left me to stew in the juices of my own fear, to make of me a more savory meal." He grinned. "Or perhaps I am simply unimportant."

"Why did he kill Abel?"

The Fat Man twitched nervously, but the opiate kept the fear to a distant clamor at the back of his memory. "Abel was a bad man."

"Why is he trying to kill me?"

The Fat Man looked at him, watching the visitor's body stretch like toffee or a shape in a funhouse mirror as the opiates ate away at Gruebel's hold on reality.

"Morphine," the Fat Man said.

"Later. Tell me who he is."

The Fat Man shivered, aware of each pore on his body emitting a single, oily bead of sweat. "He is the blind goat with eyes of burning coal."

"What?"

"His form is albino, furred and hoofed."

Lewis leaned over and rocked the Fat Man's head with a sharp slap.

The hospital room swam around Gruebel and words began to draw out into long lines of sound.

"Whoooo iiiiis heeeee?"

"A nightmare who rides men as a man would ride a horse," Gruebel said. "Even now there is one with an empty mind wandering the streets of Vienna, having been used and abandoned. Where the bodies of the mad and empty wash up on riverbanks and freeze beneath bridges, there you know he has passed."

"Is he human?"

The Fat Man shook his head slowly. "Perhaps he is the goat-headed Baphomet. Perhaps he is the evil within your own mind. He follows the scent of your terror."

"Can he be killed?"

Again, a shake of the large, round head. "Can you kill a nightmare?"

Lewis walked away and turned back to see the Fat Man's eyes rolling like marbles as they tracked him.

"Who watches the watchers?" Gruebel whispered, straining for clarity of thought. "Ask yourself who would be displeased with Abel."

Lewis bunched the Fat Man's gown in his fists and leaned close. "Are you saying he was sent?"

"Eyes of red," the Fat Man muttered. "Fur of white." His eyelids fluttered and he grabbed Lewis's wrist with shocking strength. "Do you also work for Herr Bierce?"

"What about Bierce?" Lewis demanded.

"Morphine," the Fat Man pleaded. "Morphine before he comes."

Lewis pulled free and stepped away, rubbing his wrist before retrieving the syringe from the nightstand.

"Are you sure?" Lewis asked, and the Fat Man nodded, quietly weeping.

"He wants you fat with fear before he takes you. It is his bread and wine. Morphine before he comes for me, and for yourself as well if you are wise," Gruebel said.

Lewis re-inserted the needed into the IV tube and depressed the plunger, injecting the remainder of the drug into the Fat Man's system.

- 3 -

Lewis lit a cigarette as he passed the Belvedere Palace in Vienna's Landstrasse district, long since closed to tourists for the day. His shoes tocked hollowly on the sidewalk as he glanced around and flicked the match into the quiet street, disguising a quick look back towards the low building which contained the private hospital in which he had found Gruebel, the information broker.

The Fat Man's fear had been genuine, but his scattered thoughts reeked of opiates. Lewis wondered if the day he had spent locating Gruebel, and the time it took to infiltrate the hospital, had been wasted.

His memory conjured the clatter of hooves atop the train and he turned towards a rhythmic tapping. Only a windblown shutter banging against a wall.

Not a blind goat to be seen.

"Madness," Lewis whispered. But Gruebel knew of Bierce. "It has to be madness."

Eyes of red. Fur of white.

CHAPTER TWENTY

- 1 -

Hedde sat on the thin mattress and stared at the bars of the crib, caught in a strange current as inescapable reality coalesced around her yet became more difficult to see. The smell of Etienne, of Uncle Gerard's coffee and of sharp tobacco gained strength and developed clearly discernible outlines even as her ability to remember her home, schoolboys and the sullen tension of a mother on the verge of divorce grew into diffuse, fantastical creations by C.S. Lewis.

She did not understand that she was in shock. Having fought hard to learn so much so young, she had yet to realize that there were, and always would be, events and feelings beyond her capacity to comprehend. They would push her and shove her and roll her like a vicious breaker at the seashore.

And there she was, staring at the crib while wearing the same dress she had worn for two days now, rolling in the surf with no idea which way was up, was air. No idea that she was drowning.

"Etienne!" she said.

Hedde cocked her head as she laced up her Doc Martens, but did not hear the scrabbling crash of his charge through the house, unaware that she was already clinging to the dog as a talisman against the dark waters swirling over her head.

Uncle Gerard had left her a fresh pot of coffee as well as cigarette makings while he went off to do whatever he did on frozen mornings. Something to do with the Christmas trees. Hedde sipped and she smoked in silence. She wondered if this was what adulthood would feel like. Alone and confused in a place that was not, and could never be, a true home.

Rolling in the surf. Drowning.

Hedde wandered the sparsely furnished house trailing cigarette smoke, touching this here and that there, noting the absence of personality in the rooms and wondering if that did reflect her uncle's personality.

Cold seeped from the wooden door leading down to the basement and she heard the rumble and chug of subterranean machinery. The door was locked and she decided to save exploring that for later, instead pouring herself another cup of coffee, the cup burning her hand as she trudged up the creaky wooden staircase, running fingers along a banister made smooth by years of sliding hands.

The hall upstairs seemed built for another time, too thin and too tall for this age. It conjured images of narrow New England schoolmasters and memories of *The Crucible*, that most terrifying play. The ever-present gray of the sky, the dead, leafless trees with bony branches drooping towards the iron-hard ground, all were of a piece with her taciturn uncle and these too-thin, too-tall hallways.

She paused in her room to neaten the blankets, shifting the mattress until the corner was in tune with the corner of the room itself. The crib was slightly out of alignment and she shifted that, casting a weather eye between the never-baby's bed and her own until she was sure that they were in tune.

The door to her uncle's room was not completely closed, and

she pushed it open but hesitated to step inside. It was a dark space, the shades drawn, the smell of his sweat heavy in the air, as if it were the den of an animal. She stepped back into the hall and pulled the door firmly shut.

Shrouded in shadows at the end of the dim hallway was an incongruous red door of a tall and skinny shape, signifying through color and style that it led to no ordinary bedroom. Red. Somebody had painted it red. From the peeling state of the paint, the deed had been done long ago.

She tried the knob but it refused to turn, so she set her coffee cup on the floor and raced downstairs in a great clattering of boots, fetched a butter knife from a drawer in the kitchen and thundered back upstairs, winded by the time she returned.

Inserting the slim blade between the door and jam, she pressed and wiggled while gently trying to twist the knob until the simple lock gave way. She stepped back as the door swung open with a drawn out screech of hinges.

"Merde," she muttered.

Cobwebs hung down over a steep staircase of dark wood. There was light from above but not much, and she backed away from the open door, unwilling to turn her back on it until she reached her own room where she darted inside, emerging after a moment with the fat candle in her hand. If ever there was a place that should be explored by candlelight, it was the attic behind the red door.

She lit the candle with a wooden lucifer and licked her fingertips to pinch the match flame out, hissing even as the sulfur spat and the fire died. Holding the candle aloft before her, she ascended the stairs, dust puffing beneath her boots, the steps groaning with sounds as individual as notes of a piano. Her mind was suffused with images of séances and tapping tables where mysterious gusts blew out flames and shrill piano notes floated up through cracks in the stained floor.

All were washed away as she rose up from the floor into what she knew in her heart was a deadroom.

Faint streamers of sunlight slanted in through curtained windows set high in one wall above an unmade bed. Dust lay over everything, and when she touched the grayed coverlet, a small puff arose. She pressed her free hand over her nose to repress a sneeze as she turned in place to take in the bedroom. With its dust and vague lighting, it was no more real than the black-and-white horror movies she used to watch in the basement with her father, flickering light rendering the familiar space as fantastical as the imaginary reality on screen.

A coffee cup rested on one nightstand, the inside black with mold, and there were still hairs trapped in the brush that rested on the dresser alongside an open tube of lipstick that was slowly growing into the wood. She twined a hair around one finger, feeling the woman's presence despite the lack of upkeep.

Perhaps that was why the door was locked. The woman was still here.

In her mind's eyes, Hedde saw the stack of dusty games on the living room shelf. The long box with the Parker Brothers logo, in which lay the planchette and Ouija board.

She turned guiltily, feeling the pressure of observation.

"Is anyone here?" she asked, but there was no response. She walked closer to the dusty photographs in frames, wiping aside gray talc with her fingers to see a beardless Gerard and a woman with honey-colored hair and a wide smile.

Hedde set the picture back, its resting spot easily rediscovered in the dusty surface, imagining some other Uncle Gerard, someone who could make a woman laugh.

Blouses and pants were still folded in dresser drawers and mementos of another life were littered about. She wondered why Uncle Gerard had kept them before encountering the frightening question of whether she would be able to throw out the physical memory of a loved one. She who had never held hands, never kissed a boy.

Hedde closed the drawers, but a moldy, green smell had entered the air and she wondered if keeping these things was healthy.

The inquisitive part of her mind was keenly aware that she was trying on these emotions in preparation for radical changes in her own life, but that voice was drowned out by the shrieking furies of denial.

She bent down to look through a grate in the floor leading into a dark room she believed was her uncle's and was just able to make out another grate on the floor of that room, deciding it had something to do with heating but not entirely sure what. As she straightened she bumped a rocking chair, which obliged her with a satisfying squeak as she approached the bookcase covering one entire wall.

Her flush of excitement soon faded when she realized that every single book was a mystery. Worse, old lady mysteries. Agatha Christie. Ngaio Marsh. She imagined Uncle Gerard reading about the fussy Belgian investigator and felt an urge to grin in spite of her surroundings.

These belonged to the lady with the honey-colored hair.

Hedde ran her finger along the spines of the shelved paperbacks, smoothing them into alignment so that none stuck out farther than the other, before taking one worn volume off the shelf. She sat cross-legged in front of the bookcase, enjoying the musty smell of old paper, a welcome intruder in the stale air of the bedroom.

"They were Lucy's," a voice said.

Hedde twisted around in surprise to see Gerard's head just above the level of the floor, features unreadable.

"I'm sorry—" She started to apologize, but he held up a hand and she went silent, face flushing. She watched his eyes glitter in a slanting beam of light for the count of several breaths until he sighed.

"Want to meet her?"

- 2 -

"It's mugwort. Can't believe it survived this far into the season," Hedde said, placing the small wreath of stem and leaves atop the cold granite headstone. "Sailors used it to clear up asthma."

She was babbling but unable to stop as Gerard's silence deepened. He was crouched in front of the stone with one wind-burned hand splayed against the granite, reading the four carved lines as if unraveling a mystery. She couldn't bring herself to look at the words. The dates. All she could think about was today, maybe her father's last, an ocean away. Maybe her mother's last, gone off somewhere to help dad.

"I come here once a month or so to check in," Gerard said, so quiet she wasn't sure if the words were meant for her. "During the summer, Rich Finnegan doesn't mind if I help myself to his rake and clippers, keep things neat." He drew in a big breath and blew it out. "Good guy, Rich."

He stood and cast a long shadow over her so she stepped to the side, back into the sunshine. "I know you're lost at sea, Hedde, and I'm not much for offering comfort."

"I—" Hedde bit off the rest of her words, realizing she had nothing to say. It was true. She was lost and Uncle Gerard was about as comforting as a rock.

Gerard plucked a twenty from the pocket of his jeans. "Less than a half mile that way is Annie's Book Stop. Might find yourself something better than one of those Agatha Christie's."

She took the offered money and looked at it, then at him. "Will you be okay?"

"Yes," he rested his hand on the stone again. "Gonna talk with Lucy for a little while. I'll come get you at the bookstore."

"Okay."

"Take Etienne with you." Gerard stuck two fingers in his mouth and let out a piercing whistle, but they heard no answering bark. "Okay, never mind the dog. I'll see you in a little bit."

Hedde crunched across the snow, careful not to slip where it had been packed down hard on the small road leading into the cemetery.

Alone.

Hedde never did make it to Annie's Book Stop.

- 3 -

There wasn't much to downtown Flintlock, and much of what was there sported boards over the windows and futile FOR RENT signs. It looked to her suburban eye like a place that the future had passed by, but it didn't quite know it yet.

A van motored past, Pink Floyd trailing from half-opened windows, and she turned her face away from flying road debris. The street and sidewalks were gritty from salt trucks, and even the wall of snow along the curb was ashy with dirt. A little kid in a hand-me-down snowsuit sat on the ridge of snow, breaking off chunks which he winged side-arm at a house, presumably his. A tuft of insulation escaped from a tear in his sleeve with every throw, floating in the air like an out-of-season milkweed puff.

Hedde wondered why the kid wasn't in school and why his mother didn't tell him to stop throwing ice at the house. He didn't turn or even seem to notice her as she walked past him, even though she was close enough to snatch off his hat, if she had wished.

She passed a bar and a place called the Blue Jay Café, Boston Bruins banners in the windows and a row of pickups snuggled up to the curb like so many suckling pigs. Everything was painted in grays or yellowy whites that had all the dirty appeal of nicotine-stained teeth, as if the idea of color were against a local ordinance. She thought of the red door that led to a once-happy attic and knew it had been Lucy's doing. Color brought into her uncle's grim world.

She kicked a chunk of ice ahead of her as she passed an insurance office, the towering two stories of a brick municipal building and the brightly lit Flintlock House of Pizza.

A poster board sign had been affixed to the building next door. Written in black marker with an arrow pointing at the pizza joint, the sign read PLEASE RESPECT NEIGHBORS AND KEEP NOSE DOWN. Yes, *nose*. Written in soap inside the House of Pizza's plate-glass window was TURN IT UP! Score one for pizza and spelling. Hedde suspected she knew who was winning Flintlock's civil war.

She stopped to look at the place, inhaling the odors of baking crust, red sauce and cigarettes, all scents of which she approved. It couldn't be good, definitely not up to New York standards, but she thought she might try convincing Uncle Gerard to pick up a pie for dinner.

Two boys were smoking cigarettes and leaning against the windows of the pizza joint, faces dotted with acne below shaggy hair cuts, wearing hooded sweatshirts beneath denim jackets. They held themselves as if immune to the cold in the way that New Englanders do, working towards the sullen indifference of folks who have seen other people's lives on TV while knowing it's not for them. Even with all of this going for them, Hedde would have normally passed on by, but they were near enough to her age that it satisfied some need for normalcy.

And they had real cigarettes.

"Can I bum a cigarette?" Hedde asked as she looked up at them. Tall, rawboned types with narrow features, one clean shaven, one with dark wisps of hair on his upper lip.

"You smoke?" Peach Fuzz said.

"My Uncle's got me smoking his hand rolls, but I'm craving a real one."

"Who's your uncle?" he asked.

"Gerard Beaumont."

The two townies exchanged looks, and the clean-shaven boy held out a pack of Camels. "Knock yourself out." She noticed that the skin below his right eye was a faded purple and yellow.

Hedde lipped a cigarette free and leaned in as the boy held out a lighter, hands cupped to protect the flame. She drew in smoke and let it trail from her nostrils with a sigh of relief.

"Thanks," she said.

"You gonna be going to FHS?" Peach Fuzz asked.

"What?"

"Flintlock High School."

"No, I'm just visiting."

"Gerard Beaumont," Black Eye said.

"Yes, do you know him?"

Black eye nodded. "Everybody does."

"Flintcock ain't too big," Peach Fuzz added and both boys snickered.

"So, you a Mormon?" Black Eye asked, and she shook her head. "You dress like a Mormon."

"Or a Jehovah's Witness," Peach Fuzz added.

"No I don't," Hedde said.

"So what are you then?" Black Eye asked.

"I'm wiccan."

"What?"

And because she thought it would shut them up. "I'm a witch."

The two boys glanced at each other again. "No fuckin' way," Peach Fuzz said.

"Yes fucking way," Hedde said.

Black Eye pushed off the House of Pizza. "My sidekick here is Ray Childers."

"Meetcha," Ray said, also straightening.

"I'm Hedde."

Black Eye looked her up and down. "So, you wanna see a haunted bridge?"

"Is it far?"

"It's close, and it's pretty cool," Ray said.

"Okay," she said, falling in beside the two boys as they set off down the sidewalk. She tapped Black Eye on the shoulder.

"You didn't tell me your name," she said.

He slid the cigarette to the corner of his mouth with a movement of his lips and grinned. "Dickie LaChaise."

- 4 -

They took a turn onto an unplowed road and the walking grew harder, all three of them huffing and puffing from the effort, pushing aside small, whippy branches of trees from the overgrown woods on either side. She studied the towering pines scattered throughout the woods, so unlike the trees back home whose branches became as skeletal as fingers denuded of flesh in winter. Instead, these kept their furry needles and spread over the road like wide green hands gloved in powdered sugar. When they dropped their load of snow, it made a soft thump on the ground.

Hedde paused and ran fingers along a thin branch sporting bright red berries, considering their attractive coloring and what she was doing out in the woods until Ray said, "Them are poisonous," and she moved on.

They took turns crossing a rusty chain hanging across the road with a sign reading NO ENTRY. Dickie offered her a hand but she ignored it, flashing a little too much leg and feeling the chill as she crossed the barrier, wondering if she should just turn around and go back.

"Is it much farther? My uncle will be waiting for me." She spoke to the prematurely balding spot on the back of his head, and he didn't bother to turn as he responded.

"It's right here," Dickie said.

"Don't be a wuss," Ray said.

She heard a car crackling over ice not far behind her and could smell wood smoke, so she knew she wasn't far off the main road. Still, she felt isolated amongst the trees, sounds muffled by the snow, breath steaming in the air. In the shade of the trees the cold became more pronounced, slipping fingers into every gap of her clothing. She wished she had a hat. She wished she had gloves. She wished she hadn't decided to follow two boys to a haunted bridge.

"So this bridge has been closed for like, fifteen years, right before we were born," Dickie said. "They were gonna make it into a historical thing—"

"Landmark," Ray added.

"Right," Dickie continued. "Then it happened."

"Fucked up the whole town," Ray added.

"There was a big lawsuit but because they were drinking, it got thrown out," Dickie said.

They trudged on until Hedde picked up a chunk of snow and threw it past Dickie.

"What happened?" she asked.

Dickie turned around and grinned on one side of his mouth as he tossed his cigarette butt into the snow.

"Six kids died."

"Zut alors," Hedde said.

"High school kids partying and the bottom collapsed. They hit the river and went right through the ice. Not a single one of them made it out," Dickie said.

"They froze," Ray said.

"They drowned," Dickie said.

"One kid floated all the way to Portsmouth," Ray said.

"And it all happened right here," Dickie said with a sweep of one arm, and Hedde saw it, a long, covered bridge like something from a wall calendar. Its walls were a faded red, with open spaces in place of windows and a cap of white frosting the gently peaked roof. The river gurgled over rocks some twenty feet below, and while it wasn't terribly wide, it did look deep. A grim fascination tugged at Hedde and she moved past the boys, dislodging small clumps of snow as she pushed aside branches until she was close enough to see into the shaded interior, letting her eyes adjust until she could see the gaping wound in the flooring.

"No way," she said.

"Yes way," Dickie said.

"Every kid in town has to go across it, like it's a secret rule," Ray said.

"A ritual," Dickie said.

Hedde forced a laugh, shaking her head. "Count me out."

"Every kid does it," Dickie said, and Hedde turned to take in his smirk, his crossed arms.

"Ah, that would be a nope," she said.

"Then show us your tits," Dickie said, and Ray laughed.

Hedde felt something cold gather in her middle as she realized she was trapped between a murderous bridge and the two boys.

"That's not funny," she said.

"That's 'cause I'm not fuckin' joking," Dickie said, his eyes glittering like black beads.

"Christ, you barely even got any," Ray said. "You should be happy someone wants to see 'em."

"Fuck you," she said and moved to pass around them, but Ray stepped into her path.

"Open up your coat," he said. "C'mon, you know you wanna."

Hedde's vision narrowed as, by some miracle, her mind accelerated to warp speed. She saw herself meeting the boys, relived their brief journey to the bridge, berating herself for being so stupid even as some part of her spiraled down like the drill of an oil well, tapping the darkness in her core. She felt that she could see every greasy pore on their faces, could hear the pulmonary expansion and contraction of the alveoli in their lungs, could feel each one of her own nerve endings like metallic pricks against her skin.

"Take it off," Ray said, stepping forward.

"Your breath stinks," she said, and shocked both boys when she lunged at Dickie.

Ancient signals traveled from her brain to her hand and she hooked her fingers into a claw, tearing red furrows down Dickie's cheek as she charged into him, all the while emitting a siren shriek as she butted him back and bit the hand he used to fend her off, slashing at his eyes but catching an ear as he jerked his head to the side. His eyes bulged with terror, and a string of spit hung from his gaping mouth as he retreated and Hedde overwhelmed him.

The blow to the back of her head felt strangely soft, and she felt not so much pressure as warmth on her skull as she fell face down in the snow. Something—a boot—struck her side but was largely absorbed by her winter coat as hands grabbed her and flipped her into her back. She looked up with slowly gathering cognition to see Ray shoved aside by a bleeding Dickie, who straddled her and pinned her arms, lips peeled back from his teeth in an animal sneer.

"You fuckin' whore," he hissed. "We was just gonna scare you, but now you're gonna get it good."

It may have been the tears of pain blurring her vision, or maybe it was simply the animal's speed, but Hedde had only a millisecond's awareness of a moving, liquid shadow before snarling fury swept over the fighting teenagers and she felt Dickie's weight leave her.

"Hel—"

Dickie's plea was cut off by the simple expedience of Etienne planting wide paws on his chest and leaning a dripping muzzle down over the boy's terrified face. The Shepherd's lips had drawn back to reveal a great expanse of dark gums and yellowing teeth, and a sound so low as to be almost inaudible rumbled from deep in his chest, more like the base coming from a neighbor's apartment than a growl.

It was the single most terrifying sound Hedde had ever heard and she reveled in it, even as Ray left his friend without a second thought and fled.

Hedde sat up and rubbed the back of her head as the cobwebs drifted from her mind. Dickie tried once more to say, "Please," but the rumbling machinery in Etienne's chest grew louder. Hedde saw an expanding darkness at the crotch of Dickie's jeans.

She stood, brushing the snow away, struggling with the awareness of power. She touched blood gathering beneath her nostrils and looked at the red beads on her pale fingertips, darker than she would have imagined.

"I should let him kill you," she whispered, and Etienne's ear twitched. "Etienne, come here, boy. Good boy."

Etienne stepped almost daintily from the teenager and trotted over to Hedde's side where he leaned his heavy warmth against her. Dickie made as if to sit up and the dog let loose a ripping snarl that froze the boy in place.

"Come on, boy," she said as the trees around her flashed red and blue and she saw a police cruiser grinding towards her through the snow.

- 5 -

The cop in the forest green uniform had introduced himself as Officer Wannamaker, and he had a large nose on a crinkly, brown face and kind eyes beneath a cap of curly, salt-and-pepper hair. In his uniform and Smokey hat he looked more like a park ranger than a cop, but Hedde had decided to withhold that opinion. This was fortunate, if only for his pride, because Officer Wannamaker's first name happened to be Richard, and the Ranger Rick jokes had long since worn thin.

"Show me your tits or walk on that bridge that killed those high school kids," Hedde told him. "I barely have any tits, so I should be happy they want to see them."

Officer Wannamaker looked back at the idling cruiser with smoke curling from the tailpipe. Dickie and Ray waited in the back seat, and the cop's expression was hard to read as he studied them.

Unlike Uncle Gerard's.

His face didn't so much as twitch, but his eyes never left the teenagers in the back seat as he waited, one hand on Etienne's collar.

After going over the events at the bridge a few more times, Officer Wannamaker took off his gloves and gently probed her face and the back of her skull. He asked her if she had a headache or hurt anywhere else, and when she said no, he straightened up and patted her shoulder.

"Gerry?"

"Rick," Gerard said, his eyes never leaving the boys. Hedde saw the same animal focus in her uncle that she had seen in Etienne. "That LaChaise's kid?"

"Now, Gerry," Officer Wannamaker said and turned down his belt radio when it began squawking.

"They said they knew you, Uncle Gerard," Hedde said.

It was the eyes, Hedde decided. Her uncle's eyes were so cold they burned, and when she said what she said it was if a glacier had calved an immense hunk of ice.

"Okay now," Officer Wannamaker said, patting the air. "I'm going to take these boys in and process them, and I'll want a formal statement from both of you. But I think it's best if you and Hedde come down to the station tomorrow. Best for everyone, you included, if you do that tomorrow. You understand?"

Gerard nodded.

"Now the boys are saying that they were attacked by the dog."

"Don't even start," Gerard warned.

"Hey now, you know how much I like Etienne, but that's what they're saying and he wasn't on a leash, so I have to sort this all out and listen to them too."

"Listen to Buddy LaChaise's kid," Gerard said.

"I listened to Dickie," Hedde said. "He called me a whore and said I would get it good."

Officer Wannamaker's mouth opened as if to speak, then he shut it and shook his head. "What a Christing mess. Tomorrow at four, okay? Be there at four."

The officer stomped to his cruiser and shot a quick look back at Gerard, as if afraid the other man would make a sudden rush for the vehicle.

The cruiser backed down the trail it had cut into the snow, not turning off the flashers until it was out of sight. Then it was just the three of them in the cold woods as the shadows lengthened and the river gurgled behind them.

"I'm sorry," Hedde said in a small voice, afraid to look up until she felt her uncle's big hand on her shoulder.

"For what?"

"I don't know what I was thinking."

"It ain't on you. That shit between LaChaise and me goes back. Looks like his boy is as much of an asshole as his dad."

"I shouldn't have gone off with them," she said.

A shrug. "Probably not."

For a while only the wind spoke.

"I'm really scared, Uncle Gerard. Not about this thing, I mean, it was scary, but I can't...I'm more scared..."

He stepped around in front of her and waited until she met his eyes. "I know you are." He looked around as if he scented something. "This thing has a messy feel to it. You keep Etienne with you from now on."

"I will."

CHAPTER TWENTY-ONE

- 1 -

The house whispered to itself in the smallest hours of the night as Hedde slipped away from the warm bulk of the German Shepherd and rose from her mattress.

She shivered, wrapping a blanket around herself as she crept quietly downstairs, pausing at every creaking step to listen for her uncle. She wasn't exactly sure what the rules were regarding the attic room, but thought prudence wise.

Quiet in her wool socks, she pulled a pencil from a coffee mug near the phone as she skated in a kind of sliding walk past the iron bulk of the woodstove and into the dimness of the living room, with its scalloped drapes and soft furniture. This had been *her* room, as much as the attic had been hers, Hedde decided.

She knelt in front of the shelves and reached above the stack of game boxes to pull a notebook down onto the thick rug. She lit a match, holding the tiny light close as she flipped through marked up pages until she reached a blank sheet and tore it free.

She hissed as the flame burned down to her fingers, and she flicked the match into the cold fireplace.

Paper and pencil in hand, she leaned closer to study the titles on the boxes, nodding as she saw what she thought she had seen on her earlier exploration.

Etienne was a black shape waiting for her in the upstairs hall, and Hedde slapped her free hand to her chest in fright. The big dog chuffed at her and she waved him away. "Go back to bed," she whispered. She crept quietly past her uncle's closed door and paused at the red portal to the attic, juggling the candle and paper until she was able to pull the door out towards her, wincing at the squeal of hinges.

A glance back showed Etienne still watching her from the hallway, and she shushed him before ascending the steep staircase.

- 2 -

Gerard lay atop his blankets in the gloom, unable to sleep while his niece crept around the house. He thought about rousing himself to put a kettle of tea on the woodstove but knew from experience that these long, lonely hours often needed to be spent alone, when thoughts pushed aside during daylight made themselves known.

The kid certainly had enough on that front.

He felt a mix of discomfort and pleasure when he heard her creaking ascent into the attic. It was a room he himself had trouble with to this day, still so alive with Lucy. If it brought Hedde comfort, that was a good thing. A space for the girls to hang out would have made Lucy smile.

Her quiet words were clear enough through the heat vent overhead, but he forced himself to roll over and tune them out.

He was a man who understood privacy.

- 3 -

Hedde unfolded a blouse from the dresser and draped it over her shoulders like a shawl, wrapping herself in the musty comfort of the dead woman's clothes as she lay on the bed, placing the flickering candle on a nightstand. It was as if she rested in a small tent of warm light that shielded her from the dark.

She held her palm over the dancing candle flame and lowered it slowly until she felt the heat on her skin, breathing through her nose and biting her lip as the pain grew and drove thoughts of the day from her mind. She lowered her hand further until she smelled something burning, and a sound escaped her as she mashed the wick flat and plunged the attic into darkness.

"Is there anyone here?"

The pungent stab of sulfur invaded her nostrils as she struck another match and relit the candle with her throbbing hand.

She picked up the pencil and began tracing the tip across the paper beside her.

"Hello. I know you're here," she whispered. "Will you speak to me?"

Hedde cocked her head at a faint *tick-tick-tick*. It reminded her of the noise the electric heat made in their house in Westchester, a sound Hedde had been convinced was approaching footsteps when she was a little girl.

Motion from the corner of her eye made her twist in place as the curtains overhead riffled in a non-existent breeze. She glanced down at a crackling sound and saw the candle flame leaning over as if pushed.

"Is someone here?"

The candle hissed once and went out, but Hedde forced

herself to remain in place, slowly scratching the pencil tip across the paper.

She awoke sometime later, sneezing from the dust that covered one side of her face. She didn't look at the piece of paper until she was back in her room, a sleepy Etienne rumbling at her to put out the light.

Written in jagged strokes that tore the paper across her scribbling, Hedde could make out what she thought were two words.

HERR WEISS.

Her sluggish mind struggled to process the meaningless words, but her eyelids felt weighted with stones, and she was soon curled up next to the dog and snoring gently.

CHAPTER
TWENTY-TWO

- 1 -

GRANGER. Cat had been so certain she would never again drive past the black mailbox on its carved stone post. A sense memory of alcohol and his musky stink struck her as she rolled her Jeep slowly up his long driveway. It conformed to some inner logic for her, that she should roll the dice in a foolhardy attempt to save Lewis, in a place that would hurt him deeply.

His house was on a remote acre with miles of conservation land behind it, his neighbors too far away to be seen through the trees on either side.

Jim was a dark silhouette standing in the doorway as she emerged from the Jeep and slammed the door closed. He was a big man who worked with his hands, who had carved the stone of his mailbox post and laid the brick on his own front walk. A swaggering man who went out every deer season and bragged about bear hunting in Canada.

"Hey baby, this is a surprise," he said, leaning against the doorframe. So outwardly different from Lew in every regard.

Fuck him.

"Let me in, Jim. It's cold and we need to talk."

- 2 -

Evening had turned to night outside the living room windows and she sat in a reading chair near the woodstove, which had, naturally, been installed by Jim. He was careful to always look right for his role, tonight in jeans and a checked lumberjack shirt with the sleeves rolled up. His beard was thick and curling, adding to his costume, but she knew he had it trimmed twice a month at the barbershop downtown.

"Wait a fuckin' minute," he was saying. "You told this guy to meet you here? Your husband's boss?"

"I needed a safe place, and you're always bragging about hunting, so I know you have guns."

"Wait a minute—"

"Unless I'm just a cheap piece of ass to you," she said, sipping her beer without taking her eyes off his.

"Of course not," he said, but his expression read more like, *you used to be a piece of ass, now I don't know what the hell you are.*

"It will be fast. I just need to talk to him and look him in the eye, in a place where someone has my back, someone who can kick his lily white tail."

She leaned forward in the rocking chair he'd made, a twin to the one in his bedroom, extending her hands towards the woodstove to ward off a chill that was settling over her. He had once wanted to screw her in the chair, but the armrests had turned the effort into a farce instead of a fuck. *Now is not the time*, she chided herself.

"I need one of these at home," she said with a nod to the stove. "Maybe you'll give me a rate to put one in?"

It was hard to keep the contempt for him from her voice, her eyes, when her heart seethed with so much contempt for herself.

"Shit, Cat, I've been thinking for a while that it's time we got a few things straight, and maybe that time is—" He cocked his head and a quizzical expression moved across his face.

"What is it?" she asked.

"I…" He paused again, listening. "Sounded like someone was up in the bedroom."

She rose and crossed to the window, peering out but unable to see much. Abruptly aware of how visible she would be from the outside, she stepped back behind the curtain.

"Who is this guy you're meeting? You got another boyfriend? This asshole sneak into my house?"

"No, it's Lew's boss. Lew did something at work and I need to talk to him," Cat said, voice suddenly tight with fear. "He's a suit. He wouldn't break into—"

They both heard a wooden creak from upstairs and their startled eyes met.

"Hallway," Jim said.

"I think—"

He cut her off with a slash of his hand.

"Screw this," he said, and lifted a couch cushion, pulling a squared-off automatic pistol out from beneath it. Her eyes flashed to the needlepoint on the wall in red, white and blue threads, a homey piece that read WE DON'T CALL 911, and sported the outline of an old cowboy-type gun beneath it.

"Don't…" she said.

Jim racked the slide and shot her a heavy browed look. "You stay right here. If that's your pal upstairs, there's gonna be hell to pay for him and then you. Got it, babe?"

He turned away before she could respond, rolling his shoulders. Cat picked up her purse from the table and took out the .38, head tilted back as if she could see through the ceiling above. She didn't know if she should run or wait to see what Jim found until the urgency of Lew's note came back to her.

"Shit," she said, stepping lightly as she hurried onto the Spanish tiles of the kitchen floor towards the back door.

She heard a muffled voice from above but caught only pieces of what was said, like listening to an AM radio station as it goes out of range. She heard, "All right, if there's—" and "anybody" and "gun," and then the faint rumble of words without meaning.

And then nothing.

After half a minute had passed she opened her mouth to call out, but the words tangled in her throat.

Shit shit shit.

Cat started for the back door again, ears still straining to catch any sound from above, so attuned to sound that when the lights went out she stumbled and had to bite back a cry. She caught the countertop with her free hand and realized that the entire house had gone dark.

She saw the faint outline of starlight in the panes of glass set into the door and tip-toed towards it, feeling nervous and ridiculous. The knob was winter cold to the touch but she paused, ignoring the discomfort as caution and a sense of responsibility warred within her.

Ultimately, the reality of decades won over the experiences of the past forty-eight hours and she walked back into the living room, eyes picking out shapes in the darkness as they adjusted.

"This is so stupid," she murmured, but whether it was directed at herself or her erstwhile lover, even she didn't know. The idea that he was playing a trick to punish her crossed her mind more than once, and she clung to it as both comforting and annoying. Well, Mr. Tough Guy would be surprised as hell to see that he wasn't the only one who had a gun.

The second floor hall was dark as pitch, and she held the .38 before her in both hands like she was a cop on a TV show.

She lifted her foot onto the first step and left the warmth of the crackling woodstove behind her.

- 3 -

The white phantom flutters of curtains at the end of the upstairs hall caught her eye, and she felt goosebumps crawl across her skin. A quick glance into the bathroom revealed movement and she saw that window was open too. An exceedingly rational inner voice wondered why the hell two windows were open in November. She glanced through an open doorway into the moonlit guest room and saw the curtains dancing there as well. She paused to push the door all the way open, ensuring there was no one behind it.

"Jim?" she whispered, ears straining until she rounded the bed in two long steps and saw nothing but sliding dust bunnies.

She stepped back into the hall, increasingly convinced that Jim was doing this to frighten her. She had met Mr. Bierce on more than one occasion, and he was a humorless type, not one to play games. This wasn't his work.

Jim on the other hand…

"Jim," she hissed, waiting for a response.

The next open door led into the room where he had his workout gear—a weight bench and treadmill. Without the moonlight, it was darker on the backside of the house, but unoccupied.

Both of the windows had been pushed up and she bared her teeth against the cold.

What had they heard upstairs, really? The house settling as interior heat and exterior cold shrank and expanded the wood? Had the windows already been open? Maybe he had been staining something and needed ventilation? She had felt the cold in her bones even inside, even next to the woodstove.

Or was the son of a bitch waiting for her in the master

bedroom, thinking he'd bully her into a goodbye fuck before he threw her out?

"Jim!" A whisper loud enough to make whispering pointless. Still, her vocal cords weren't quite ready to relax themselves yet. Maybe when she saw him, maybe when it was time to tell him exactly what she thought of him...

She heard the shifting drapes before she reached the open door to the master bedroom and paused. These were of heavier material and didn't flutter like the gossamer things in the other rooms, designed to keep him in unlit hibernation on weekend mornings when he needed to sleep it off. Instead, they shifted and rippled enough that she knew the windows behind them were open, but details beyond that sense of movement were hard to make out.

She pushed the open door against the wall and knew he was not waiting for her there. "Jim," she whispered, "You better not be screwing around." The smell struck her then, meaty and moist.

She stepped inside and held her gun out, turning at the waist to track the weapon around the room as she felt for the wall switch, finding the wet plastic plate and flicking it with no re-sult. She wiped her hand on her shirt and took another step inside, opening her mouth to call out, loudly this time, when the darkness shimmered to her right.

She jumped back and jabbed her pistol at the motion as her fist tightened on the weapon and it bucked in her hand with a deafening bang.

Stunned, she froze in place for a moment as her ears rang before she ran to the heavy drapes and jerked them aside to let in the moonlight.

A piece of glass tumbled free from the standing mirror in the corner and she realized she had been fooled, spinning wildly to jab the shaking revolver at the man sitting in the rocking chair.

"Jim? Oh shit, I didn't mean to pull…"

He was looking up at her from the chair holding something wet and glistening against his belly. She stepped closer, aware of the thickening smell as she struggled to understand that the wetness he held *was* his belly.

"Are you all right? What happened?" she asked.

"Cat," he said, and his voice came to her as if through a congealing liquid.

She looked around the room warily and moved until she could see into the adjoining bathroom.

Empty.

"Get up," she hissed, grabbing his arm. He moaned as she pulled him, and the chair began to come up with him before she let him fall back with a crash.

"What happened?"

"You…you…" Thick tributaries ran from the corners of his mouth and she touched him, pushing aside squeamishness as she patted his torso for a wound amidst the liquid, the blood warmer than she had imagined blood would be. Her fingers strayed across a knobby piece of wood in his gut, and she stepped around the chair with mounting horror as she saw the shining end of gardening shears pinning him to the rocker.

Her mind went white as she backed away, forgetting the gun as she clapped a hand to her mouth to hold back the rising scream.

When the backs of her knees bumped into the mattress she did scream, long and howling, and bolted for the door like a woman gone mad, never seeing the pale hands that lunged from beneath the bed, clamping onto her ankles like cruel manacles of ice as she fell headlong. The floor was carpeted, but even so the breath exploded from her body. She was incapable of anything other than mindless writhing as she was dragged by the feet into the origin and endpoint of every childhood nightmare.

CHAPTER TWENTY-THREE

- 1 -

A man named Clark Lorraine stepped off the jetway from Lufthansa flight 772, Vienna to Montreal. He made his way through the bustle of the busy Pierre Elliot Trudeau International Airport, passing through customs easily and pausing to buy a black coffee after waiting in line at a Tim Hortons in the terminal. He looked much the same as the other businessmen emerging from the flight, tired eyes beneath hair cut so short he was nearly bald. Round, steel-rimmed spectacles, a London Fog raincoat and carrying a slightly battered briefcase with a nylon bag over his shoulder.

Though he had checked two suitcases in Vienna, Lorraine made no effort to retrieve them from the baggage claim. Instead, he checked himself into a downtown hotel, the Intercontinental, and made a reservation—with the assistance of a helpful concierge—at the excellent Tocque restaurant, after which he retired to his room.

The shower was an indulgence, one of few he allowed himself, and the over-priced cashews from the minibar were necessary fuel for his badly fatigued body.

Lorraine emptied the contents of the nylon bag onto the soft, white coverlet of the queen-size bed, ignoring the pang of regret that he would not be sleeping in it. He stripped down to his socks and stale boxer shorts before pulling on creased Levi's and a black Boston Bruins hoodie. A blue windbreaker went over the hoodie and he pulled on a black knit cap also sporting the gold, black and white Bruins logo.

He left Lorraine's belongings in the room when he departed and dropped the glasses in a curbside trash can. Lorraine was burned. Gone. He would never walk the earth again, and the paperwork that Lewis Edgar had retrieved from a locker in Frankfurt had no more value.

Sean Finnegan headed for the train station on foot, grinning at the occasional catcall from Montreal locals and pausing to banter with two Montreal cops who gave him a bit of good-natured shit about the score that night, and the season in general, before he entered the station and queued up for the train south.

US Customs was stern and militant in comparison with their Canadian counterparts, but the Bruins sweatshirt brought the right sort of derision from the New York-based agent, and threats about keeping Boston fans where they belonged—outside the borders. They talked about the score for a moment and how damned good the Montreal Canadiens were, and Finnegan commiserated about the plight of the Islanders.

After ten hours aboard the train, without incident beyond a truly heinous microwaved cheeseburger from the café car, Finnegan emerged in New York City's chaotic Penn Station. He pushed down the crowded sidewalk on Thirty-Second Street, pausing to offer his sweatshirt to a bearded homeless man who said, "Bruins? C'mon, man," before finding the Avis rental office a block south on Thirty-First Street.

The gold Kia was not his choice, but it was what they had on short notice, and he ground his way through honking traffic to the Westside Highway where he headed north.

He was in a realm well past fatigue by this point, his mind stretched out of shape by tension, violence and repeated blows to what he thought of as reality.

But he was close. He had crossed a continent and an ocean already, and knowing that it was only a matter of hours before he would see his wife and daughter filled him with a golden flame that fed his starved circuits and kept him functioning.

Lewis kept his speed even as he headed north on Interstate 287. He would drive up through Vermont before hooking east into New Hampshire.

The hours in transit had given him time to assess what he had experienced and gain some measure of acceptance with the idea of an unnatural or supernatural event. Understanding that he had witnessed some collision of supernatural powers was a step he could climb up to, but the kind old monk's talk of God and the holiness of the nonnen grew harder to hold onto the farther he went from the man. Still, he could reconcile himself to the idea of a territorial collision. Whatever was pursuing him had entered into the realm of the nonnen and, like predators in the wild, the two powers had clashed.

Lucien had said, "It is not important that you believe in what happened the way I, a Catholic, believes. Only that you accept that it was real."

Lewis could work with that.

He did not believe, and neither did Lucien, that his pursuer was destroyed, only temporarily vanquished. In preparation for meeting his hunter again, Lucien had taken Lewis's confession and blessed him in the name of God and the four brave nuns. The monk confessed his own ignorance to the nonnen's ability to extend their protection across the Atlantic, but begged Lewis to find a church in America and take of the blood and flesh, confessing again if he felt able.

Lewis knew of a small Catholic church in the next town over from Flintlock, and he would stop there. Strangely, though Lewis had made a profession of deception, he found himself unwilling to break his promise to Lucien.

He would seek a blessing, hoping for some benefit despite his doubts, after which he would find his wife and child.

"I'm coming, guys," he said in a voice so coarse as to be unrecognizable. He glanced in the rearview mirror at his red-veined eyes and willed his thoughts outward.

After ascertaining his family's safety he would head south again. He expected Bierce would not be happy to see him.

- 2 -

Cat awoke in pain, suffocating, struggling to move but unable, pressed between a sandwich of wood mashing her nose, breasts and hips from above and her shoulder blades and buttocks below. Naked and crushed in a claustrophobe's nightmare, the needle-sharp teeth of panic tearing into her mind.

Her scream was an animal thing, no more hers to call back than was the summer, and her mouth was filled with sawdust and fibers. She coughed, triggering violent eruptions as she convulsed in the great vise holding her until the motion subsided and she stilled, weeping quietly.

She could feel footsteps approaching, hard-soled shoes on a hardwood floor like the one in their bedroom at home. The steps drew closer, measured as a heartbeat, until they seemed to stop directly above her and she felt as if a weight was added to the pressure on her rib cage.

She heard the grunt of someone kneeling and then something tapping on the wood until a slim board was pried up with a great screeching of nails. Cat greedily sucked in air, bloodied nose throbbing in relief.

A familiar brass candlestick was lowered to the floor next to the opening, and in its uneven yellow light she saw a man in a neat business suit lean down, his face drawn by leering shadows into the villain from a black-and-white movie.

"I honestly don't know what advice to give you," the man said, pained. "I don't know if you should tell him what he wants to know immediately, or hold out as long as you can. I believe he will make this last no matter what you choose. Your horror is his sustenance. And this will be horrifying."

"Mr. Bierce," Cat strained to say, her voice constricted.

"I fear he will toy with you as a cat with a mouse. I…" Bierce looked away, turning back with a thin board in his hand. Tiny red flames danced in his eyes. "I have been *instructed*…" And his pause gave silent voice to the horror of this instruction. "I have been instructed to give you this."

He held up a square of shiny paper and lifted the candle closer until she could make out the three of them: Lewis, beaming; Hedde, young enough to grin; and herself, hair blowing across her own face.

"Why?" she managed.

Bierce moved the edge of the picture into the dancing flame and the photo caught alight. He dropped the flaming meteor of her family onto her bared skin and she gasped at the contact.

"Don't—" Cat tried to scream as he slapped the board down into place and began hammering nails into it while she thrashed. She cried out when she felt the sharp bite of steel in her left breast and in her ribs. A small blessing, the flame was smothered and she was left with the pulsing afterthought of burned flesh.

By the time she stopped weeping his footsteps were long departed, and she accepted the granite reality on which her life rested.

Escape or die.

She sucked in two slow breaths, inflating her lungs, imagining oxygenated blood racing into the big muscles of her arms and legs. She exhaled and held the image of her muscles glowing with strength and then, when the image was solid in her mind, she repeated the process, ignoring the tickle in her throat as she let her lungs inflate slowly, demanding that the air flow down into her diaphragm.

Again.

And again.

She felt the vibration of footsteps ascending a nearby staircase and knew she was out of time.

Catherine Edgar fought.

She gritted her teeth and banged against the board over her head, ignoring the hot agony of the nails tearing into her flesh as she slammed her hips down and bucked them up, drumming her heels and digging them in as she tightened the long muscles of her thighs and pressed her knees into the floorboards over her. Her elbows dug in below and she reversed her hands, pressing with the heels of her palms overhead in one long, protracted push that made her dizzy with effort until she felt the impossible.

It gave.

She redoubled her effort, panting and coughing against the sawdust as she snarled.

The surface beneath gave way with shocking suddenness and she fell through the ceiling below in a rain of plaster dust.

It could only have been moments, but Cat awoke to a body screaming in pain. She sat up amidst great shards of plaster and fell back with a moan as pain gripped her like a vice.

But dregs of her fury still burned and she pushed herself up with her unbroken arm, grabbing hold of a wooden chair and staggering upright, only to see herself in the mirrored wall of her own dining room, her naked body coated with white dust and streaked with dark blood. A winter demon with howling eyes.

She lurched on stiff knees from her living room, uncertain and uncaring of how she had arrived in her own home.

Bloody feet made sucking sounds as she staggered across the tiled floor of her kitchen, stepping into the sticky remains of the orange juice she had dropped when she read the note from Lewis.

HEADBAND.

When had that been?

Who had she been when she read that note?

She banged into the kitchen counter and braced her good arm. Like a bargeman poling across a marsh, she moved sideways until she reached the wooden knife block and pulled free eight inches of gleaming, razor-sharp steel.

The staircase creaked, familiar house sounds fraught with menace. She grunted in pain and defiance as she limped towards the door leading from her kitchen onto her back deck. From the deck she would push straight through the line of shrubs that separated their house from the Cavanaugh's backyard. Glad, so glad that she had not yet prevailed upon Lewis to install the wooden fence that she wanted to keep their neighbor's Labrador from using her yard as a bathroom.

Her breath fogged across the glass panes and she felt her skin crawl with goosebumps. Nipples tightening at the sudden chill, she clamped the knife blade between her teeth. She tugged at the doorknob until she remembered the deadbolt. Leaned against the door as she ran her hand up the wood until she felt the cold metal and struggled with numb fingers to work it free.

The quality of the air shifted.

Her name whispered.

Leaning against the wood she turned her head to the side, straining her eyes to see the white moon of a face floating towards her from the shadowy womb of the hallway. Pale birds fluttered on either side of the featureless oval until she realized they were hands, raised as if conducting a symphony.

Cat turned her body completely, crying out around the steel between her teeth when her broken arm banged against the doorknob. Then her shoulder blades were against the wood and she took the kitchen knife from her mouth.

"What do you want from me?" was what she meant to ask, drawing in her last true breath.

Instead, she screamed, "This is my house!"

She lifted her knife and darkness closed around her.

- 3 -

Gerard closed the front door behind him, trailing clouds of breath as he crunched over to the hanging tree. He glanced up at his niece's window. Even without much in the way of furniture, he had begun to see it as her room, and saw the wavering light of her lantern.

Etienne had been pacing the house and growling, enough so that Hedde had kicked him out of her room.

Tough kid, he thought. *Smarter than me.*

But he worried about her. Worried that he was out of his depth.

A wind from the northwest dragged a caul of clouds across the face of the moon, and the silver light grayed, the shapes of the Christmas trees spread over the hillside growing diffuse until they were poised like ranks of soldiers preparing to storm the house.

Like Etienne, Gerard was uneasy and unable to sleep, unwilling to put himself down with whiskey as was his custom on such nights.

He adjusted himself on the stump and held the question in his mind, releasing it on his breath. Then he lowered his head and closed his eyes, hoping to hear the ghosts.

Instead he heard a dangerous rumble from the barn and rose, yanking the axe from the stump and banging through the snow until he reached the door. He fumbled the keys from his pocket, cold with only his thermal shirt on, and unfastened the padlock, slipping the chain from the hasp. He jerked the big door to break the ice and slid it aside just enough to slip inside.

"Easy, girl. Easy, Sophie," he said, baritone carrying into the dark barn as he took in the musky smell of animal and old blood. He pulled a flashlight from its hook near the door and flicked it on, panning it around the interior.

Several sets of eyes blinked into existence and the growl grew louder.

The den was in the rear of the barn, a low, open-faced structure looking like nothing so much as a manger stolen from a nativity scene. Its floor was lined with straw and old blankets, and Sophie had pulled herself to the front, facing Gerard where she lay growling.

The puppies began yipping and squeaking and several charged out to meet him. He set the axe aside and scooped them up, warily approaching the female Shepherd while maintaining a constant, vocal reassurance.

"What is it, girl?" he asked, kneeling several feet away. He held out his hand and she nosed forward, whining. "What is it?"

He spent several minutes scratching her ears and reassuring her, taking time to check the stitches on her belly and prod exploring pups back into the straw behind her. Sophie's tongue lapped at his wrist and he touched her nose, warm and dry when it should be cold and wet. "You keep resting and get well, hear?"

He picked up her metal bowl and refilled it from a faucet low on the wall. He saw that there was still plenty of dry food if she grew hungry.

"Okay now, Sophie, okay."

He backed from the barn with his axe and pulled the door closed, re-attaching the chain and padlock. He panned the flash-light beam over the crusted snow and cursed when he saw what he had missed earlier.

The snow had been churned by something outside the barn door. Keeping the yellow circle of light on the tracks, he followed them towards the Christmas trees until he could make out the shape of hooves. Large hooves.

He swept the beam of light across the trees and their shadows danced on the snow, but he saw no other movement. The tracks were a clear line of dark holes punched in the snow, leading into the firs, but there was no way in hell Gerard would go into the Christmas trees in pursuit of whatever had upset Sophie. Not in such close quarters. Not at night.

CHAPTER
TWENTY-FOUR

- 1 -

The sun was yet to rise when something banged down onto the floorboards next to Hedde's mattress, and she cracked open her eyes to see the scarred wooden stock of a rifle.

"Get up. There's trouble."

Hedde struggled up off the mattress, kicking herself free from twisted blankets. "Is it mom?"

Her uncle was a dark shape, but she could make out the shake of his head.

"Something nosing around the barn last night, really pissed off Etienne and Sophie."

"Sophie?"

"Come out to the barn," he said, clomping downstairs while she pulled on her socks and shoes and grabbed up her coat.

Outside, she shivered, warming her hands on the hot coffee while Uncle Gerard scattered handfuls of salt crystals across the smooth snow to make a path between house and barn. He set down the big salt sack and undid the chain before sliding back the door. She remembered the growl that had issued from the cavernous interior.

"You look in here yet?" he asked.

"I did, but I couldn't see anything. Why is it locked?"

In answer, Gerard led her inside and took down the flashlight, aiming it at the den in back where Sophie guarded her pups.

"Need to keep her and Etienne apart," Gerard said. "She had a hard birth, lost two of the pups. She's hurt and too scared to think straight. If he comes near, she'll attack him. She'll tear herself open if she does."

"Merde," Hedde whispered, studying the fixed eyes of the dog until Gerard backed out of the barn, herding her behind him.

Back inside the house Etienne paced the kitchen, his claws scratching on the floor. Hedde scratched his ruff and he whined.

"What's wrong with him?" she asked.

"He wants out. Etienne owns this ground. He'll go after anything that comes onto it, any predator. He's killed a coyote, a wild dog and, once, a bobcat. That's what got his ear."

"Really?"

"He won't fuck around. He'll go right after it and attack, so we need to keep him inside."

"But he's strong."

"This thing is big, maybe too big for him. We need to kill it before Etienne gets out and hunts it down."

Uncle Gerard opened the door to the basement and she remembered the meat-locker cold that flowed up and around her ankles.

"What's down there?"

"Safe," he said.

"What's in the safe?"

He reached into the dark and tugged a string until a bare lightbulb glowed.

"Guns."

- 2 -

The snow was gently falling, fat flakes easy to track as they drifted to earth, unlike the granular snow of deep winter, which rode in on fierce winds and stung like blown sand.

Wrapped around his lower face, Gerard's scarf was icing from his moist breath in the dawn temperature. He wore layers on layers and two pairs of wool socks under water-proofed and lined hiking boots. He wore a small backpack containing various necessities and mittens over fingerless gloves. He carried a long arm in each fist.

His eyes watered in the tiny slit between his scarf and hat as he scanned the forest, still dark beneath the naked trees and even darker when they pressed into growths of tall evergreens. Snow muffled the sounds of the forest, and the crump of their boots barely disturbed the quiet.

Even anticipating the danger ahead, Gerard liked the woods at this time. In this season. They were far enough from the road to escape the growl of Ray Gleason's snowplow and the salt trucks following behind. It was too cold and remote for idiots who thought hunting meant sitting in a blind with a six-pack and a rifle, and the animals who weren't hibernating were wary and clever. The strong ones.

The fact that it wasn't hunting season also meant he wouldn't get shot by a weekend warrior from Massachusetts looking to bag a buck.

His niece struggled along behind him, too winded to complain. Her scarf, hat and shoulders were dusted with white, as if she had plunged face first into a bowl of powder donuts.

As smart as she was, it was abundantly apparent that she was quite out of her element.

Gerard stopped and held up a hand. Predictably, the girl stumbled right into his back and bounced off.

"Merde."

Gerard heard a muffled voice, turning to see his niece sitting in the snow. The kid was bundled up as heavily as Gerard was, in Lucy's old gear.

"Why'd you—" Hedde started to say, yanking the scarf down from her face.

"You need to learn to pay attention. This…" Gerard held up his hand, "means stop. And this…" he made a flattening gesture, "means get down behind the nearest cover, or go flat if there's nothing."

Their breath was already clouding in the cold. He watched her blink against the snow landing delicately on her eyelashes.

"Awake yet?" he asked.

"I'm too cold to tell," she said.

The big man held out a hand and hauled Hedde to her feet. "Everything is done quietly. If you fall, don't say anything, just try to do it quietly."

He looked her up and down, waiting until she stopped brushing off snow to meet his eyes.

"Are you ready for this?" Gerard asked.

Her well-covered head nodded.

"This is bigger than a nod," he said. "Say it out loud."

"I'm ready."

She took the .22 bolt action clumsily in her mittened hands.

"You told me you're not a kid and I believe you. Today you prove it, understand?"

Hedde nodded and after a beat said, "Yes."

"Have you shot before?"

"Twice with my friend Carol. They were .22's like this but not with the bolt."

Gerard nodded. "Have you hunted?"

Hedde shook her head. "No. I mean…it's not what people do in Westchester and mom hates the idea. Dad…" She shrugged.

Gerard nodded again and produced a gleaming, brass bullet from his pocket. He took her rifle and loaded the round.

"One bullet?" Hedde asked.

"One round makes you careful. Do not screw up your shot."

Gerard pulled several larger rounds from another pocket and loaded them into the .30-06 hunting rifle he held.

"You follow me and do exactly as I tell you. You only shoot if I tell you, got it?"

Hedde nodded. "Yes."

"Now sling your rifle across your back and follow me. I don't want you to trip and shoot me in the ass."

Gerard pulled the scarf back up over his mouth and worked his way through the unbroken snow between the trees. Hedde imitated her uncle and pulled up her scarf, following in his wake.

- 3 -

A shelf of snow fell off a pine bough and triggered a minor avalanche. Gerard held up his hand and gestured. Hedde dropped into a squat as the snow cloud settled.

A few big flakes continued to fall and Hedde looked up between the branches to watch them swirl and drift. She remembered watching an old movie with her father, back when they did things like that. Robert Redford was a mountain man, fighting Indians in the snowy Rockies. Her uncle looked like that, part hunter, part moving pile of snow.

The barrage of emotional changes over recent days had left her strangely bereft of feeling. In that void where resentment normally curled in on itself, she felt an unusual awareness creeping in. So much so that this morning the snow and the quiet was something special. It was an out-of-place absurd thing to think, but somehow Hedde didn't believe it was wrong.

Her uncle looked back, breath clouding around his head, and gestured Hedde forward. She rose into a crouch, like she had seen in the movie, and moved forward, trying not to pant or make too much noise.

"Snowing is good," Uncle Gerard said so quietly Hedde almost couldn't hear him. "Screws up the sight picture but muffles noise. You sound like a herd of cows."

Hedde shrugged and snow slid off her shoulders.

"See up there?" Gerard said, and she followed his pointing finger. "Those marks on the snow are from a hare. I believe this is a regular run, so we're gonna sit here and wait for him. Unsling your rifle. He will hear and see movement, so we sit still like two boulders in the woods."

Hedde nodded and unslung the .22, wincing at all the noise. She settled down into a cross-legged position next to Gerard, butt sinking several inches into the white carpeting.

"The hare is your shot, so pay attention when I give you the signal," he said.

Hedde nodded, holding the slim rifle at port arms, tired and cold and exhilarated all at once.

- 4 -

Hedde had fallen into a semi-doze, the cold transforming into a gentle warmth that made her eyelids droop.

She awoke to a gentle tapping on her hand and opened her eyes to look over at her uncle who appeared to be a simple feature of the forest covered in a blanket of new fallen snow. She looked ahead at the tracks.

And there it was. A lean, brown hare not even twenty feet away, huge ears up and twitching. *Holy crap*, she thought, only by force of will catching the words before they came from her mouth.

Carefully she slipped her hands free of the mittens one at a time and slid the index finger of her right hand through the trigger guard. The metal was so cold she almost hissed at the contact but fought it back.

Hedde lifted the butt of the rifle to her well-padded shoulder but couldn't aim properly down the barrel, so she twisted her hips slightly.

Snow crunched beneath her seat.

The hare twitched and was gone. She jerked the rifle after it and fired, the high pitched *crack* of the weapon unbelievably loud in the quiet woods.

"I missed," she said, lurching up to her feet.

"Stay still—" Gerard began to say in the split-second before snow-covered underbrush to their right exploded and a snarling *something* came boring at them, wings of white kicking out to either side of its charge.

Hedde was flying through the air before she knew it, her uncle sweeping her bodily off her feet as if she weighed no more than a rag doll. She landed on her back in a detonation of snow and, for a moment, couldn't see anything.

The .30-06 roared and a massive wave of air seemed to press Hedde backwards. She fought up to see a dark, bristling form disappear into the trees as her uncle sat up, rifle held in both hands. The big man jacked another round into the chamber.

"What was that?" she asked, voice cracking.

"A boar. Wild pig."

"That was a pig?" Hedde clapped a hand over her mouth but couldn't hold back sudden hysterical laughter. Even Gerard smiled and made the harsh, barking sound that passed for his laugh.

"Come on," he said, clambering upright. "I hit him good, left chest, I think, and he's leakin' like a faucet."

Hedde picked up her rifle and then herself, shaking off snow. She saw a trail of scarlet splotches like brightly blooming roses leading into the brush.

- 5 -

The boar was hanging from a branch by its feet and Gerard's big knife jerked across the pig's throat with a sound like tearing plastic. A waterfall of black blood sprayed out and he placed a funnel beneath the wound to direct it into a plastic water bottle.

Hedde thought she might vomit. When her uncle held out the half-full bottle to her and said, "Drink," she was fairly sure she was about to embarrass herself.

Instead she took the dripping bottle, held it up in front of her eyes and turned until she was facing east, where slanting rays of morning sunlight cut through the trees.

"Horned God and Green Man, Father of the East, we honor you," she said, splashing bright drops onto the snow at her feet and placing the bottle to her lips before she could think. The hot liquid filled her mouth with a taste of pennies and meat before burning a path down her throat. She held the bottle back out to her uncle who took it and swigged deeply. Red drizzled into his beard, and Hedde could feel it staining her own pale chin. She imagined her blood-smeared face staring up at Susie-with-a-heart and her lips parted in something close to a snarl.

Gerard tipped a few drops of blood onto the snow in the direction of the dawn.

"Do you know why we drink?" he asked.

"To honor him?"

Gerard nodded. "You drink so you know what you've done and who he was. This one was a fighter, most likely escaped from some farm and took on every comer. He was old, tough and mean. He's a part of you now."

Hedde nodded, looking at the fresh bloodstains on her mittens. She had the feeling of something Indian happening. Something important.

"But I didn't make the shot," she said after a moment's reflection. She felt a little drunk.

"Your partner's shot is your shot. We hunt together."

"I get it."

"Do you?"

"I think so."

Gerard looked down at her. "You were interested in the gun your father left for your mother. This is what guns do."

He dug around inside his thick coat and produced a key on a chain. Hedde accepted it from him, the dull metal chain draping off the side of her palm like a dirty icicle.

"This was Lucy's. It opens the door to the cellar, and the safe opens with her birthday," Gerard said. "Tomorrow we'll start working with the other guns to get you used to them."

Hedde said nothing as she worked the chain over her head and tugged her hair free, unzipping her coat and loosening her scarf to shove the chain down inside her sweater.

"Good," Gerard said.

He twisted the cap back onto the bottle and set it in the snow before turning back to the boar and ramming his knife into its sternum. Using both hands, he jerked the knife straight upward, and a bucket load of guts fell steaming into the snow.

Hedde said, "Yep," and staggered away before vomiting forth a bright crimson spray. She felt ashamed and turned back to her uncle.

The big man seemed not to have noticed.

Hedde crouched and stuffed a handful of snow in her mouth to wash out the taste when he spoke.

"Go in my pack and pull out the garbage bag. I want you to stick in the liver for Sophie. She needs it. Throw in the heart for Etienne so he doesn't get jealous."

Hedde walked back to the blue-black pile of steaming guts and thought, *they sure look like guts.*

"Stop thinking about it as a pile of guts and look for shapes," Gerard said.

She knelt in the snow and pulled off the mittens, wincing as she reached into the pile and started to separate the organs.

"This and this?" Hedde asked, holding up a slippery liver and surprisingly heavy heart.

"Yep. Leave the rest, something will come along for it."

Hedde stuffed the organs in the bag while Gerard laid out a canvas tarp and lowered the carcass onto it.

"Uncle Gerard? Why did we chase it? I mean, it was a dead pig walking after you shot it."

Gerard tied the tarp around the pig and looped some rope through metal rings in the edge of the canvas. "Two reasons. We didn't know it was shot dead, and if it was alive, it would've been dangerous to anything near these woods. More dangerous than ever. Second, best thing to do when you know there's trouble is go out and meet it."

"Then why did mom bring me to hide up here?"

He stood and looped the rope over his shoulder. "Because we don't know where the problem is yet."

- 5 -

Gerard dragged the boar in the canvas tarp out of the trees and into the field, enjoying the burn in his thighs. He could see the ghosts of previous paths where he had dragged the trees he felled, always dead wood, to his chopping spot under the hanging tree.

Hedde had asked to drag the carcass and Gerard had given her the ropes, watching as the teenager struggled to move the boar half a foot before stopping, eyes wide in surprise. He took the ropes back.

"Pig weighs near two-hundred pounds, even with its guts out," Gerard said.

"Whoa."

"Grab some snow while we're stopped and wipe off your chin."

Hedde's face darkened. "It's my first kill."

He grabbed a handful of snow and wiped at his beard, the snow coming away pink in his hand. "It'll be your last if your mom thinks you got hurt out there."

Reluctantly Hedde bent and copied her uncle's actions. "You think she'll be back today?"

He nodded. "Or call." He set off hauling the boar again and heard Hedde start up behind him.

The girl had done well for her first time. Didn't matter that she puked because every time she was asked, the kid stepped up and met the challenge. Find her things to do, keep her learning, and she might sit on her fear and anger until Cat came back.

CHAPTER
TWENTY-FIVE

- 1 -

Bud Light. Schlitz. Michelob. Not a single one of the neon signs in the smoke-filled bar were lit.

Buddy LaChaise had been drinking since noon at the Red Red Rooster, Flintlock's one and only purveyor of suds. To say he was sober upon entering R-3, as the locals called i, would be ambitious to the point of optimism, what with his useless progeny held overnight in one of Ranger Rick's jail cells for an offense that would undoubtedly cost Buddy a wad of hard won cash.

"Redneck," Buddy said with a raised finger, to which Dave Baillie grunted and, Buddy would swear, farted in response from where he sat watching a corner-mounted television. Still, for the fifth time since Buddy had placed his considerable backside on the cracked vinyl of his preferred stool, Baillie placed the Budweiser and shot of Canadian Club on the faux-wood bar without spilling a drop. Buddy carefully studied the contents of his wallet in the dim, red glow of the holiday lights strung over the mirror behind the bar before laying down a wrinkled five spot to cover it.

"Grassy ass."

Most of the shot hit the back of Buddy's throat with a satisfying burn, and he brushed a few errant drops from the oval nametag on his blue jacket. BUDDY it read with a cursive flourish. He had a habit of turning his left side towards people as he spoke so they could see his name, this in spite of the fact that everyone he talked to at R-3 knew who he was.

"Dog's a menace," Sam Stout said from two stools down as he tapped his cigarette into a plastic ashtray.

Everyone in town also knew about Buddy and Gerard Beaumont and a few, like Sam, might have texted a pal with the knowledge that Gerry Beaumont was due at the jail to file a report against young Dickie LaChaise, whose father had been drinking rednecks at the bar next door to the municipal building all afternoon.

"Little Miss Fingerbang," Buddy said without slurring, a skill acquired after years of semi-functional alcoholism. He grinned around a mouthful of nicotine-stained teeth and belched. The replacement teeth installed by the dentist after his one and only dance with Beaumont were still factory white. The contrast with his natural beauties invited folks to compare his grin to an ear of two-toned corn.

"Probably not even his niece," Jackie Strong said from his stool on the far side of Stout. Bored and out of work, he had walked over when Stout told him there might be some fireworks downtown, if things went just right and Buddy kept on drinking. Not above a little egging on, Strong pulled off his camo cap and wiped at his slick comb-over. "Probably some Russian gal he met over the Internet."

Russian gals who could be ordered over the Internet were a subject of great interest to Strong, and he had long since promised himself to get one if he was ever gainfully employed.

"Little Miss Fingerbang," Buddy repeated with the air of a debater delivering the coup de grace.

"Dog bites your kid. Ain't right that your kid got picked up," Stout said, worried that Buddy was too drunk for subtlety.

The door was pushed in and a reluctant shaft of light pressed into the smoky interior. The two newcomers were carrying a flat, greasy box from the Flintlock House of Pizza next door and they set it down at one end of the bar.

"Saw Beaumont's truck pull up to the town building," one said to nobody in particular.

"Son of a bitch," Buddy said and pushed against the bar, sliding his ass backwards off the stool with a jangle from his overloaded key ring. His boots smacked down on the stained carpet and he straightened. "Don't touch my beer," he said over his shoulder as he lumbered for the door with his trademark limp.

The men in the bar gave it a moment for propriety's sake before filing out after Buddy.

"You know Gerry Beaumont will kick his ass," Baillie said.

Jackie Strong glanced back. "So what? Buddy's a jerk."

Baillie shook his head and lifted the cardboard lid of the pizza box, plucking free a dangling length of mozzarella and placing it on his tongue. He used the small key on his keychain to secure the cash drawer on the register behind the bar while he picked up the slightly greasy counter phone to make a call. "Yeah, Aaron, get your ass down to the bar. You got a shift." He hung up the phone, snagged another piece of mozzarella and headed for the door.

The television continued its murmuring about Bruins hockey to an empty room.

- 2 -

It was a one-room police station with two holding cells and a small cubicle that served as an interrogation room or nap room, depending on how business was going. A small bank of radios murmured in background conversation.

Business was booming today.

"Well shoot, Bill, if you think it was rabid you gotta take it with you to the doctor's office," Officer Rick Wannamaker was saying into the phone. "No, don't cut off the head, bring in the whole carcass." He listened while rubbing his eyes. "No, just forget the vet. Let the doctor worry about that part. Take your body and the animal's body right over to Dr. Saunders."

He hung up the phone as Gerard Beaumont and his niece entered. He already had a headache.

"Gerry," he said and nodded at the girl, struggling for her name. "Hedde."

"Lot going on?" Gerard asked.

"Crazy stuff," Wannamaker said. "That was Bill Evers. Said he just ran down a goat who charged his bumper out on Route Thirteen. When he went to check on it, the animal bit part of his thumb off. And an hour ago Reverend Lawson at the Methodist called to say a flock of crows barged straight through the storm windows at the rectory. Killed themselves trying to get in." He looked at Gerard and cocked an eyebrow. "Ronnie Chasen said you killed a boar."

"That loudmouth son of a bitch," Gerard said. "Don't give me any shit about seasons, Rick. The pig was trying to get into my barn and after Sophie."

Wannamaker held up a placating hand.

"Who's Ronnie Chasen?" Hedde asked and Wannamaker silently thanked her.

"He'll butcher an animal for quarter of the meat," Wannamaker said.

"And blab out his ass," Gerard said. "Damned animal could've killed Etienne."

"That'd be a shame," Dickie LaChaise called out from the cell where he lounged alongside Ray Childers, the both of them chewing through the contents of a McDonald's bag. "Be an even worse shame if the mutt ate some poisoned bait."

"Now goddammit," Wannamaker said, rising and thrusting a finger at the boys. "No more out of you."

It wasn't Gerard who moved, however, but Hedde taking a step towards the boys, eyes narrowing. She stopped when her uncle's scarred hand rested on her shoulder.

"Gerry, ignore those two," Wannamaker pleaded, switching gears. "I ain't worried about hunting seasons. I'm worried that I've heard about three damned weird animal incidents and thinking about rabies."

Gerard held his gaze on the occupied cell for a beat longer before nodding to Wannamaker. "I'll tell Ronnie to cut off the head and run it over to Saunders."

"That's good, and tell him to freeze the meat until Saunders gives us the all clear."

"Okay."

"And I want some chops off that pig," he added.

Gerard's mouth moved into what Hedde took to be his smile. "You got it."

The phone rang again and Wannamaker glanced at the incoming call before letting it go to voicemail. "Martha Leroux, probably complaining about the UN trying to steal her land." He looked at Hedde and unconsciously adopted an Officer

Friendly tone of voice. "Now hon, we need to go into this room over here so I can take your statement down. Just you, not your Uncle Gerry."

"Okay," she said with a shrug. "But that's a cubicle."

Wannamaker sighed. "It's what we got." He looked at Gerard. "Gerry, how about you go downstairs and smoke a cigarette or two. I'll walk her down when we're done."

"I'll stay."

"Gerry, dammit, I've been listening to these two bitch and whine all night and they finally ran out of steam. I don't need you getting them going again." He paused. "Actually, you could do me a favor and pick up a bottle of Tylenol at the store."

Gerard looked at his niece, and Wannamaker thought he was going to ask if she'd be okay, or offer some assurances about his proximity, but what he said was, "You be nice to Ranger Rick here, he's having an Excedrin kind of day."

"Tylenol," Wannamaker said as Gerard clomped across the hardwood floor to the doors. "Excedrin has caffeine." Wannamaker shrugged at Hedde.

Gerard's boots were banging down the stairs outside when Hedde said, "Ranger Rick?"

Wannamaker sighed.

- 3 -

Because the store was in the opposite direction from R-3, Gerard didn't notice the man lumbering towards him or the small crowd gathered in front of the bar. He paused to light a cigarette, leaning into his cupped hands to shield it from the wind and trying to recall what he knew about rabies.

By the time Gerard heard the phlegmatic breath of an obese man running, he had just enough time to glance back before Buddy LaChaise swung a fistful of tire chains at his head while bellowing something that was more spit than words.

It should be noted that the crowd of men who had egged Buddy on did protest when he pulled the chains from his truck bed, and Jackie Strong had a genuine *Oh shit* moment when he saw that Gerry Beaumont would be caught unawares, but the taciturn son of a bitch was quick. Gerard threw up his left hand and slowed the blow, but the swinging chain whipped around his wrist and struck his forehead even as he hurled himself backwards and went "ass over tea kettle," according to Dave Baillie. The momentum of the swing caused Buddy to stumble to one knee.

"Get up, Beaumont," someone shouted, and both men did.

"Kill you, motherfucker," Buddy slurred and drew back the chain as Gerard leapt in with an overhand right, more power than grace, but it dropped Buddy onto his ass in the street.

Buddy looked up from where he sat with a red welt already swelling on his forehead, and Gerard paused to touch his own wound, studying the fresh blood on his fingertips for a moment as the tenor of the shouting audience changed and they felt the shifting of the ice across the distance.

Gerard lashed out with a short kick that rocked Buddy's head back and then stomped hard on the crotch of the man's blue Dickie's. He turned and spit, stepping around the writhing man on the ground until he was no longer standing on slippery ice.

"Gerry, don't!" Baillie called out, running forward even as Gerard Beaumont went to work with his boots.

CHAPTER
TWENTY-SIX

- 1 -

Martha Leroux drew a stick-thin finger back and let the faded drapes fall over the darkening window as she backpedaled, piloting her gangly form around furniture and stacks of magazines with a skill born of long experience.

She rarely left the house anymore; it was too frightening out there. So long had she been inside her home that the absence of its comforting smells—equal parts vegetable soup and eau de litter box—triggered an almost Pavlovian panic, flooding her mind with horrific headlines.

A godless communist was in the White House, scheming to sell American land to the United Nations. Waves of foreigners were carrying new and unheard-of diseases across the borders, and the streets were filled with drug-fueled rapists who preyed on good Christian women. These things, and others she knew from her research, filled her with dread.

When the hem of her lank dress caught on a stack of tabloids and sent several thumping to the floor, she nearly screamed. Instead, she held her hands over her damp eyes and prayed quietly that someone would answer their phone when she called.

Her heart was beating fast, too fast, and Dr. Woolrich would have put her on bed rest immediately if he knew. She pressed a hand against her drawn-in stomach as the acid burned at her middle. There was so little she could eat these days that wouldn't upset her system.

Martha glanced around to make sure every light in her three room double-wide was still blazing brightly—no energy saving light bulbs for her, thank you very much—and all of the drapes and shades had been pulled to keep out prying eyes.

And they were out there. Hundreds of them.

Even with all the lights in the trailer burning bright, the brown faux-wood paneling was squeezing inward like a vise. She hurried once more to see that the door was deadbolted. There had been no other sound from outside since the dreadful *tap-tap-tapping* had interrupted her favorite afternoon program, *General Hospital*. She had unfolded from the couch, letting loose an unladylike curse as she opened the two doors and prepared to give whomever was outside looking for a handout a double-barrel load of hell.

Her first shock had come when she saw her unmoving cat on the ice-covered walk leading up to her door. "Leo?" She hadn't even known he was outside.

When she had noticed all of those terrible eyes watching her from the woods, she moved back inside with uncanny quickness before locking the doors.

She skirted a couch-side magazine bin and scooped up the receiver of her princess phone, her long finger spearing the dial.

As the phone at the other end of the line rang in her ear, Martha caught sight of a framed watercolor of *The Last Supper*, and said another silent prayer until the ringing ended and the voicemail recording began.

"You have reached the Flintlock Police Department. If this is an emergency, please hang up and dial 911 immediately. If it is not, please wait for the tone and leave a message."

Beep.

"I pay taxes, Ranger Rick! I pay your salary, and you'd better answer your damned phone!"

She slammed the receiver back into the cradle and planted her hands on her narrow hips, unconcerned that she had not left her name or number. That Ranger Rick knew who she was, all right, and if the idiot had somehow forgotten, she'd already left him five messages to remind him just who he worked for.

Her eyes strayed to the front door. Locked. To the well-lit kitchen. Empty. To the bathroom and doorway to the bedroom. Closed. As she weighed her options, her eyes strayed again to the painting of the Savior on the wall and she had an inspired thought.

She picked up the phone again and straightened in place as she composed herself, her hair nearly brushing the low ceiling as her lips turned down and began trembling.

"It's Martha Leroux. Thanks so much for answering," she said, pausing as the greeting ritual was repeated at the other end. "I didn't know who else to call. I can't get anyone at the police station and I need someone to come over right away." She paused again. "Something came to my door and terrified me. Terrified me, I tell you. I can't go outside and I've locked myself in with all of the lights on. Oh, ple—" She paused and then gushed, "Thank you, thank you."

And hung up.

When Martha was younger she could make herself physically sick on days that she wanted to miss school. Even now, despite her genuine fear of all those eyes on her home, she didn't give a second thought to using the same skills to get what she wanted.

She glided over to the window and peeked between the drapes one more time, but recoiled immediately.

She was beginning to understand the meaning of real fear.

- 2 -

Father Messina pushed aside the heavy velvet curtain and stepped from the cramped confessional into the airy openness of his church, humble by Catholic standards but suited to the spartan nature of his congregation. As he paused, the white walls were washed in a rainbow of colors as the setting sun sent its orange rays through the stained glass windows in a wonderful reminder of God's grace, a sight that rarely failed to lift his spirits.

Messina sat in the first row of wooden pews and looked at the wonderfully wrought cross on the wall behind the pulpit as he struggled to comprehend what the stranger had told him in the dim anonymity of the booth.

He glanced at the silver-plated watch on his wrist and looked away again without noting the time, a nervous gesture left over from his youth.

Infidelity. Physical abuse of wives and children. Theft. Lies and lust. His purview was a domain of vapid and petty evil. Confronted by this stranger's monstrous tale, he was also confronted with the atrophy of his spiritual muscles, the puniness of his belief.

He scratched his black beard and rubbed the bridge of his nose beneath his wire-rimmed glasses, eyes resting on the closed curtain concealing the stranger.

Stranger.

Stranger still was his tale of flight and murder and what could only have been a spiritual confrontation of significant magnitude in the German countryside.

Messina shifted on the uncomfortable pew, an unfortunate Protestant infiltration of his church, and read again the note by the German monk.

> *"Now faith is the assurance of things hoped for, the conviction of things not seen."*

Hebrews 11:1.

The message was not lost on Messina.

Believe this man.

"Are you all right, my son?" He spoke quietly and the acoustics of the wonderfully constructed church carried his voice as on wings.

The curtain stirred and the man appeared, his face gaunt from the effort of his telling.

"I'm sorry, Father."

Messina held up one thick hand, tiny curls of black hair foresting each scarred knuckle. The people in these parts expected a working priest.

"Come sit."

The man sat, clad in a pair of heavy jeans beneath a white sweater. On his feet he wore unmarked but sturdy Timberland boots, and over his arm he carried a long coat of gray material, a coat only a stranger to these parts would wear.

In his eyes he carried the weight of his truth.

"I must ask you these questions before we continue," Messina said. "Please do not take offense."

"I won't."

"Are you currently on any medications, or should you be?"

"I'm not."

"Are you currently under the care of a psychiatrist or any kind of doctor?"

"No."

"Are you..." Messina hesitated. "Are you wanted for any criminal activity?"

"Murder, theft, drug trafficking and illegal border crossings are all that I can think of," Lewis Edgar said.

Messina watched his eyes and waited before continuing. "Do you love your wife?"

"I do, but damn me for forgetting for so long."

"And your daughter, you love her?"

"I do. I love her so much, but I'm a terrible father."

"And Gerard Beaumont, do you love him?"

A flicker of life in the stranger's eyes and a twist of his lips before he said, "If he took my gals in, I'll take back everything I've ever said about him and kiss his hairy French ass."

Messina barked a short laugh and patted the stranger's knee.

"And all these things you have told me, you understand they sound…"

"Crazy?"

"They are difficult to accept. Are they all true?"

He met Messina's eyes, and the country priest was struck at the power in them.

"Everything is true, I swear it." Lewis paused. "I have memorized a number for Lucien if you would like to call him, though he said his phone service is *unzuverlassig*. Unreliable."

The conviction of things not seen.

Messina shook his head.

"You have confessed your sins and you will take the host—" Messina cocked his head as he heard the telephone ring. "Excuse me for one moment."

He rose and strode quickly to an inconspicuous door on a side wall, a short, sturdy man in black with unruly hair salted with white.

Lewis liked him and was surprised. Not at liking the man, but that such a thought would even cross his mind now.

He heard the murmuring of a distant conversation before Messina reappeared, his open face wearing a torn expression.

"I… That was a member of my church. A virtual shut in. She

sounded quite panicked and has asked me to go to her immediately."

Lewis stood, the small hairs prickling on the back of his neck. "What frightened her?"

Messina took in the man's stance, and by God he indeed looked like a man capable of fighting across Europe and the Atlantic to reach his wife and daughter.

"She was vague," the priest said. "She is not always entirely lucid, I'm afraid, but she has few friends. Fewer still who would go to her aid."

"Then go."

"Will you wait for me here?"

"I'll come with you if you need me."

Belief in things not seen. A blossoming flower in Messina's chest.

"Stay here so we may complete your armament in the Lord's Grace," Messina said. "I believe your daughter is safe. I was told that an out-of-town girl had a scuffle with two local boys—"

"Hedde? Is she alright?" Lewis interrupted, stepping forward.

Messina patted the air. "Yes, yes. But I know she is scheduled to give her statement at the police station right around now. She is certainly safe there." He grabbed a winter coat from a hook near the door. "I will be back very soon. Martha Leroux has many problems, but she is comforted quickly."

And with that the priest stepped out into the cold gloom of a New Hampshire twilight, passed the ridiculous little gold car and climbed into his Dodge 4x4. The headlights splashed across the stained glass at the front of the church and cast the room in molten tones.

Lewis heard a honk followed by the crunch of tires over ice as the vehicle backed out. He sat in a pew, looking around the kind space and knowing that he could not wait.

- 3 -

Father Messina turned left at Percy Street, accelerating to blow through a small snowbank left by plows passing on the main road. The homes here were modest, a mixture of single-story ranch houses and both single- and double-wide trailers separated by great swathes of trees on empty lots.

He was anxious to return to the church and to the mysterious Lewis Edgar, for in the man he sensed he might be exposed to, and be a part of, the most clearly defined struggle between good and evil he had ever imagined. It awoke something in him that he had not felt since the heady days of a young man at seminary. A battle against fire, not the slow decay of poverty and despair.

And so it was that when he turned into Martha Leroux's short driveway, the only thing he noticed amiss was that nobody had bothered to plow it clear.

He threw the shift into PARK and turned off the ignition, sitting for a moment as his engine ticked and thinking of the steps he might take to further aid Lewis. Realizing that a no-longer-quiet voice within him had already decided he would accompany the man into Flintlock to retrieve his family. And if the shadow remained over the Edgars after today, Father Messina would accompany them further.

A curtain twitched in the trailer, and he noticed that every drape had been drawn, but light blazed around the edges of each small window.

Martha must have every light in the house on, he thought.

Father Messina pushed open the door with a squeal of hinges and stepped out into the shin-deep snow, wishing he had paused to don his boots.

The dead cat came as both a shock and something of a relief.

Poor Leo had met his match at last. The priest crouched slightly, straining to make out wet details in the fading light, face tightening in distaste. Ugly, what had been done to it. Judging from the amount of damage, probably not another cat.

Perhaps a raccoon?

If the sight shook him, it would nearly have unhinged poor Martha.

He stepped over the mangled body of the cat and pressed the faintly glowing button beside the door, hearing the chime inside.

"Who is it?" a tremulous voice asked from behind the door.

Messina paused, realizing she really *was* shaken. "Martha, it's Father Messina."

In the silence that followed, he heard the whisper of wind in the trees.

"When I open the door, you come in quick," Martha said from inside. "No 'how are you' or 'nice to see ya,' just Johnny-on-the-spot and in you go."

"Of course."

Messina heard the rattle of locks as the inner door was opened, and then the deadbolt was thrown and the outer door swung towards him. He pushed it wider with one hand and took the single step up and through onto the mustard-colored carpet.

"I'm so sorry about Le—" he was saying when she shouldered him aside and slammed both doors, throwing the locks immediately.

- 4 -

Lewis hunched over the wheel, following the Kia's meager headlights and forcing himself to drive at a measured pace. Sliding off the road on a patch of black ice would slow him down.

On the seat next to him was a Bible taken from the rack on the back of a pew, and an inner pocket contained a metal flask he had stolen from Messina's desk. He had regretted pouring the amber liquid down a drain in the bathroom, but he needed it for other things.

The flask had gurgled like a living thing when he pressed it down beneath the surface of the holy water in the granite stoup. He hoped he was not committing some kind of blasphemy in doing so, or diluting the agency of the holy water if it came in contact with alcoholic remnants in the flask, but it was all he could think of to do.

Strange weapons, he thought. Yet they comforted him. He hoped it was not the placebo effect of a desperate man needing to believe in something, but didn't have the luxury of dwelling on the idea.

Downtown Flintlock was too poor to warrant many streetlights, and he struggled to make out the shape of the municipal building as he crawled through town. He saw it looming slightly over its neighbors and cut the wheel too late, pulling into a slot between trucks and SUVs in front of a bar called the Red Red Rooster.

Emerging with the Bible tucked under his arm he slammed the door with an unimpressive *whack*, suddenly nervous about seeing his wife and daughter, some tactical part of his brain deciding to talk to Gerard first, to thank the man while giving himself a chance to sense the lay of the land with his family.

Inside the front door was a small window with the shade pulled down. The hours stenciled on the glass indicated it closed at 4:00pm.

"Fine, then. Here I come, unannounced."

The stairs creaked beneath him as he climbed, and while he imagined that Cat would be cautious in her response to the sight of him, at least publicly, his daughter was another matter. Hedde was a girl who spoke her mind. Silently he prayed that he would not see disappointment on her face, or anger. He desperately wished for a chance to make things right.

The outer door of the police station was half wood with pebbled glass on top, and he could hear raised voices as he steeled himself and turned the knob.

"Not what I expected," he said aloud at the sight of Gerard Beaumont behind bars, a bandage wrapped around his head, no less, arguing with a uniformed officer who looked suspiciously like a park ranger.

Both men paused in their exchange to stare in surprise at the newcomer, and Gerard lifted a hand in greeting, but it was the officer who spoke first.

"Sir, we are very busy at the moment as you can see. If it's not an emergency, come back later. If it is, take a damned number and sit down."

"What the hell's going on?" Lewis asked, stepping towards the cells and ignoring the cop who was approaching with a hand out.

The two teens in the adjacent cell looked at the newcomer with rapt attention.

The officer stopped and glanced back at Gerard. "Gerry, who is this guy?"

Lewis caught motion at the corner of his vision and saw Hedde in an overlarge winter coat emerging from a cubicle. Her face went pale and she dropped the pen she'd been holding. Words caught in his throat and Lewis saw his daughter's eyes well with tears as her lips curled with the awful completeness of a child in pain.

"I—" Lewis began, and she spoke over him, her whisper decimating him.

"Daddy?"

He nodded, feeling the sandy prickle behind his eyes that meant he was moments from weeping.

"Dad?" She wailed, face twisting with disbelief and accusation. And then she was charging, hair streaming out behind her. He staggered as she hit him without any effort to slow, and then she was squeezing him hard enough to push the wind out of him.

When did she get so strong?

His hands were moving over her arms and head as he kissed her hair, and they both tried to say what had already been said with their eyes, words tumbling over each other to create a jumble of sound that meant nothing and everything.

Officer Wannamaker stepped closer to Gerard and leaned against the cell. Gerard leaned forward from the other side of the bars and said, "That's Hedde's father."

And Wannamaker got off a good one, as his friends would say. "I didn't think it was her husband."

Gerard Beaumont grabbed the cell bars in both scarred fists and threw back his head, roaring with laughter. After a moment, Wannamaker joined in with a little less volume, laughing as much out of surprise as anything else.

"Gerry, this is some strange day," Wannamaker said.

Gerard patted him on the shoulder and looked at the hugging family.

"Lew," Gerard said.

Lewis lifted his watering eyes and walked in a clumsy two-step towards the cells with Hedde, unwilling to release his grip. He wiped his eyes with his free hand and then offered it to Wannamaker, who took it.

"Hi, I'm—"

"This is Lewis Edgar," Hedde interjected and stepped away, eyes searching her father's face.

"Meetcha," Wannamaker said after the shake.

"Dad?" she said. Lewis turned just as Hedde slammed the heels of her hands into his chest.

"Hey!" Lewis said, backpedaling as Gerard and Wannamaker shouted in surprise, and the town boys whooped.

"You merde," she said, tears streaming. "Where have you been?"

- 5 -

"Thy kingdom come, thy will be done!" Martha Leroux shouted from another room.

As Messina stuffed kitchen towels into the crack growing beneath a bedroom window, some giddy, spinning part of his mind noted that he had never heard the Lord's Prayer shouted quite like Martha Leroux could shout it.

Then again, she was terrified and so was he.

A staccato blast raked across the metal roof as if they had been strafed by a fighter plane. Just then, the trailer rocked as a mighty *BOOM* sounded, and Messina raced into the apocalyptic nightmare of the living room, gaping as chunks of faux-wood paneling tumbled from the wall and the trailer shook again from a mighty blow that dented the outer metal.

"What is happening?" Martha shrieked from her kneeling position on the liquid-smeared kitchen floor. She was covered in flour and cooking oil. Soda bottles rolled as if they were on the deck of a ship.

"Keep praying, Martha!" Messina shouted back and leapt over shattered glass and furniture to scoop up a magazine rack and hurl it at the shape bulging inward through a window curtain.

"Though I walk through the valley—" the panicked woman wailed, and Messina ran to the door, throwing his bruised bulk against it as something heavy crashed into it from the other side.

He had been sipping a cup of tea while Martha described the eyes outside, watching her trailer all day long. He had been in the midst of explaining, ever so rationally, that he had seen nothing outside when the lights went out and all hell broke loose.

"Father!"

He wheeled at a shriek and saw another curtain bulging inward as if some great, amorphous shape were trying to climb through. He fought down a groan of terror and swept a lamp off the floor, shoes crunching over glass as he hurled the fixture with great force.

The curtain slapped against the window once more and Messina whirled in place, eyes darting everywhere at once. His breath was the ragged gasp of a marathoner in the last mile.

He had yet to lay eyes on a single one of their attackers.

BOOM!

The trailer shook again and he fell to his knees, screaming as glass tore through his pants and into the meat of him. Martha was screaming as he put down a hand, crying out again as his palm was impaled, and rose, fighting to pull the shard free.

How arrogant had he been just moments ago, eager to do battle against EVIL while armored only in his unbreakable faith.

A crash sounded from the bedroom and he sprinted for it, droplets of blood flying in his wake.

His battle had come. Not in a blaze of white light at the center of things, but with the town pariah in a dismal trailer on the edge of everything. Hell, in all honesty, even *he* didn't like Martha. There were no trumpets or choirs of angels singing his praises. His battle against genuine evil had arrived and his inadequacy was laid bare.

There was nothing in the gloom of the bedroom, nothing at all. He leapt to the closet and ripped the mirrored door aside hard enough that it tore from its runners and smashed into the wall.

Clothes. Debris of a lonely life stuffed inside to make room for visitors who never came.

He sprang onto the creaking mattress of her single bed and tore open the drapes to scream at the empty night.

"Where are you? Show yourself!"

The hollow dark mocked him silently.

From the kitchen Martha screamed, "Oh my God, Father, help me!"

Messina staggered back in drunken exhaustion, falling from the bed as it shifted beneath him. His head struck the doorframe with an audible crack and the darkness spun around him.

"Father, please!"

He pushed himself up and crawled back into the living room across debris, feeling the heat of the fire even as he beheld the flames racing in jagged lines across the counter and floor.

"What happened?" He croaked as she staggered towards him, a scarecrow silhouette outlined in blazing light.

"They were coming up! Coming up through the drain in the kitchen sink so I...I..."

"What?" He roared, surging upright and grabbing her stick-thin upper arms. "What did you do?"

"I burned them," Martha sobbed, falling against him, and for a moment he felt himself in the grip of a horrible urge, the desire to shove her back into the growing conflagration.

"I'm sorry," she blurted, and he was repulsed by her teary, soot-stained face. "I'm so sorry." A great bubble of snot grew from her nose and popped.

Smoke was already boiling across the ceiling and they began to cough.

"I'm so—"

A bleeding finger was pressed across Martha's lips, silencing her.

"No, Martha. No more," Messina said hoarsely. "It's me who has failed. I've failed you as your priest and friend."

Martha lifted her eyes, shining and black in the crazed half-light. "You're the only one who ever comes." Her thin chest hitched. "And now I've killed us. We can't stay inside because of—"

It took his whole hand this time but he silenced her.

"Maybe I've been wrong. Maybe we shouldn't stay inside." He paused, covering his mouth with a fist to hide a cough. "Let's go outside and see this thing face-to-face."

Her mouth formed a nearly comical O of fear.

"After all," Messina continued, "they have knocked ever so politely."

A sound blatted from her and it took Messina's tired brain a moment to process it. Martha Leroux was laughing.

He walked with an arm around her shoulders, her body so thin he could feel her shoulder blades, like dinner plates sliding beneath her dress.

"I'm frightened," she said.

Messina nodded his understanding, only then realizing that the banging and smashing from outside had ceased.

"The Lord God has made us such a beautiful sky tonight. A million stars shining against the black. I suspect he would want us to see it, don't you?" He was aware that he was using his Sunday school voice, but it seemed somehow appropriate.

They were at the door when she said, "Thank you for always coming."

"After we get this place fixed up, you'll have to invite me over for tea," he said, undoing the deadbolt and thumbing off the lock on the knob. "I insist."

Father Messina pushed the outer door open and they descended down into the snow as the fire roared behind them.

"Look up at the stars, Martha. Do it now," Messina said, and she did. He slid his hand from her shoulder to the side of her jaw, gently guiding her gaze still higher.

There was no need for her to see what was coming.

"It…it's so beautiful," she sobbed.

"He made it just for you because he loves you," Messina said, fighting her a bit as she tried to look at the apparition gliding towards them.

"Oh, I'm so frightened," she cried and tried to wrench away, to look upon the horror. He would not let her and held her in his powerful, workingman's arms.

"Look at the stars and think about His love," he said, his voice deep with the training of years before congregations. "Do you give Him your love? Do you love God as much as He loves you?"

"Oh yes! I love Him!"

The sound of approaching footsteps announced the emptying of the hourglass and he held her head rigidly aloft. But for himself, Father Giancarlo Messina, born in Boston's North End forty-eight years ago and drawn to the priesthood as a boy of seventeen, *he* watched the approaching wraith with defiance in his heart.

There came a blurred moment, as if several frames of film had been removed, and the evil stood close enough to touch.

"Our last moment is not yours," he whispered and looked up at the sky, pressing his head alongside Martha's.

Shining brightly above, such beauty.

CHAPTER
TWENTY-SEVEN

- 1 -

The car smelled like kitchen grease and Marlboros, and so did the driver. The radio was screaming about a highway to Hell, and Hedde closed her eyes, trying to sort out a whirlwind of conflicting emotions.

"Better tips at R-3, but I get a shift meal at the Blue Jay, so it sorta evens out," Amber was saying as she drove Hedde back to Uncle Gerard's house. Officer Wannamaker had begged the favor of the bored girl after she delivered a sack of burgers for the prisoners.

"I'm done with my statement," Hedde had said, laying the papers on Wannamaker's desk and studiously avoiding her father's entreating look. "Etienne needs to be fed," she said to her uncle, who shook his head.

"He'll be fi—"

"Sophie won't get better without food, she needs it on time. I should go while you figure this out."

"No," Lewis said, but Gerard reached through the bars and patted his arm.

"We won't be much longer, and she'll be fine with the dogs to watch her. She knows how to take care of herself. Just ask those two assholes." Gerard said, jerking a thumb at the other cell.

Hedde remembered her father's face as he looked between her and Gerard. Cut out of their conversation, something had deflated inside him.

Hedde had to fight down the urge to run back to her father and hold tight to him, something she hadn't done since she was in grade school. Instead, she left without saying a word.

"Fuckin' song has been playing since Halloween," Amber said, turning the station away from a commercial set to "Here Comes Santa Claus." She took a greedy suck on her cigarette and shot Hedde a sidelong glance as if the younger girl might demand a drag. "I'm already sick of Christmas and it ain't even Thanksgiving."

"Me too," Hedde said, needing to fill the gap in conversation. *Thanksgiving? Christmas?*

Did those things still exist somewhere?

How could she have walked out on her father?

Hedde scratched the side of her nose and surreptitiously wiped moisture from her eye.

"That how they dress in New York now?" Amber asked, and Hedde shook her head. Not exactly on the cutting edge of chic herself, she was still aware of the girl's bangs. The hairspray. The bangle earrings straight out of a music video from the dawn of MTV.

"So it must be cool living in New York," Amber continued. When she was introduced, the girl's accent turned the name Amber, which was pretty in a stripper kind of way, into "Am-buh," which wasn't pretty in any fashion.

"We don't really live in New York City," Hedde said. "It's a small town outside of the city."

"Oh," Amber said, blowing a jet of smoke up at the small opening in the window. "So it's just like here."

No, never like here, the town that time forgot.

"Yeah," Hedde said.

The night was an anonymous thing outside the window, and Hedde was surprised when Amber put on her right blinker and pulled her little car up and into Uncle Gerard's driveway. The car's headlights dragged a small part of the looming old house into view, but the rest of the unlit property was just a humped shadow against the night.

"Creepy fuckin' house," Amber said, smoke tumbling out with her words. "Wouldn't catch me in there alone."

- 2 -

Creepy? No. But Hedde was aware the very moment the house became haunted.

She could hear the clack of Etienne's claws on the kitchen floor as she built up the fire in the living room fireplace, stuffing wads of old newspaper beneath dry pieces of wood before bringing a match to it. Her eyes watered as the paper blackened and curled inward, outlined in orange until licks of flame sprouted like spring blossoms.

Hedde knelt before the fireplace, her face lit in flickering orange, watching with bright eyes as shadows danced on the walls. Her own shade expanded up and out as she stood, racing up the wall and flooding across the ceiling. Huge. Dark. She spread her arms and it appeared to embrace everything—the couches, the bulky block of the never-used TV and record player.

She remembered Susie-with-a-heart telling her about the burning of witches and her lips peeled back in a grin, white teeth catching the firelight.

"They hanged us," Hedde said to invisible others as she picked up a stick from the fireplace and swung it in fiery loops until the flame at the tip was extinguished.

A bark sounded in the doorway and she turned to see Etienne's black shape beneath the arch, glittering eyes fixed on her.

"It's all right, boy," she said, but he backed away when she followed him into the kitchen. She began scribbling on the floor with the charred point of the stick, muttering words she forgot as soon as they were spoken.

The dog lunged, paws scraping at the ashy lines as he snatched the stick from Hedde's hand and backed away, shaking it violently.

"Stop it! Give it to me!"

Etienne backed away, whining.

"Then go outside," Hedde said, pushing past the dog to open the door.

Etienne whimpered and circled, but she pointed and, after a moment, he fled outside.

When the old phone on the wall rang, Hedde answered it, cord stretching out behind her as she meandered back to stand over her charcoal writing. A minute passed and she hung it up without saying a word before returning to the living room where she knelt on the thick rug beside the dusty shelves and pulled the stack of board games free. Risk. Monopoly. She set them aside and lifted the third in both hands, smiling at the faded cover of the box. *Mystifying Oracle Talking Board Set! Ages 8 to adult!* Parker Brothers indeed.

She tucked the box containing the Ouija board under one arm and lit a fat candle from the open fire, enjoying the sizzle of falling wax when she held it too long in the flame.

Holding the candle before her, Hedde mounted the old staircase, following the burning will-o'-the-wisp atop the wick up into darkness.

CHAPTER TWENTY-EIGHT

- 1 -

Dave Baillie led a small group of inebriated and chastened men down the stairs of the municipal building and out into the cold, where they paused for the ritual of zipping and buttoning.

"Colder'n a witch's tit," Sam Stout said.

"How would you know?" Baillie asked.

"Know what?"

"How cold a witch's tit is."

"Fuck you. Let's go drink."

"I'll second that," Jackie Strong said and led off with the men trickling behind him. "Ranger Rick was wicked pissed, huh?"

"Yuh," Baillie said. "Rightly so. We shouldn't have egged LaChaise on."

"Fuckin' Beaumont didn't have to kick him like that."

Baillie stopped and looked at Strong, wondering, not for the first time, how he wound up stranded among these knuckle-heads. "Wouldn't you?"

Stout reached the door first and they could hear the strains of Bob Seger's "On the Road" through the door. "Hope fuckin'

Aaron didn't burn the place down," he said with a laugh as he opened the door and loud music flooded the street.

They filed in, stomping and tossing coats on barstools, resuming their accustomed spots at the bar. Baillie heard what he thought was one of the guys saying, "Is that sausage?"

Indeed, what looked to be several feet of link sausage was draped over the lazily spinning ceiling fan which spun all year long because the R-3 was one bar where a man could still smoke. He was thinking proprietor thoughts about getting the stepladder from the back room and a re-emergence of the backyard hibachi idea he had been toying with. Guys needed more beer with their dogs and hotdogs were cheap.

"Where's Aaron?" Strong asked.

The insistent ring of a phone drifted from the back office.

"Smokin' a little bud in back?" an expert named McNeil commented, wandering over to the jukebox.

"Goddammit," Baillie said. "Aaron! Where the hell are you?"

Stout wrinkled his nose. "What's that smell?" He was leaning over the bar when the jukebox lost power and the song wound down to a halt.

...ROOOoooaaaad.

"The fuck you do, McNeil?" Baillie asked as the lights went out and everyone started cursing.

"Didn't do nothing," McNeil was saying, and it took a moment for Stout's frightened voice to cut through all the bitching.

"Oh my god," he said. "Get the light on. There's something behind the bar."

In back, the phone was still ringing.

"What?" Baillie said.

"I think it's Aaron," Stout said.

"Open the door," Strong shouted.

A moment later a crack of dim light from the street filtered in to create a muddy gloom. McNeil was holding the door open, trying the switch on the wall.

"Must be a circuit—" he was saying when he was snatched off of his feet and pulled outside. The door banged shut and plunged them again into pitch darkness.

The rustle of clothing and scraping of flints heralded the appearance of several tiny flames, pinpoints of light in the black.

"What just happened?" Strong asked.

"Aw Jesus," Baillie said from behind the bar, backing up fast enough that his lighter flame went out and he slipped. "Aw Christ, that's blood! I slipped in blood!"

The door swung slowly open and Jackie ran over only to skid to a stop. In an oddly high-pitched voice he bleated, "You're not McNeil," before something bright punched through his back and splattered Stout with blood.

Strong rose into the air as if levitating and shook like a man with palsy as he floated inside. In the moment before the door slammed closed again, Stout saw something that made his bladder release.

"Get the shotgun." Stout's voice carried across the dark before he screamed.

- 2 -

A black wave of exhaustion crashed over Lewis and he sat heavily in the chair. He would have rolled back on the casters if Gerard had not reached through the bars and caught his lapel. Lewis looked at the other man's outstretched arm before letting his eyes wander. Individual seconds ticked past on the wall clock as his gaze settled on the pebbled glass of the front door.

He mused on how odd it was that the words FLINTLOCK POLICE DEPARTMENT stenciled on the glass read TNEM-TRAPED ECILOP KCOLTNILF from the inside...

"What?" Lewis asked.

Why did he let Hedde go when he stayed to argue for Gerard's release? She had every right to be angry with him, but she was his daughter. What kind of father did that? His mind was filled with billowing fog. His thoughts moving in jagged, confused lines. Had he been away so long that he forgot his most important job?

Officer Wannamaker—not a bad guy, all things considered—had walked away from the cell and Lewis's persistent argument for Gerard's early release in exasperation, saying he had to "Deal with the radios."

The boys in the next cell had complained about the television volume, and Wannamaker had stopped by the little black-and-white set perched on a desk before slapping it with his hand. "You boys are in jail, for Chrissakes. Don't push your luck."

Over at the radios, Wannamaker was heard talking about a fire at the trailer park when Gerard had motioned him to the far corner of the cell, away from the boys. Lewis rose and pushed his rolling chair over.

"She'll be with Cat," Lewis said under his breath, and Gerard flinched.

"Lew," Gerard said. "I don't know how to tell you this, but Cat ain't at home."

"What?"

"She left a note, snuck out in the middle of the night," Gerard continued, watching Lewis's expression fold inward like a collapsing tart. "Said she was going to speak to someone who could help you."

"There's no one at the house?"

Gerard shook his head. "Hedde is safe. She's armed and I've

taught her. And she's got the dog. You get the hell outta here if we can't budge Rick when he comes back over."

"Oh God, have you heard anything from Cat since she left?" Lewis asked.

Gerard shook his head.

"All hell's breaking loose at the park," Wannamaker said as he returned to his desk.

He frowned down at Hedde's statement on the desk blotter and mouthed words silently before asking, "Hedde speak German?" He held up the statement and Lew blanched as he saw HERR WEISS scrawled across the neatly printed lines.

Wannamaker's phone shrilled and he wondered why the call had come in on a direct extension as he reached for the handset.

"Shit!" He exclaimed, snatching back his hand as the after image of a blue spark faded. "You see that?"

Lewis stared at the ringing phone. "Don't answer it!"

"Huh?" Wannamaker gave him an odd look as he gingerly picked up the receiver and said, "Flintlock Police Department, Wannamaker speaking."

Wannamaker squinted, as if focusing his vision would help him understand the caller. He looked quizzically at Lewis.

"For you," Wannamaker said. "Bad connection. Sounds like long distance."

"Who knows you're here?" Gerard asked.

"Who is Mister White?" Wannamaker asked, carrying the wireless receiver over to Lewis.

"Hang it up!" Lewis said.

"What?"

"Hang the damn phone up!"

Wannamaker put the phone to his ear and shrugged. "Caller already did."

The overhead lights went out and plunged the room into darkness, the fluorescents maintaining a ghostly afterglow for a moment as the incarcerated boys began shouting and Wanna-maker yelled back, "Shut up!"

In the quiet dark, they heard sounds from outside.

A gunshot.

Screams.

- 3 -

Rick Wannamaker was very cold by this point, cold and confused in the dark of night. He shivered and hugged himself, teeth chattering uncontrollably.

So many tears had been shed that the creases in his dark cheeks had frozen, the cracked plain of dry country after a sudden rainfall, a myriad of tributaries become veins of ice that gleamed in the moonlight, raining down so that a passerby might think his face was glowing.

His uniform had frozen and as he walked, red bits of ice flaked free. If he had looked behind him he would have seen a blood trail in the snow, moonlight darkening the scarlet spatters to black.

Here comes Santa Claus, here comes Santa Claus. The damned car commercial had been using the Christmas tune since before Halloween. Since before…

Before…

He shook in a whole body shiver like a mink shaking off water and fell to one knee. The radio on his belt squawked at him but it was another language. Farsi. Martian. He had no idea what the words meant, only…

A low moan slithered from his parted lips as he remembered running out the door of the police station after the two panicked boys. A sight that made his thoughts explode in static even as his foot slipped on something jellied and he was sliding down the stairs in the red waterfall of remains that were once Dickie LaChaise and Ray Childers.

Right down Santa Claus lane...

Wannamaker wobbled upright, internal gyros struggling to keep him on feet he could no longer feel. Up ahead he made out glowing rubies and amethysts and thought of the lights he would string on the tree this year. He no longer put up a tree at home; it felt maudlin after Gladys left. But at the department he liked to fill the place with the smell of Douglas fir and the glow of colored lights. Gladys, a purist, had liked only the tiny white bulbs. Each year, Mrs. McMahon would bring the first and second graders on a field trip from school and they would hang ornaments and strings of popcorn—eating much of it—while they sang carols.

When the police station lights went out, Lewis had done something in the dark, some jiu-jitsu bullshit straight out of the movies, and Wannamaker found himself unlocking both cells with his own gun aimed at his considerable belly.

The town boys panicked and fled out the front door, sounding like a herd of elephants slamming down the stairs in their work boots. And Gerry Beaumont was saying, "You have to come with us," when Wannamaker heard the boys screaming. They had all heard it—high, terrified sounds like calves subjected to a particularly cruel slaughter.

And he, the fool everyone called Ranger Rick, especially townies like Dickie and Ray, had started after them.

"He'll kill you," Lewis said.

And this was the kicker because the town fool, the court jester with a badge, had said, "They're my boys."

Lewis had spun the Glock around with some trick move and held it out to him butt first. Nothing to say, Wannamaker took the gun and tossed his car keys at him. Two kids trading baseball cards.

"Even Steven," he said and went after the boys.

He remembered slipping in so much blood it was as if the staircase had been doused with a fire hose. Then he saw that thing…

Static.

Wannamaker pushed himself up, trailing an anguished cry.

"Vixen and Nixon and Blixen and that other one…" Determined to speak, to stay conscious, all he could think to say were the absurd lyrics to that idiot song that played over and over on the radio.

And now he was freezing and walking towards those spinning Christmas lights, all red and blue.

Hands were on him and he heard words he knew he should understand, but it was just too much effort. Someone threw a jacket around his shoulders and led him to sit in the backseat of a squad car.

"Rick, Rick, are you hurt? What's all this blood, man? Tell me about this blood."

Wannamaker tried to focus, but the frozen liquid on his eyes made it hard. "I told…" he said, making a futile effort to clutch the lapels of the man in front of him. "I told…"

"Told what?" the voice asked. "Talk to me man."

"Told…" Wannamaker mumbled.

"Get him to the hospital," another voice ordered, and someone carefully tucked his legs into the car. In the moment before the door closed, Wannamaker heard someone say, "Did you see his hair? It was totally white."

CHAPTER
TWENTY-NINE

- 1 -

Gerard stomped on the accelerator and the police 4x4 skidded from the lot, slamming on an angle over the hard snow packed beside the driveway and blowing through in an explosion of white shards. The vehicle slid sideways into Main Street going too fast, but Gerard wrestled it under control and hit the gas again.

"What the hell was that thing?" Gerard asked, voice tight with fear. He had seen it in the doorway and every hair had stood on end. Lewis had fired the police twelve-gauge up at it from a range of no more than twenty feet from the bottom of the back staircase. Gerard heard the spackle of pellets against the hallway inside, but Lewis hit *nothing*.

"Just go!" Lewis barked.

"Tell me what it was!"

"It knows about Hedde," Lewis shot back. "Somehow, the damned thing knows about her!" He pulled the crumpled statement from his pocket and smoothed it out on the dash.

"I can't read it," Gerard said, flicking buttons until the flashers overhead began to strobe and the few cars on the street pulled aside as they roared past.

"'Herr Weiss,'" Lewis said. "She wrote 'Herr Weiss.'"

"So what?"

"It's German," Lewis whispered. "She wrote *Mister*—"

It happened quickly. Two glowing lumps of coal rose up from the road ahead and Gerard had just enough time to think *eyes!* before the snowy body of a goat struck the windshield with a horrific crash, driving the safety glass into driver and passenger as the big vehicle slid broadside and flipped, flinging metal and glass through three revolutions before it planed across the snow on its roof.

Stunned and bleeding, Lewis struggled to orient himself, reaching through the empty passenger side window to dig his fingers into the snow as he struggled to drag himself from the vehicle.

Gerard hurried around to the passenger side and gripped him by the wrists to pull him free, tearing a shriek of pain from Lewis.

"Ribs," Lewis gasped as the big man knelt down, the right side of his face gleaming black with blood.

"What was that?" Gerard asked.

"It's him," Lewis said. He reached out and grabbed Gerard with desperate strength. "Get to Hedde. Please, get to Hedde."

Gerard made his decision with the speed of a wild animal. No sooner had Lewis released his grip than Gerard was up and bulling across the open field of snow until he pushed his way through snowy branches and into the trees.

Lewis rested in the snow for a moment before he lifted his head and dragged himself from the wreckage.

- 2 -

Alone in the deadroom, Hedde sat in a tiny dome of light thrown by a single candle set beside the board. Despite her sophistication, she was a little girl to the world of spirit, her fourteen years the blink of an eye to a ghost.

The dust she disturbed swirled to form shapes and patterns that she dared not look at. Despite her courage, she was afraid. She whimpered as she rested the fingertips of both hands atop the plastic planchette with the gentleness of sparrows alighting on a branch.

Around her the building groaned in the secret language of houses and tried to make her stop, but the little girl did not listen, could not listen, as the air thickened with mold in this attic where a happy couple once lay together.

"Hello," Hedde's voice punctured the silence. "Is anyone there?" She felt like a rabbit beneath a circling hawk. "I know you're here."

She glanced at the spill of shadows in the corners of the room and shivered as they pooled on the dusty floor. Had they come closer?

"I know you're here," she said, and inside her mind she screamed *no* even as she said aloud, "Herr Weiss."

The curtains over the bed undulated in an imaginary breeze, and she groaned at the creaking movement of the red door below.

"Do you want to talk to me?"

The planchette slid under her fingers and goosebumps broke out on her skin as the plastic scraped against cardboard. She leaned over the board as it stopped above a letter.

"J," she said. The planchette slid left along the arc of letters until it rested on another. "A."

"J-A," she repeated. "Ja?" she asked with passable pronunciation. "Are you German?"

This time the planchette slid up and to the left, past the ornate image of the sun to rest on the word YES.

There was a slithering sound from the hallway below and her head whipped around, hair flinging wildly. She almost blurted out, "Are you here?" but caught herself just in time and went still. Her eyes darted to the grate on the floor and she carefully dropped to her belly.

She inched carefully across the floor, leaving behind the tiny dome of light until she was in shadow. Placing her head on the floor, Hedde listened for several long seconds but heard no further sounds of movement. Realizing she could delay no longer, she held her breath and lifted her head until she could see down through the grate into the room below.

The white blur of a face stared up at her.

Hedde screamed.

She scuttled away from the grate in a crablike movement, whirling clumsily as a sudden gust shook the room. The candle blew out and she was left with the terrifying image of the blankets on the bed swelling and rising. A child's image of ghosts, of a father playing tricks on Halloween. But Hedde knew this was no illusion, and she sprang to her feet, body suffused with panic.

It was in the room.

Getoutgetoutgetout.

She darted around the thing beneath the blankets as white hands stretched from the half open closet to clutch her in an impossible grip.

Hedde fell headlong on the floor. The Ouija board went flying as she fought and twisted, shrieks tearing at her lungs even as she clawed at the rug which bunched and came with her, the nightmare of every child come true as it dragged her into the closet.

An answering howl rent the air, and she felt the thunder of his charge even during her struggle, her head and shoulders all that remained free, the rest of her body screaming against the impossible cold and she flung out her arms.

"Etienne!"

And he was there, her savior, his mighty jaws gripping her wrist hard enough to send blood spattering as he dug in his hind legs, his growl vibrating the floorboards. Hedde felt a moment of clarity and bright, shining hope.

A moment later she was sucked into darkness, and Etienne was dragged after.

- 3 -

Breath was whistling in and out of tortured lungs and his thighs burned from effort as Gerard broke from the tree line and staggered up the hill.

The house was a great blot against the starry sky. Once the sight of love, more recently the sight of loneliness, never before had the sight of the big house struck him numb with fear.

He made out an orange glow wavering in the attic window and paused to wipe at the tears streaking from his half-frozen eyes.

"Hedde," he croaked, hands on his knees, wanting nothing more than to collapse into the snow.

His right boot broke through the icy crust, followed by his left. In a moment he was moving at a dogged trot, blowing like a bellows as he passed the hanging tree and he slowed, breaking stride to wrench the axe from the broad stump.

The kitchen door was open in unwholesome welcome and he paused, skin crawling as his eyes sought to pull detail from the dark interior. His upper lip curled at a rank smell that brought to mind dead things rotting in a crawlspace.

A scream careened like an object thrown wildly down the stairs, and Etienne's answering howl galvanized Gerard into action as he charged into the kitchen and broke for the stairs, taking them two at a time.

- 4 -

Lewis ran awkwardly with one arm clutching his ribs, stumbling into branches and pressing through cascades of tumbling snow as he tracked Gerard's passage with a powerful police flashlight.

Exhaustion was a physical weight pressing down on his shoulders and his head hung low, blowing like a horse pushed to breaking. Blind in the woods. Blindly trusting the trail.

Anything. Anything. Anything.

His mantra offered to whomever might listen. To the nonnen for strength. To God for salvation. To Mister White for mercy where he knew none would be found.

He was a lurching thing beyond fear, though he suspected not beyond one, final horror. Failure as a father. As husband.

Anything.

He was an undeserving fool.

Pain had replaced time in his universe when Lewis pushed past a pine bough and staggered up the hillside. The moonlight rendered the landscape as a boldly drawn work of pen and ink as he marched past the silent rows of Christmas trees, an incongruous sight in his personal hell.

There were no lights on in the house.

He labored up the wooden steps and leaned against the doorway, aiming the flashlight into the interior and halting at the black mess of ash scribbled in great sweeps across the linoleum. The words HERR WEISS marked in slashing strokes.

Footsteps blazed a path through the ashen writing.

Lewis caught his breath in the doorway until he could find his voice and called out, "Gerard!" He paused as a numbing blackness pressed in at the edges of his vision. "Hedde!"

He stepped inside, groaning at the sharp pain in his ribs as he braced his hands on the kitchen table. They peeled free with a sticking sound when he was able to move deeper into the house towards the base of the staircase.

He had the sense of movement from above even as he heard the thud of boots against hardwood. He aimed the light upward to see Gerard wavering at the top of the stairs, eyes wide with horror until he fell forward with no effort to catch himself, the impact that of a hammer against meat. Gerard slid face first down the stairs as Lewis hobbled backwards. The big man came to rest at the bottom, an axe buried between his shoulder blades.

Lewis knelt and pressed two fingers to Gerard's neck, knowing the futility. A groan of pain escaped him as he rose, hand on the round finial at the base of the banister to step over the body before making his way upstairs, following the wobbling circle of light.

Anything. Anything. The word echoed in his mind as he pulled himself up the cliff face of each single step. Eighteen times anything.

He had some dim idea of offering Mister White a trade, himself for his daughter. *Take me to the glass room and reap pain and fear until you're full to bursting.*

Lewis made out the trail of reddish footprints along the hall and followed them, dragging a hand along the wall for balance, dislodging several framed pictures that fell with a crash.

The red door was half open and he nudged it further with the flashlight before aiming the beam upstairs where it caught dust motes floating like the flakes of a gentle snowfall.

"Hedde," he croaked, aware of a rhythmic noise from above. He felt something in his middle give and used his free arm on the railing to pull himself up, his light panning across the tacky spill covering the floorboards until he saw the furred carnage twisted into a bunched rug in front of an open closet. He covered his nose against the sewer stink of disembowelment.

"Oh…" The sound might have grown into a wail if not for the gentle creak of wood and he turned, sweeping the flashlight around until he saw her in the rocking chair.

"Hedde?"

Her eyes were overly wide and white in the red smear of her face, as if registering surprise. She neither flinched nor turned as his light struck her, and though he saw the pupils react, the eyes didn't track when he passed a hand in front of them.

"Hedde?" he said gently, stretching the fingers of his right hand to touch her chest, assuring himself of the rise and fall. "It's dad, hon, I'm here."

She continued to rock back and forth as he slid to his knees and felt the bump of the metal flask in his pocket. He pulled the flask free and unscrewed the lid, splashing water into his cupped hand before gently wiping her face.

She twitched and he nearly dropped the flask.

"Hedde?" he said, wiping more water on her face until she turned her head like an infant avoiding a wash cloth. She whispered something.

"What?" Lewis leaned closer. "Oh, Hedde."

"He's inside me…" So low he almost imagined the whisper.

Lewis recoiled back onto his haunches, but his daughter made no move except to turn her blank eyes towards him again, rocking back and forth. He glanced at the flask in his hand as an idea floated across his desperate thoughts.

"Drink this, honey, just a sip."

He gently pushed her bottom lip down with his fingers and held the flask to her mouth, wincing as it clacked against her teeth.

Lewis filled his daughter's mouth with holy water.

The reaction was immediate. Hedde arched her back, sliding from the chair into the mess on the floor while her eyes rolled wildly in their sockets. He straddled her writhing form and she fought him, scoring his cheek with her nails as he forced the flask into her mouth, splitting her lip. "Drink! Drink!"

She went limp beneath him and her eyes blinked in confusion. "Daddy?"

He was leaning down when she began to buck and she screamed, "He's inside me, Daddy! Oh God, he's inside me!"

"How do I help you? Tell me how!" Lewis said, pinning her wrists. "How do I get him out?"

"You don't," she said.

Lewis pulled back to look at the thing staring up from his daughter's eyes.

"Drink," he said, jamming the flask into her mouth again as she fought until the water was bubbling out between her teeth and she went limp in his arms.

Fighting his own pain, Lewis lifted Hedde into his arms and carried her downstairs into the bathroom off the hall. He washed her face and hands as best he could in the sink while her head rolled loosely, and she blinked up at him with the gaze of an aging barfly wheedling free beer.

"Gonna need more of that stuff," Hedde slurred.

"Is it making him go away?" Lewis asked.

She shook her head.

"Marrow in my bones. Nightmare in my mind. My nightmare now." A limp hand pawed at his lapel. "But...it quiets him. Can hear myself."

How long Lewis wept on the bathroom floor, holding his daughter to him, he did not know. But when she touched the scratches on his cheek and said, "He's coming," Lewis roused himself and carried her downstairs, setting her down before the fireplace. "I'll be right back," he whispered and returned to the base of the stairs.

He moved woodenly, as if he had no joints. Kneeling beside Gerard took an effort of will. Touching the cooling body took even more. He had so many things to say to this man. Too many things. In the end, he said nothing.

Lewis saw the kitchen door open and shuffled outside, fear mounting until he found Hedde wandering in a fugue, unsuccessfully trying to slide the ice-crusted cover from the Camaro. He hoisted her into the passenger seat and would not remember until much later that her hands were newly wetted with blood.

Before they left he broke the lock off the barn door and took the time to dump a bag of dry food on the dirt floor at Hedde's insistence. Sophie's mournful eyes followed his every move, but she made no sound.

Lewis settled into the driver's seat and guided the old hunk of Detroit rolling iron carefully down the driveway, heading for Father Messina's church.

- 5 -

Lewis found Messina arranged about the interior of the church in red dismemberment, lit by the headlights of the still running car just outside the open doors.

He struggled to find some word or gesture of atonement, but in the end simply refilled the flask with holy water, the bubbling of liquid the only sound.

- 6 -

Too tired for clever routes, Lewis picked up Interstate 95 in Massachusetts and drove south, watching the broken white lines disappear beneath the car. Hedde lolled in the passenger seat nuzzling the flask, equal parts degenerate drunk and overgrown infant.

She was nestled in an aura of that horrid butcher-shop stink, and his stomach churned at her proximity.

"I've come so far," Lewis pleaded with childish desperation.

"You never should have gone," she said without great concern.

In her listlessness he saw her future as predicted by Gruebel. When Mister White was finished with her, she would become another nameless waif discovered frozen beneath an overpass or, if she were lucky, wandering mindless until she was picked up and institutionalized.

The idea to travel south was hers, or possibly Mister White's, but Lewis agreed to it as he came to understand there would never again be joy for him in this life. All that was left, all that he might earn, was red satisfaction.

They drove through most of the day and arrived in Alexandria, Virginia as dusk lay across the town.

Lewis followed her directions to a neighborhood of stately homes with wide, front lawns and driveways sporting BMW's and Mercedes in equal measures.

He pulled up in front of a well-kept dwelling with bright, bay windows and cut the ignition. The engine ticked as Hedde took a last hit from the flask and handed the empty container back to him.

"Won't need it after tonight," she said.

The dome light threw its radiance down over them when she pushed open the passenger door and paused with one leg still in the car, one leg outside, disheveled and possessed and all of fourteen years old.

Halfway gone.

"I want you back," he said.

"You can't have me back."

Lewis clutched her knee through the long skirt but recoiled, nerve endings transmitting the undeniable truth of what she was becoming.

He looked at the house and spittle flew from his lips when he spoke. "Then you make him pay," he snarled. "Make him suffer."

"Yes, Daddy." His daughter smiled at him from beneath tangled hair. "You run when I close this door," she said, and he saw a curl to her lips that belonged to Mister White. "You go someplace that I'd never think of, that he'd never think of, where no one who knows you would ever think of. He will never stop looking for you. Understand?"

Lewis nodded, trying to fight through the blockage in his throat as tears streamed freely down his cheeks. "I love you," he whispered, but she swung outside and a door slammed shut between them.

He threw himself across the car, hands slapping against the window. She looked back, her expression writhing with confusion, and he knew that fear was the only thing left of his daughter. He wept openly, the warmth of his sobs fogging the glass as his dark girl walked away, somehow evading the motion-sensitive security lights that shined daylight on the front lawn. She danced into shadows and became insubstantial.

Lewis sat back in the driver's seat and wiped the tears from his wet face before keying the ignition. He revved the engine, flinging hatred from his eyes at the comfortable house before shifting into gear and dropping the hammer. The powerful car fishtailed until he wrenched it under control.

Anything, he had promised.

It was her last wish, so he headed south.

CHAPTER THIRTY

Bierce was seated alone at his dark wood dining table clad in nothing but a silk robe as he sliced a thin piece of squab in a red wine reduction, the gentle strains of Vivaldi reaching him from the stereo in the living room. The electric chandelier overhead cast a dim yellow light over his meal.

He was, as a rule, fundamentally opposed to the idea of business dinners and had ignored a request from the FBI man, Chambers, to meet him at the historic Tabard Inn this evening. Dinner was a time to let the senses play and mind work undistracted by social interactions.

Besides, the blue pill dissolving under his tongue meant he wouldn't be going anywhere for a while. He felt a warm drop in his middle as the narcotic took hold. He had been near to a twitching wreck after the past several days, and it was time for him to withdraw into his well-appointed shell and pull himself together.

The disastrous reports from New Hampshire had not yet been connected to Lewis Edgar, though he expected the connection to Catherine Edgar would be revealed eventually. Though Lewis Edgar's corpse had yet to be discovered, several of the bodies would require dental examination for purposes of identification, and Bierce was certain that the quarry had been run to ground.

More importantly, it seemed that the European operation was finally concluded without dangling ends and his connection with Abel was no longer visible.

He pierced a baby russet potato and chewed thoughtfully, exhaling to release some of the heat as he considered the propriety of backing a container truck loaded with kerosene up to the old Millhouse and running a hose inside to the escalator. He grinned, his too-small teeth briefly visible.

Not a practical solution but—

The music ceased and he lifted his head, perturbed when it didn't resume. Still chewing a mouthful, Bierce walked past the glass cases of his liquor cabinet onto the soft Persian rug in his living room, cocking his head when he saw the PAUSE button pressed on the CD player. He pressed PLAY and the music resumed as he returned to the dining room.

Bierce lifted his face, nose wrinkling at an unpleasant smell.

He was slow to register the scrape of cutlery against plate and paused on the threshold, gasping when the lights flickered overhead.

A filthy little girl was seated at the table, eating his dinner. She was dressed strangely and her hair was matted with some tacky substance.

"Who are you?" he demanded. "What are you doing here?"

The girl looked up at him, cheek stuffed full of his squab as she chewed.

"Don't you know your old friend?" the girl purred, and Bierce placed a hand to his temple as a pain knifed through his skull. He thought quickly of the black leather case and its eyedroppers upstairs in his personal safe.

"Hey, you don't have my book here at your home, do you?" she asked.

He took a step back, exhaling sharply through his nose at the sensation of gnats buzzing in his face. The girl rose from his seat and the lights flickered again before they went out completely. Bierce blinked, thankful for the wash of illumination from the streetlights through his large windows.

The girl stood in front of him.

How did she suddenly get so close? he thought as he was enveloped in a rank, organic odor. He flinched but was unable to tear his eyes away from the pale shape of her face, her features an indeterminate smear, save for her mouth. Her teeth.

"Who...who are you?" he asked.

"Lewis Edgar sends his regards," she said, and he wondered when her fingers had grown so long.

"What?"

"You know who I am," the girl said.

A filth-encrusted fingernail touched his breastbone and slid down to his belly as a voice slithered through his mind.

Who am I?

His bladder released and his moan was that of the damned.

"You can't..." he said.

"You were always going to be mine," she said as he backed into the wall and slid to the floor, a marionette with his strings finally cut.

"Say my name," she said as she leaned over him and he gagged at the corruption she exhaled.

"God help me," he whimpered.

"Say my name," she murmured in a lover's voice as her nose touched his in an Eskimo kiss. Her palms found either side of his head and began to exert pressure, squeezing his weak whisper into a shrill scream.

"Mister White...

"Mister White.

"MISTER WHITE!"

EPILOGUE

It was a bright day and the shade of the overhanging poplars was a welcome cover for the two old men seated in front of the combination gas station and general store.

"Got a live one," Henry said from his wooden chair on the porch, tapping ash from his pipe.

Leonard glanced at his white-bearded friend, his seamed, brown face like old leather. "Whyn't you earn yourself the price of those Cokes you keep stealin' from my cooler and pour the man some gasoline."

The old Camaro was road dirty and its overloud engine rumbled to a stop as a cloud of dust settled around it.

"White boys and they cars," Henry opined, bringing a wooden match to the pipe's bowl.

"You really ain't gonna go help this boy?" Leonard griped, hawking an impressive loogie into the dirt.

"You offering insurance?"

"Nobody would insure your grizzled ass," Leonard said, pushing up from his chair with a grunt. "I pay you more'n you're worth in Cokes as it is."

Leonard stepped carefully down from the wooden porch and walked over to the Camaro as the driver's door opened. He dragged his foot to a stop as the gray-faced man with the red-rimmed eyes emerged.

"Haunted," he would tell people later. "Man had haunted eyes."

"Fill her up," the stranger croaked.

"You all right, son?" Leonard asked.

The man nodded and cleared his dry throat. "Tired."

Leonard hobbled around the back of the car and felt for the gas cap. "Henry, get this boy a Coke if you can bring y'self to share one. Boy's throat sounds like sandpaper."

Lewis nodded thanks and slumped against the car as Leonard inserted the gas pump and flipped the lever. Numbers rolled and the pump dinged dutifully.

"New Hampshire plates," Leonard said in the uneasy silence. "You a long way from home."

"Where is this?" he asked, and Leonard snuck another look to make sure his customer wasn't drunk or high.

"Roke, Alabama," Leonard offered after a bit, waving the air at a stink that seemed to be coming from the car.

"Drink this," Henry said, approaching with the aid of a cane. He fixed Lewis with his gaze and said with his typical lack of manners, "Son, you look like the Devil hisself been bitin' your tail."

Lewis jerked and nearly dropped the glass bottle, but Henry steadied him with a gnarled hand and exchanged a glance with Leonard, both men sharing the same thought. *This man shouldn't be allowed back behind the wheel.*

"What's your name?" Henry asked.

"Lewis," the customer replied.

"You hit something with your car? Stinks like maybe you got a rabbit or something underneath." Leonard used his hands to lower himself, palms in the dirt, and glanced underneath, but shook his head when he rose.

"Something in your trunk? Get y'self a deer?"

Lewis straightened and pulled the keys from his pocket, face twisted in confusion. He stepped over the gas hose and Leonard shuffled aside to let him turn the key in the lock. The old man said nothing about the dried, brown handprint he spotted on the trunk, smaller than this stranger's own.

"Lord," Leonard said, throwing an arm over his face at the powerful stench.

Shiny flies buzzed around a hat box resting next to a spare tire and greasy jack.

"What you got in the box?" Henry asked, coming around to the back.

"I don't know," Lewis said in a dead voice.

Henry and Leonard exchanged another look and Henry asked, "You mind I open it?"

Lewis shook his head and reached down to do it himself, waving aside the fat flies crawling on the box.

He lifted the lid and both old men stumbled back, Henry losing his balance and falling to the dirt.

"Oh Lord!" Henry said, and Leonard bent to pull his friend back away from the haunted man and the horror in the trunk. "Call the sheriff!"

The customer seemed not to notice the two men as he reached into the box and gently lifted a woman's severed head in both hands.

His pained moan rose like a foghorn until Lewis screamed, "Cat!"

He sagged to the dirt, staring down into his wife's stiff expression, hair crusted brown with blood. Her eyes were frozen wide in terror and eternal in their accusation.

"Cat!" Tears burst from his bulging eyes as the two old men hurried inside the store with all the speed their arthritic limbs allowed, the horrible shrieks continuing behind them.

Lewis laid back in the dirt, the bright sky above a dazzling blur through his tears as he cradled his wife's head against his chest and wept.

THE
END

ABOUT
THE AUTHOR

John C. Foster was born in Sleepy Hollow, New York, and has been afraid of the dark for as long as he can remember. A writer of thrillers and dark fiction, Foster spent many years in the ersatz glow of Los Angeles before relocating to the relative sanity of New York City where he lives with the actress Linda Jones and their dog, Coraline.

Foster's short story "Mister White" appeared in the Grey Matter Press anthology *Dark Visions: A Collection of Modern Horror – Volume Two* before inspiring the novel of the same name. His short fiction has appeared in numerous magazines and anthologies.

Foster released his first novel, *Dead Men*, in 2015. *Mister White* is his second novel. A third novel, *The Isle*, is coming soon from Grey Matter Press. For more information, please visit JohnFosterFiction.com.

ACKNOWLEDGEMENTS

Several years ago I submitted the short story "Mister White" to Grey Matter Press and they were kind enough to publish it in the anthology *Dark Visions: A Collection of Modern Horror - Volume Two*. That process was such a wonderful experience that I knew wanted to work with them again somewhere down the road, and when the idea to expand the story into a novel hit me, I had only one home in mind for the book. Fortunately they liked the novel as much as the short story and the rest, as they say, is history. I'd like to offer my sincere thanks for the generosity, patience and friendship of Anthony Rivera and Sharon Lawson. This book would not be what it is without your talent. The next round of margaritas is on me.

Thanks are also owed for the unwavering support of Carol and Duane Jones, who have welcomed this ne'er-do-well writer into their family. While I question your judgment with regard to vagabond novelists, I will never question your heart. You are still not allowed to read the book, however.

To my mother, sister and brother, I'm glad you're always in my corner.

Writing would be a lonely business if not for Linda Jones. I am a lucky man indeed to have not only your love, but access to your keen eye on each and every fledgling draft. Reading a first pass requires a delicate touch and your imprint lingers on each and every story.

MORE DARK FICTION FROM
GREY MATTER PRESS

"Grey Matter Press has managed to establish itself as one of the premiere purveyors of horror fiction currently in existence via both a series of killer anthologies -- *SPLATTERLANDS* (2013), *OMINOUS REALITIES* (2013), *EQUILIBRIUM OVERTURNED* (2014) -- and John F.D. Taff's harrowing novella collection *THE END IN ALL BEGINNINGS* (2014)."

- FANGORIA Magazine

GREY MATTER
P R E S S

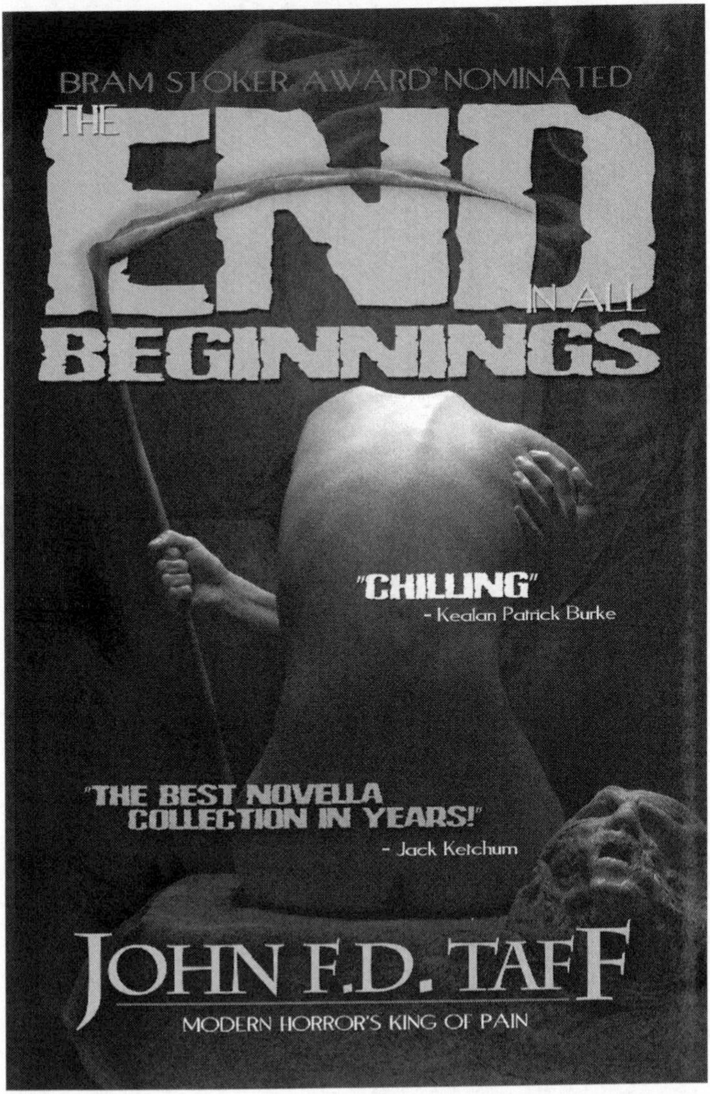
BRAM STOKER AWARD® NOMINATED
THE END IN ALL BEGINNINGS
"CHILLING"
- Kealan Patrick Burke
"THE BEST NOVELLA COLLECTION IN YEARS!"
- Jack Ketchum
JOHN F.D. TAFF
MODERN HORROR'S KING OF PAIN

THE END IN ALL BEGINNINGS
BY JOHN F.D. TAFF

The Bram Stoker Award-nominated *The End in All Beginnings* is a tour de force through the emotional pain and anguish of the human condition. Hailed as one of the best volumes of heartfelt and gut-wrenching horror in recent history, *The End in All Beginnings* is a disturbing trip through the ages exploring the painful tragedies of life, love and loss.

Exploring complex themes that run the gamut from loss of childhood innocence, to the dreadful reality of survival after everything we hold dear is gone, to some of the most profound aspects of human tragedy, author John F.D. Taff takes readers on a skillfully balanced emotional journey through everyday terrors that are uncomfortably real over the course of the human lifetime. Taff's highly nuanced writing style is at times darkly comedic, often deeply poetic and always devastatingly accurate in the most terrifying of ways.

Evoking the literary styles of horror legends Mary Shelley, Edgar Allen Poe and Bram Stoker, *The End in All Beginnings* pays homage to modern masters Stephen King, Ramsey Campbell, Ray Bradbury and Clive Barker.

"*The End in All Beginnings* is accomplished stuff, complex and heartfelt. It's one of the best novella collections I've read in years!" – JACK KETCHUM, Bram Stoker Award®-winning author of *The Box*, *Closing Time* and *Peaceable Kingdom*

"Taff brings the pain in five damaged and disturbing tales of love gone horribly wrong. This collection is like a knife in the heart. Highly recommended!" – JONATHAN MABERRY, *New York Times* bestselling author of *Code Zero* and *Fall of Night*

GREY MATTER
P R E S S

greymatterpress.com

A NIGHTMARE OF SUPERNATURAL, SCIENCE & SOUND

DARK FICTION
INSPIRED BY MUSICAL ICONS

HARD ROCK
HEAVY METAL
ALTERNATIVE
PROGRESSIVE
CONTEMPORARY
ELECTRONIC
CLASSICAL
BLUES
AND MORE

SAVAGE BEASTS

FROM BRAM STOKER AWARD-NOMINATED EDITORS

ANTHONY RIVERA AND SHARON LAWSON

SAVAGE BEASTS
A NIGHTMARE OF SUPERNATURAL, SCIENCE AND SOUND

SAVAGE BEASTS is a volume of contemporary dark fiction inspired by some of the greatest artists in musical history. A thrilling and thought-provoking nightmare of devastating supernatural experiences exploring darkly introspective science fiction and fantastical alternative realities, each accompanied by the sound of the music that defines your life.

The short stories in *SAVAGE BEASTS* shine a light on eleven dark worlds with fictional work inspired by Nine Inch Nails, Pink Floyd, The Cranberries, Genesis, Tom Petty and The Heartbreakers, Pestilence, Grace Jones, Underground Sound of Lisbon, School of Seven Bells, Wolfgang Amadeus Mozart and Johann Sebastian Bach and more.

FEATURING:

Edward Morris	Daniel Braum
Karen Runge	Maxwell Price
John F.D. Taff	E. Michael Lewis
Shawn Macomber	T. Fox Dunham
Konstantine Paradias	J.C. Michael
Paul Michael Anderson	

"The tales in *SAVAGE BEASTS* are as varied as their inspirations. Many of the contributors don't just use music as their muse, they place it front and centre in their narratives. Here, music has the power to save and to kill, and nothing buried in the past stays buried forever, regardless of how frightening it is."
– *RUE MORGUE*

GREY MATTER
P R E S S

greymatterpress.com

A COLLECTION OF MODERN HORROR

DARK

VISIONS 1

VOLUME ONE

EDITED BY
ANTHONY RIVERA AND SHARON LAWSON

DARK VISIONS ONE
A COLLECTION OF MODERN HORROR

Somewhere just beyond the veil of human perception lies a darkened plane where very evil things reside. Weaving their horrifying visions, they pull the strings on our lives and lure us into a comfortable reality. But it's all just a web of lies. And this book is their instruction manual.

The Bram Stoker Award-nominated *Dark Visions: A Collection of Modern Horror - Volume One* includes thirteen disturbing tales of dread from some of the most visionary minds writing horror, sci-fi and speculative fiction today.

Dark Visions: A Collection of Modern Horror - Volume One uncovers the truth behind our own misguided concepts of reality.

FEATURING:

Jonathan Maberry

Jay Caselberg

Jeff Hemenway

Sarah L. Johnson

Ray Garton

Jason S. Ridler

Milo James Fowler

Jonathan Balog

Brian Fatah Steele

Sean Logan

John F.D. Taff

Charles Austin Muir

David A. Riley

"This compilation of stories acts as a guide book for the evil minions that lurk within humankind and try to destroy it. Think of *The Twilight Zone* introduction from the popular TV series, and you will get the idea that this compilation is more than just a series of short fictional works." – *HELLNOTES*

GREY MATTER
P R E S S

greymatterpress.com

A COLLECTION OF MODERN HORROR

DARK
VISIONS
2
VOLUME TWO

EDITED BY
ANTHONY RIVERA AND SHARON LAWSON

DARK VISIONS TWO
A COLLECTION OF MODERN HORROR

Dark Visions: A Collection of Modern Horror - Volume Two continues the terrifying psychological journey with an all-new selection of exceptional tales of darkness written by some of the most talented authors working in the fields of horror, speculative fiction and fantasy today.

Unable to contain all the visions of dread and mayhem to a single volume, *Dark Visions: A Collection of Modern Horror - Volume Two* is now available from your favorite booksellers in both paperback and digital formats.

FEATURING:

David Blixt

John C. Foster

JC Hemphill

Jane Brooks

Peter Whitley

Edward Morris

Trent Zelazny

Carol Holland March

David Murphy

Chad McKee

C.M. Saunders

J. Daniel Stone

David Siddall

Rhesa Sealy

Kenneth Whitfield

A.A. Garrison

"There is something for every horror/sci-fi aficionado in this collection of modern and speculative horror. Fourteen incredibly terrifying stories varying in degrees of horror." – *HELLNOTES*

GREY MATTER
P R E S S

greymatterpress.com

SPLATTER

REAWAKENING THE SPLATTERPUNK REVOLUTION

LANDS

COLLECTED AND EDITED BY

ANTHONY RIVERA AND SHARON LAWSON

SPLATTERLANDS
REAWAKENING THE
SPLATTERPUNK REVOLUTION

Almost three decades ago, a literary movement forever changed the landscape of the horror entertainment industry. Grey Matter Press breathes new life into that revolution as we reawaken the true essence of Splatterpunk with the release of *Splatterlands*.

Splatterlands: Reawakening the Splatterpunk Revolution is a collection of personal, intelligent and subversive horror with a point. This illustrated volume of dark fiction honors the truly revolutionary efforts of some of the most brilliant writers of all time with an all-new collection of visceral, disturbing and thought-provoking work from a diverse group of modern minds.

FEATURING:

Ray Garton	Michele Garber
Michael Laimo	A.A. Garrison
Paul M. Collrin	Jack Maddox
Eric Del Carlo	Allen Griffin
James S. Dorr	Christine Morgan
Gregory L. Norris	Chad Stroup

J. Michael Major

Illustrations by Carrion House

"Grey Matter Press delivers with a delightfully disturbing anthology that will render you speechless. As a fan of horror for some thirty plus years I have never read anything quite like this and regret not a moment of it." – *HORROR NEWS*

GREY MATTER
P R E S S

greymatterpress.com

OMINOUS REALITIES

THE ANTHOLOGY OF DARK SPECULATIVE HORRORS

EDITED AND COLLECTED BY

ANTHONY RIVERA
SHARON LAWSON

OMINOUS REALITIES
THE ANTHOLOGY OF
DARK SPECULATIVE HORRORS

Ominous Realities: The Anthology of Dark Speculative Horrors is a collection of sixteen terrifying tales of chilling science fiction, dark fantasy and speculative horror.

Prepare to travel through an ever-darkening procession of horrifying alternate realities where you'll explore shocking post-apocalyptic worlds, become enslaved by greedy mutli-national corporations that control every aspect of life, participate in societies where humanity is forced to consider perilous decisions about its own survival, experience the effects of an actual Hell on Earth and discover the many other disturbing possibilities that may be in our future.

FEATURING:

John. F.D. Taff	Bracken MacLeod
William Meikle	Gregory L. Norris
Ken Altabef	Alice Goldfuss
Hugh A.D. Spencer	T. Fox Dunham
Martin Rose	Eric Del Carlo
Edward Morris	Jonathan Balog
Paul Williams	Ewan C. Forbes
J. Daniel Stone	Allen Griffin

"This is what happens if the works of Ray Bradbury, Isaac Asimov, H.P. Lovecraft, and Stephen King consummated and had a baby. Excellent anthology!" – *HORROR NEWS NETWORK*

GREY MATTER
P R E S S

greymatterpress.com

"A tenacious attempt to hold on in a world out of control."
THE HEART OF DARKNESS AWAITS
"Startling and terrifying."
"A killer anthology."
EQUILIBRIUM OVERTURNED
A VOLUME OF APOCALYPTIC HORRORS
FROM BRAM STOKER AWARD NOMINATED EDITORS
ANTHONY RIVERA
SHARON LAWSON

EQUILIBRIUM OVERTURNED
THE HEART OF DARKNESS AWAITS

The end is coming. But how will it arrive?

From alien civilizations bent on human destruction, to demonic incursions from beyond the event horizon, to the dangerous malevolence that lives within us all, *Equilibrium Overturned* drags you into the heart of darkness to explore brutal personal and worldwide apocalypses and the lives wavering on the brink.

Survive destroyed worlds and terrifying dystopian societies. Experience a prison of the future and the whitewashing of a horrifying past that threatens our very existence. From preventable transgressions, unavoidable doomsdays and personal calamities both near and far, *Equilibrium Overturned* offers shocking revelations into what life may be like at the end.

FEATURING:

John Everson	JG Faherty
Tim Waggoner	Jay Caselberg
Tony Knighton	Geoffrey W. Cole
Sean Eads	Jeff Hemenway
Rose Blackthorn	S.G. Larner
Josh R. Vogt	Roger Jackson
Martin Slag	Stephen T. Vessels

"The stories in *Equilibrium Overturned*, are solid and the thread of desperation and survival is present. Most deal with a bleak sense of survival, the settings change and the details and characters, but every one involves a tenacious attempt to hold the fuck on in a world uncontrolled." – *SHOCK TOTEM*

GREY MATTER
P R E S S

greymatterpress.com

DEATH'S REALM

THE ANTHOLOGY

FROM BRAM STOKER AWARD NOMINATED EDITORS

ANTHONY RIVERA
SHARON LAWSON

DEATH'S REALM
WHERE THE HERE
AND THE HEREAFTER COLLIDE

Something awaits you on the road ahead. It's here, at the intersection of this existence and the next, where the forces of the Living and the Dead converge in a terrifying place known as Death's Realm.

And it's here that the forces of the living and the spirits of the dead meet to wage an everlasting battle for control. *Death's Realm: Where the Here and the Hereafter Collide* contains sixteen stories from these wars written by an acclaimed selection of masters from the horror and speculative fiction genres.

FEATURING:

Stephen Graham Jones

Hank Schwaeble

John F.D. Taff

JG Faherty

Rhoads Brazos

Aaron Polson

Jay Caselberg

Gregory L. Norris

Brian Fatah Steele

Karen Runge

Simon Dewar

Martin Rose

Jay O'Shea

John C. Foster

Jane Brooks

Matthew Pegg

Paul Michael Anderson

"*Death's Realm* is a triumph, pressing a universal experience through a refracting prism and revealing to us bold colors and nuanced hues of form and experience we had not hitherto dreamed existed. It is provocative and challenging without ever succumbing to the temptation to deliver a narrative kick to the head." - *FANGORIA Magazine*

GREY MATTER
P R E S S

greymatterpress.com